Memorial Day's Escape

A Larry Macklin Mystery-Book 19

A. E. Howe

Books in the
Larry Macklin Mystery Series
(in order):

November's Past

December's Secrets

January's Betrayal

February's Regrets

March's Luck

April's Desires

May's Danger

June's Troubles

July's Trials

August's Heat

September's Fury

October's Fear

Spring's Promises

Summer's Rage

Autumn's Ghost

Winter's Chill

Valentine's Warning

St. Patrick's Cross

Memorial Day's Escape

Independence Day's Search

CHAPTER ONE

It was a Tuesday near the end of May and the temperature was already close to ninety with the humidity right behind… and it was only ten in the morning. I wiped sweat from my forehead as I watched my friend and ex-partner, Pete Henley, shoot and reload his Glock 17 from a wheelchair.

Two months earlier he'd been in a crash where his car had landed on a guardrail, crushing the driver's door and breaking multiple bones in his left arm and leg. His arm was mostly healed, and he'd progressed to being able to take a few steps with the aid of a walker or a crutch, but he still relied on the chair for a lot of his navigation. I'd come with him to help him get around the department's sandy range. He had a lot of frustration to release on the targets at the end of the shooting bay.

"Another hundred rounds and I'll be done," Pete assured me as he tried to shift the chair closer to the table where he could reload his magazines. "Would you mind?"

I pushed him the rest of the way, then nodded toward the table. "I can help with that."

Pete scooted two magazines over to me. "Can you pick up the brass too?" he asked with a smile.

I liked seeing flashes of his old humor. There had been

less and less of that during the last month as depression over his injuries had settled in.

"Sure, I'll do all the grunt work," I said, passing him the full magazines.

"At least I can reload ammo while I'm sitting around the house." There was a hard edge to his voice as he set the empty gun down on the table with the slide locked back. "You can reset the targets too."

"Fine. But you have to look at a couple of cases for me," I said, knowing how much he loved the chance to do some real work, even if it was only in an advisory role.

"Deal," he said, handing me the roll of adhesive squares to paste over the bullet holes in the paper targets.

I was halfway back from the targets when my phone pinged with a text alert. As I pulled it from the case on my belt, I saw Pete reaching for his as well.

All deputies report to your supervisors, read the alert. Pete and I looked at each other, then I involuntarily glanced up at the sky. The only other time I'd seen an all-deputies alert had been for a weather emergency, but today the sky was bright blue and clear.

I called my supervisor, Lieutenant Phil Eccles, as my phone began to blow up with messages from the investigators under me.

"What's up?" I asked when Phil answered.

"First, promise me you won't go off half-cocked. I'm angry enough for both of us." I could hear him grinding his teeth through the phone. "Manning was being transported today and there was an accident. He's missing."

I let out words that would have made me burst into flame if I'd been in a church. Neil Manning was a Machiavellian sociopath who'd kidnapped a woman, orchestrated several deaths and, most damning in my eyes, engineered the stabbing of my father.

"How…" Having used up my four-letter-word vocabulary, I was now at a loss for words, though my anger was still stomping around inside my brain as I tried to come to grips with the situation.

"Apparently, it was a planned escape. With the help of the highway patrol, we've already set up blocks on all the roads leading out of the county."

"Why weren't we told they were moving him?" I was still stuck in *how-could-this-happen?* mode.

"You need to let all of that go for now. Not only did Manning escape, but there were two other prisoners with him. Catching them needs to be our focus," Phil said with surprising calm.

I took a deep breath. "Right. Where do you want me?"

"Head for the crash site. It's south of town at the forest cut-off between Old Plank Road and Alligator Point Highway."

"I know it."

"We've circled the area out for a mile, but there's a lot of forest and whoever helped them had at least a ten-minute head-start on us, so they could be beyond the perimeter by now. We're going to move it out to five miles as soon as we have enough deputies. I want you to head up our end of the investigation."

"Our end?"

"All the prisoners were under federal indictments, so this is going to be multijurisdictional with the FBI and the U.S. Marshals involved."

"Okay." I had mixed feelings about all the help. I was glad for the assistance but concerned that they'd try to sideline us. "I'm ten minutes from the scene and will be on my way in five."

"Good," Phil responded and disconnected the call.

"I heard." Pete was looking at me with just a touch of envy in his eyes. I knew that not being a part of this would eat at him. "Go!"

"I can't just leave you here," I argued.

"Don't worry about it. I'll call Sarah to come get me. Go!" he barked.

"I'll keep you in the loop," I promised, already running

for my car.

Driving south, I could see a small column of smoke in the distance. My grill lights were flashing so I barely slowed as I waved at the deputies working the first roadblock and drove around it. The closer I got to the scene of the accident, the more blue lights there were.

At the cut-off, Deputy Andy Martel had his car blocking the road. I parked on the shoulder beside two other patrol cars and a red pickup truck from the fire department.

"I think that's evidence," Martel said after we greeted each other. He was pointing to a "Road Closed" barricade that I had assumed was ours. "We're thinking it was used to keep anyone from driving down the road after the accident."

"Don't let anyone touch it," I told him.

"I got this," he said and gave me a casual salute as I headed down the road.

The narrow, paved cut-off road wound through the corner of a large wildlife management area used for hunting and recreation. On both sides of the road were palmettos and longleaf pines as far as the eye could see. A hundred yards in front of me, the rear end of the prisoner transport van was sticking five feet up into the air. The words *Coastal Security & Transport* were printed on the back door of the van. The vehicle appeared to have fallen hood-first into a hole in the middle of the road. *A sinkhole?* I wondered.

Then my attention was drawn to the red engine and other fire department vehicles surrounding a smoldering yellow backhoe near the transport van. I wondered if it was county equipment being used to fill in the sinkhole.

I headed toward Julio Ortiz, one of our investigators who was standing in the middle of the road and watching the firemen work. As I got closer, I could see that the backhoe had been used to tear a hole in the passenger side of the van, explaining how the prisoners had escaped.

"They've taken the driver to the hospital." Julio turned to look at me, his grim expression mirroring my own feelings. "The other guard is dead."

I walked past him, carefully trying to avoid the mess created by the firemen, who were rolling up their hoses and stomping through the mud. I couldn't blame them. Their job was to put out fires. Preserving a crime scene was only a secondary consideration.

"Sorry for the mess," the deputy fire chief said as I approached. "Fire's a hundred percent contained. You can smell the gasoline. My guess is someone wanted to add confusion by burning the backhoe and getting us to douse it with water. We'll be out of your way in about half an hour." He looked down at the muddy prints surrounding the vehicles. "I'll get my guys to record their bootprints so you can compare them later."

"Any idea how long ago the fire was set?" I asked.

"We got here about twenty-five minutes ago, just after we got a call about the smoke. I don't think it had been burning more than fifteen minutes. As soon as we saw the van we called dispatch, but they'd already been alerted."

"We got a call from the company transporting the prisoners when they noticed that the van's GPS had stopped moving and they couldn't reach the guards on the radio," Julio spoke up from behind me.

I peered through the jagged hole in the side of the van and saw a female guard with her head covered in coagulated blood.

"Question is, did she die because of the crash or did someone kill her?" I frowned.

"This trap is like something out of a Roadrunner cartoon," Julio said, stopping at the side of the hole and looking down at the cab of the van.

The front half of the van was down in a five-foot-wide hole that ran the width of the road and was at least four feet deep. I looked around and saw where the backhoe had slung the dirt and tarmac from the hole down into the ditch. Several large painter's tarps had been pulled into the hole with the van.

"Wow!" I said as it all came together in my head. Julio

was right. Whoever was responsible for this had clearly raided the Acme Evil Plan Department.

"They dug the hole and covered it with the tarp. You can see where they nailed it down to the road." Julio pointed at the nails, then nodded toward the yellow machine. "That's my backhoe."

"What?" I thought for a minute that he literally meant it was his.

"I took a report on it four days ago. It was stolen from a job site on the north side of town."

"County's?" I asked by way of confirmation, looking at where the words *Adams County Road Department* had been stenciled in black on the door of the cab.

"No. It wasn't even yellow. It's been spray-painted and someone stenciled the words on the cab."

Looking closer, I could see yellow paint specks on the seat of the cab.

"This has to be Manning's doing," I said angrily. "I don't know how he did it, but it has to be him. Maybe with the help of his father… We need to secure all the footage we can from cameras aimed anywhere along the Alligator Point Highway or Old Plank Road going in both directions."

"We're a couple of miles out of town. The coverage won't be good," Julio warned.

"I know. But we need to shoot at all the targets and hope we hit something."

I started walking along the side of the road, looking into the ditch. Unfortunately, May was one of our driest months. It had been a couple of weeks since we'd had any significant rain and the sand in the ditch wouldn't hold a print. Fifty feet in both directions didn't give me anything, though I did find where the backhoe had been parked off the road. Maybe we would find a piece of paper or a cigarette butt that we could pull fingerprints or DNA from, but all of that would have to wait until crime-scene techs showed up.

When our crime-scene van finally did arrive, it was followed closely by one from the Florida Department of

Law Enforcement. They all parked on the other side of the barricade and, after checking in with Deputy Martel, the techs started hauling their equipment toward the prisoner transport van. Martel would be taking meticulous notes of who came in and out of the crime scene. With such a major investigation, the last thing the Adams County Sheriff's Office needed was to come off looking like bumpkins.

"We have lots of help on this one," said Shantel Williams, the head of our crime scene and evidence division, in a neutral tone as she walked by me.

I nodded, hoping that there wouldn't be any jurisdictional tit-for-tat stuff. I didn't want any other department calling the shots on this case but ours.

Shantel and her partner, Marcus Brown, started processing the van alongside the techs from FDLE, leaving Julio and me with nothing to do but stand around and take pictures.

"Part of me wants to be on the search for these guys," I told Julio.

"I can handle things here," he told me with a grin. Julio had been in our criminal investigations department for about nine months, covering mainly burglaries and auto thefts, and for the last month he'd been trying to get me to assign him a crimes-against-persons case.

"Don't tempt me," I said, knowing that finding the escaped criminals and their accomplice or accomplices was the red meat of this investigation. With only a minimum amount of competence, any jury would convict them for felony murder of the guard in the van. Any additional charges would be just icing on the cake.

Every time I looked toward the barricade, it seemed that there were more cars and vans parked on the other side. Now I could see the coroner's van and a black sedan that screamed federal agency. I was proven right about the sedan when a woman I recognized came walking toward us. I'd worked with Special Agent Padilla in the past and our professional relationship had been rocky, to say the least.

"She looks like she's on a mission," Julio commented.

"Agent Padilla is always on a mission."

Before she could reach us, my phone blared with Dad's ringtone.

"Where are you?" he asked.

"At the crash site, and I have federal incoming," I told him.

"Special Agent Padilla will be taking the lead for the FBI. Since the three prisoners were charged with federal crimes and were being transported to the federal prison in Tallahassee for arraignment, the FBI put on a strong argument for jurisdiction." I could hear the tension in Dad's voice. As sheriff, he would be in the center of the multi-agency pig pile.

"I don't like it," I said as Padilla made eye contact with me.

"Let me be clear. The FBI is taking the lead on the search for the missing prisoners. The murder of the guard is *our* investigation." Dad was emphatic.

"At least that's something."

"And even though they're in charge of the search, they're going to need us to do the real work. Leon County has sent one of their helicopters, and I've already told Bob Muller to notify our mounted posse to get ready."

"Got to go," I said, hanging up on Dad as Padilla stopped just inside my personal space.

"Deputy Macklin." Her dark hair was pulled into a severe bun, and she wore a poorly disguised smirk.

"*Sergeant* Macklin," I responded. "Agent Padilla, we meet again."

"Special Agent in Charge," she said, placing a lot of weight on the last word. "I hope this goes more smoothly than the last time we worked together."

"I'm sure it will," I said with my own share of sarcasm. "I thought there'd be more of you?"

"Other agents are setting up the mobile command center at a crossroads a quarter mile north of here. Our main mission is the recapture of the three prisoners." She said all of this as if she were briefing the media. "With that in mind, I'd like to look at the scene."

"Look but don't touch, and try not to leave too many footprints." I gave her a fake smile and she responded with a deadly glare.

I watched as Padilla walked around the van, looking at the jagged hole in the side. She leaned in as far as she could, and I knew how badly she wanted to crawl inside to pick through any evidence left behind. Then she walked over to where the scorched backhoe was sitting in the mud created by the firehoses. Again, I could tell that she had to restrain herself from crawling up onto it and looking around at what was left of the seat and console for clues.

"We'll have the scene fully documented and fingerprinted in a couple of hours. FDLE is here to assist," I said when she came back over to me.

"I'll want to see all the pictures and a list of the bagged and tagged evidence."

"You'll get them. I'll need to get your shoe size and photos of the soles," I told her, pointing to the ground around the van. "You left footprints that will need to be eliminated."

She frowned but nodded. I followed her back to the barricade where I took photos and wrote down the details from her shoes.

"We have two search-and-recovery teams en route," Padilla informed me as she put her shoes back on.

"And Dad's got our mounted posse standing by," I said, half expecting her to make some disparaging remark about us using nineteenth-century ATVs, but she only nodded.

"If this was as well planned as it looks," she said thoughtfully, "they might already be on the interstate headed out of the area."

"I know Neil Manning. Who are the other two prisoners?"

"Lester Stevens is an idiot. He's a thirty-four-year-old

white drug addict who decided that it would be a good idea to steal a mail truck. As he was driving off, the mail carrier tried to hop back into the truck and Stevens swerved and brushed him off on a tree. The mailman was crushed and died less than an hour later. The other one though, Doyle Waugh, is a real piece of work. He's fifty-one years old, black, and with a remarkable number of prison tattoos. In and out of prison all his life, mostly for assault and drug crimes. Lately he's taken to kidnapping and killing people, just for fun."

I winced. "I've heard of him. He grabbed a couple from Daytona Beach."

"That's him. He kept them alive for a week. Those are autopsy photos that you *don't* want to see."

"He tortured them?"

She nodded. "He's clearly a sadist. He would have had even more serious charges against him over the years, but most of the women he abused are terrified of him. After looking at pictures of his victims, I can understand why no one wanted to testify against him."

"And now he's loose in our county," I groaned.

"If it makes you feel any better, I doubt he's going to stay here long. If we don't catch him soon, he'll be hundreds of miles away and it might take months to catch up with him."

"So who do you think the guy with the backhoe intended to set free?"

Padilla shrugged. "Probably Manning."

"At least we can agree on that."

"Neil Manning is the only one with friends and family who might help him. Lester's family gave up on him when he was a boy, and I don't think even winning the lottery would make him popular. Doyle has lots of people who fear him, but no one who would go out of their way to help him."

"You need to talk to Manning's dad," I told her.

"We've already invited him in for an interview."

"Did he agree to come?"

"The invitation came with some caveats," Padilla said smugly. "Mostly that we'll get a warrant and be tearing his place apart by the end of the day if he doesn't talk to us."

"The subtlety of the federal government never ceases to amaze me." Seeing the look on her face, I held up my hand. "Hey, I'm not criticizing. If you're going to bring the hammer down, then Rudy Manning is definitely the right nail to hit with it."

Her phone rang and she glanced down. Turning away from me, she answered it.

"Padilla. Right, good. On my way," was the sum total of her side of the conversation. "He's at our mobile command center," she said over her shoulder to me as she started for her car.

I saw Phil Eccles walking toward us, but I ignored him and jogged after Padilla. I despised Rudy Manning and was certain he was behind this.

"I could help you interview him. I know him, and he's not going to bow down to your FBI badges."

"He has a lawyer with him," she said without turning back.

"And the lawyer is top-shelf." I knew that Rudy Manning had hired one of the most famous, and expensive, criminal defense lawyers in North Florida.

Padilla stopped and sighed. "Come on then. I learned the last time we met that you're a pain in the ass if you don't get your way."

"I'll follow you to the command center."

"What's going on?" Phil asked me as Padilla walked by him without a word.

"They're from the government and are here to help," I muttered. "They've got Rudy Manning at their mobile command center and Agent Padilla has condescended to let me sit in on the interview. Can you take over here?"

"Sure. I'll get Shantel to bring me up to speed," Phil said, nodding.

I hurried to my car as Padilla pulled her SUV around and

threw dirt and gravel in her wake as she accelerated off the shoulder.

At the crossroads was a derelict roadside store with rusty pumps surrounded by a cracked and pothole-filled tarmac parking lot. The FBI's incident command RV stood head and shoulders above all the patrol cars, pickup trucks and SUVs parked around it. Dad's truck and half a dozen of our people were off to one side of the parking lot. A couple of pop-up tents had been erected that looked low-rent next to the FBI's operation.

Dad was talking to the deputies and other members of the search teams as I walked toward the RV. Padilla had parked her black sedan ten feet from the RV and didn't even spare me a glance as she got out and hurried over to one of her sunglass-wearing compadres. They were still conferring when I caught up.

"Who's he?" the FBI agent asked Padilla. Standing a little taller than my six feet even, with wavy black hair and a square jaw, the agent looked like he could have been featured in the law enforcement edition of *GQ*.

"Sergeant Macklin is the local lead on the murder of the guard," Padilla told him. She turned to me. "Macklin, this is Special Agent Redcliff."

"Before we go in, why don't you tell me why the U.S. Marshals weren't transporting the prisoners?" I asked. Driving over there, it had occurred to me how odd it was that a private security company had been moving the prisoners.

"It's a pilot program. The federal prisons are trying to outsource to save money," Padilla said neutrally.

"Who on earth would think that was a good idea?" I shook my head.

"Number-crunchers. We're going over Coastal Security and Transport's procedures to see if there's a leak on their end." Padilla paused, staring at me hard. "Look, if you want to attend the interview, you have to agree not to interfere. We'll get your input afterward."

"Agreed." When I'd volunteered to help, I hadn't really expected them to let me participate.

CHAPTER TWO

I followed Padilla and Redcliff into the mobile command center. The sides of the RV had been rolled out, creating an impressive amount of room inside. One look around at all the built-in electronic gizmos told me this thing had probably cost more than our department's entire fleet of patrol cars and unmarked vehicles combined.

At the widest point of the RV was a conference table that could seat about ten people. Rudy Manning and a stocky, blond-haired man in his forties that I didn't recognize were already occupying a couple of the chairs. Manning glared at me.

"What's he doing here?" he growled. Manning started to stand, but the man next to him put a hand on his arm.

"Don't worry, Rudy. Macklin isn't going to give us any trouble." The man gave me a strange smile.

"He's persecuted Neil from day one. Never gave him a chance," Manning grumbled. It took all the restraint I could muster not to tell him what I thought of his evil offspring.

"Sergeant Macklin is going to sit in on the interview," Padilla said in a flat, no-nonsense tone.

"At least he's wearing clothes today," the man next to

Manning said. He was openly sneering now.

"Do I know you?" I couldn't help asking.

"I'm David Thorne. You were in my house a couple of months ago, sopping wet and half naked. My son's YouTube channel gained a hundred-thousand subscribers thanks to you. Might even pay for most of his college."

I felt a chill go down my spine. Phil Eccles and I had washed up in the backyard of the man's lakefront house after a floating gunfight. The canoe we'd been using sank, forcing us to strip down and swim for shore. A kid named Jax Thorne had used his phone to film us when we asked him for assistance. All we'd needed were some towels and a phone, but instead we got a lot of smartass comments and our butts all over the internet.

Covering my own embarrassment, I looked at Manning. "What happened to Ralph Calavera? Did he have an attack of conscience after his wife was murdered? Decided he didn't want to represent scum like your son anymore?"

Manning rose from his chair again, rage in his eyes, but Padilla held up her hands. "I don't care what's going on between you all. We need to move on."

Once we were all seated at the table, Thorne began unctuously, "My client is happy to help in any way. He's very concerned for the welfare of his son, who was in your custody at the time he was kidnapped by two very dangerous criminals."

My mouth fell open at the audacity of the man to suggest that Neil Manning was a victim in all this.

"Let's be clear," Padilla said. "We regard your client as a person of interest in the escape. That doesn't mean he's a suspect, but we have to consider his history when it comes to enabling his son."

"Who, I'll point out, hasn't been convicted of any crime."

"Let's agree that his innocence is a technicality," Padilla responded. She'd thoroughly reviewed our files on Neil Manning and there was no doubt of his guilt. He'd kidnapped a woman, held her hostage in a storage container on his property for months, then subjected her to so much twisted mind-whammy that it had led to more than one death and the attack on my father. Manning's attempt to evade capture had put a number of people at risk, including me.

"I don't trust you all to bring him in safely. The last time law enforcement went after him, he was in the hospital for weeks."

Rudy Manning looked frustrated and sounded sincere. A small voice of doubt in my head asked if I was sure that he had helped his son escape.

"We would like an accounting of your whereabouts during the last twenty-four hours," Padilla said, ignoring Manning's concerns.

The words were hardly out of her mouth before Thorne was pulling a prepared list of Manning's schedule for the last two days out of his notebook.

"I can email you an electronic copy of his itinerary if you'd like. You'll see that, next to each time and place, we've listed the name of one or more witnesses."

"Convenient that you already have this information," Padilla said, maintaining her neutral tone.

"Let's just say you all are predictable. As soon as Mr. Manning informed me that his son had been kidnapped from the transport vehicle, I suggested that he outline his movements."

"And we do appreciate your cooperation," Padilla said with a smile while setting aside the paper without looking at it.

"My question is, what are you doing to find my son and get him back from these criminals?" Manning demanded.

"We're going to do everything we can to find your son and safely return him to prison," Padilla assured him. "Your cooperation will help us. Can you think of anyone who might assist him in escaping?"

"He didn't orchestrate this!" Manning persisted. Thorne gently put his hand on Manning's arm.

"We aren't going to convince them of your son's innocence," the attorney said.

"Have you or anyone else helped your son communicate with someone outside the prison?" Padilla asked.

Neil Manning had been out on bail, but confined to his home before the Feds had pressed their own set of charges that included kidnapping, sending him back to prison. Since our investigation into his crimes had led to the discovery that he was highly skilled in the use of surveillance equipment and the dark corners of the internet, he had been forbidden from using any electronic devices the entire time he'd been on house arrest.

"No," Manning said through clenched teeth.

"Can we look through your phone and other electronic devices?" Padilla asked.

Manning turned and looked at Thorne, who shook his head solemnly from side to side.

"No."

Padilla sighed. "You've been caught aiding your son's lawless behavior in the past, so I don't think we're going to have a hard time getting a warrant."

"Then write up the request and submit it to a judge. When we see a warrant, we'll hand over what it asks for," Thorne said, clearly bored.

Padilla looked at Agent Redcliff. He gave her a small nod.

"The request was submitted thirty minutes ago. We're just waiting to hear back."

"So why did you bother to ask?" Manning stared at her.

"He knows why." She pointed to Thorne. "Sometimes we just like to measure the amount of cooperation someone is willing to give. Apparently, you aren't that concerned about your son."

As her words sank in, the blood rose in Manning's cheeks. This time, Thorne's hand on his arm wasn't enough to stop him from standing up and sputtering, "I didn't have anything to do with this! Giving you my phone won't help you find my son!"

"Mr. Thorne knows we have to eliminate obvious suspects, and the longer it takes, the longer it's going to be before we can concentrate all of our resources in directions you might feel would be more productive. His advice is what's slowing down the recovery of your son." Padilla pointed her finger directly at Thorne, who looked irritated for the first time since the interview had started.

"We're done here," Thorne said.

Manning looked at Thorne before reaching into his pocket and taking out his phone. He held it out to Padilla. "You can look through it."

"You can't take it out of this room," Thorne said hastily.

"I won't need to." Padilla started to scroll through the phone. I looked over her shoulder and watched as she skimmed through his texts and phone calls, then his various apps. Fifteen minutes later, satisfied, she handed it back to him. "Thank you. With local assistance, we're conducting an air search as well as road checks. When the helicopters are done, we'll move in and do an intensive search of the forest. We'll keep you informed."

We escorted them out in silence.

"Your thoughts?" Padilla asked as we watched them walk to Rudy Manning's Mercedes SUV.

"I would have bet money before the interview that Manning was behind the escape," I said thoughtfully.

"But now?"

"Not so sure." I hated to admit it. "Someone needs to keep track of Manning. Even if he's not involved in the escape, his son is likely to contact him."

Padilla turned to me and smiled, tapping the side of her nose. "We requested several warrants. Trust me, he's covered."

Padilla's phone buzzed. She took the call and climbed back into the RV, giving me a small wave. As the door closed, I looked at the rockstar-quality vehicle and wondered what it would be like to work for an organization that could spend that sort of money.

I intended to join Dad at our command tent, but as I headed that direction, a man I knew waved and jogged toward me.

A little younger than my dad, Charles Maxwell had been the police chief for the City of Calhoun for several years before running for sheriff against my father two years ago. Since then, he'd taken a job with Silver Security, a firm in Tallahassee that provided high-tech security for banks, businesses and people a lot richer than me.

"Macklin," he said, holding out his hand and greeting me with more enthusiasm than I thought our past association warranted.

"Maxwell, what are you doing here?" I asked, trying to keep it friendly.

"The transport was ours," he said with a frown.

"You mean Silver Security?"

"That's right."

"I thought the name on the van was Coastal Security and Transport?"

"Silver Security bought them four months ago."

"Doesn't the company just deal with high-tech stuff?"

Maxwell sighed. "For the most part. However, the bosses want to get locked into some of those lucrative government contracts. When they learned that Coastal Security had received the contract for this pilot program transporting prisoners, they thought it was a way to get their feet in the door."

"So when they bought Coastal, it came with a federal contract, and they thought they'd be able to spin that into more deals as Silver Security." I was trying to follow the logic.

"Exactly. They had me evaluate Coastal. Lucky for me, the reports I wrote pointed out several problems with the company. Unfortunately, they didn't make Coastal correct the issues before purchasing them. Now here we are, four months later, and we're just starting to make the changes that are needed."

"I didn't see any cameras on the trucks."

"And no body cams for the guards. We've just ordered them. Even when we get them, it's going to be a month before we can train the staff to use them properly."

"Great." I shook my head.

"The truck *did* have GPS tracking, which is why the Feds were notified as quickly as they were." He saw the look on my face. "I'm not happy about this either. Even if those reports cover my ass, I'm still not going to be in a good position. I'm the lead advisor who's supposed to be bringing Coastal up to our standards."

"You can't do something like that overnight," I said, sympathizing with his position.

"Especially not when they already had contracts that they had to fulfill. It wasn't like I could just pull them offline until they were up to speed."

Maxwell had always come off as a little arrogant, but now he seemed like a boxer in the middle of the tenth round.

"They wouldn't fire you over this?" I asked.

"No." He looked up as though looking for answers from above. "Though I'm not sure that would be the worst thing."

"You don't like the job?" A friend of mine worked for Silver and had offered me a job with a ridiculous six-figure salary. I'd turned it down, but not without a lot of thought.

"In a word, no. I was a lot happier as chief of police in little Podunk Calhoun. Your father beat me fair and square, but I can't help thinking about how different my life would be if I'd been elected sheriff."

"Then you would be sheriff of little Podunk Adams County," I quipped.

He shook his head. "I'm not bashing Calhoun or Adams County. Though you gotta admit, they aren't Orlando or Tampa. Like I said, half the time I wish I was back in my little office with that pittance of a salary. Now I've got all the money I'll ever need and a job where most of my time is spent writing reports that are ignored. Case in point." He waved his hand toward the activity around us.

"The money has to be some compensation."

"All the money did was give my wife delusions of grandeur. We bought a new house and now she thinks she should be dean of her college at the university. Several times a month, we have to entertain the pretentious peacocks she works for in hopes that she can play the game well enough to rise to the top of the academic heap."

"Tough," was all I could think to say.

"Enough of my problems. I need to get these prisoners back in the can as quickly as possible. Where are you on the search?"

"That's not really my job. I'm lead on the murder. What do you know about the driver? How's he doing?"

Maxwell's face fell and he took a quick breath. "His name's Willie Mathis. He's alive, but I'm not sure about the long-term prognosis. Apparently, he had his head close to the side window when they drove into the trap and the airbag deployed. The bag pushed his head sideways into the window, causing considerable head trauma. Who knows if he'll remember anything. There's a good chance he'll have some brain damage. I did a drive-along with that team a month ago. Willie and his partner, Florence Murray, struck me as good people. The owner of Silver Security has notified the families. I guess you think I'm an asshole for not focusing on them first."

"I've known you for years. Like my dad, you're able to compartmentalize. I get it. I'm having a hard time focusing on the murder when I all I want to do is chase down Neil Manning and toss him back in a cell." Even though Maxwell could be a jerk at times, I'd never thought he was heartless. "Is there any chance that the driver or the guard could have been involved in the escape?"

"Never say never, but I don't see it. Obviously, whoever was operating the backhoe could have double-crossed an insider and killed them to keep them from talking." He shook his head. "My guess is no. If they're involved, it's more likely they just ran their mouths in the wrong bar or restaurant. Or trusted the wrong person."

"Come on. Let's go see how the search is going."

Maxwell and I headed over to our tent, where Dad was talking to several members of the mounted posse. There were half a dozen horse trailers parked around the tent with men, women and horses all milling about.

"I thought you were at the wreck?" Dad said when he saw me.

"Phil is there. I came over to sit in while the FBI interviewed Rudy Manning."

Dad nodded and looked over at Maxwell with raised eyebrows.

"He works for Silver Security. They bought out Coastal Security and Transport a few months ago, so the guard who was killed worked for Silver. Maxwell is here representing them."

Dad nodded and stepped over to Maxwell with his hand out.

"No hard feelings, Charles, but you aren't law enforcement anymore," Dad said as they shook hands. "We can't share information the way we did when you were chief."

"Ted, you didn't share that much with me when I *was* the chief." Maxwell smiled to let us know he was kidding. "I just want to know enough to keep my bosses informed and to let the families of our guard and driver know that you're on the trail of the people responsible."

"You know we are," Dad said. "First and foremost, we need to catch the three prisoners. What can you give us?"

"Not much. We have the GPS tracking of the truck, plus all the records associated with the transfer of the prisoners and the employees' phone data."

"You'll give up their electronic devices?"

"Of course. All employees sign an agreement stating that the company has full rights to search any device they bring to work or use for work-related activities."

"We've collected their phones?" Dad asked, looking at me.

"Shantel is bagging evidence now. I know we collected the driver's personal effects before he was transported to the hospital. Also, I've got Lionel on the way to secure the laptop inside the truck." Lionel West was the department's indispensable technology wizard.

"You'll need our tech people to give you access to the information on the laptop," Maxwell said. "It's used for routing and keeping track of prisoner transfers and has very secure encryption protection. It's not my field of expertise, but I wouldn't suggest your guy goes mucking about with it before discussing it with our team."

Maxwell had a way of irritating me without even trying, but I knew he was right. Electronic security was Silver's expertise, so I would expect any equipment they used to be well protected. It was just a shame their prison transport wasn't as secure.

"The sooner you can get me all the information you have on the driver and the guard, the better," I told Maxwell.

"I'll get with HR and have it to you before the end of the day. I'll be glad to arrange interviews with our employees when you need them." He paused for a moment, then said, "I know in cases like this, you have to look for the inside man. I don't know these people that well, but I haven't gotten any hinky feelings at the company."

"I appreciate your assessment," I told him, though we both knew it didn't mean much. I was still going to have to dig through everything about everyone connected with the transportation of the prisoners.

"Let us know what we can do for the employees' families," Dad said, leading Maxwell back to his car before returning to me.

"I'm going to need you to help with the mounted search," he said.

"I thought you wanted me to handle the investigation of the murder?"

He held up a hand. "This *is* part of your investigation. I need you to ride out with the posse to make sure anything they find that might be evidence is properly preserved and recognized if it's important for the ongoing search."

I glanced again at the assembled horse trailers and recognized Dad's. Finn and Mac were hitched up to the trailer. Finn was looking around with curiosity while Mac was asleep, one foot cocked up and half-eaten hay hanging out of his mouth.

"The posse will move in right after the dogs," Dad told me.

I didn't envy my father the decisions he had to make. No matter what order the different teams went in, there would be criticism of the way the search for the escaped prisoners was conducted. Preservation of evidence versus the urgency of recapturing dangerous criminals were conflicting priorities.

"How long do I have before they head out?"

"An hour, maybe two. LCSO One is almost done covering the area. He's going to circle out to ten miles and then return to Leon County. The dogs will go in once he's done." LCSO One was the designation for the helicopter operated by the Leon County Sheriff's Office. They were responsible for air coverage for several counties in Florida's panhandle.

I could hear the baying of the bloodhounds, as if they were signaling their readiness to go on the hunt.

"Whose dogs?"

"Not sure. FDLE brought them in." Dad began to shift his weight from one leg to the other, a clear sign of impatience. "Did you see anything at the van that would help?"

"Whoever was operating the backhoe had to get there in a vehicle, and at least some of the prisoners probably left the scene in that same vehicle, though we can't guarantee all three of them did. If there were any tire tracks or other evidence, the firetrucks and water probably destroyed it."

"The FBI is pulling all the CCTV and security camera footage they can find in this area, which won't be much. Of course, if the convicts drove away from the scene, then we're just wasting our time hunting for them in the forest."

"The question is, who was the backhoe operator trying to release? Was it Manning or one of the others? Was it all three? If they were just after one or two of the guys, they might have left the other one or two to fend for themselves."

"As a way of distracting us."

"That *would* be one of the benefits for them and the convict they were helping."

"Great," Dad grumbled sarcastically.

"My money is on Neil Manning. I think this was a plan hatched by him or his father. In which case, the other two prisoners might be out there hiding somewhere."

"We need to know everything we can about the other two. First and most importantly, are they city or country?"

I knew what he meant. If they were city-born and bred, they'd be looking for the nearest car to steal. But if they were raised in the country, they might just run off into the tens of thousands of acres of forest and hunker down until we gave up hunting for them.

"The FBI will have access to their records," I said.

"Your buddy Padilla said she'd let us review their files, but I wouldn't count on it being done quickly. I get the feeling the FBI wants to catch these guys on their own."

"That might have to do with the fact that the prisoner transport was part of some kind of government and private enterprise pilot program. Someone's ass could be in a sling if it goes any more sideways than it already has."

"Politics are always so helpful in a public emergency situation," Dad muttered.

"Since I've got a little while before the posse heads out, I'm going back to the crash site to see how Shantel is getting along."

"We'll start the dogs from there," he said, looking over at

the four eager bloodhounds. They were sniffing around an SUV, followed by two handlers.

"I'll make sure they can get close enough to the van to get the scent," I assured him.

CHAPTER THREE

Back at the scene of the wreck, Julio was following Shantel and a couple of guys from FDLE's crime-scene unit as they went along marking possible evidence.

After letting them know I was back and asking them to finish documenting the area around the van first so the dogs could get in close, I went back to my car and read reports on a dozen other crimes that had happened in the last twelve hours. It was one of my new responsibilities as a sergeant and one that I had a love-hate relationship with. On the one hand, reading all the burglary, armed robbery, domestic abuse and other crime reports was time-consuming. And it wasn't just a matter of reading them—I also had to ask the responding investigators to clarify or dig deeper whenever I found holes in their narratives. But on the other hand, I found it fascinating to have a bird's-eye view of all the major crimes taking place in the county. The only crimes not under our purview were the ones covered by Calhoun's police force, and there weren't many of those. The city's department was so small that it only covered a fraction of the crimes that occurred.

As I read the reports, I kept my eyes open for any possible connections between them. In the two full months

I'd been a sergeant, I'd been able to piece together a few crimes committed by the same bad guy with a penchant for assaults involving stolen wallets and purses.

After about thirty minutes, I heard Shantel approach my car. "We're done if you want to examine the body."

"Find anything interesting?" I asked as I followed her back to the wreck. I valued Shantel's opinion. She'd been to more crime scenes than almost anyone else in the county, had a sharp eye and didn't jump to conclusions.

"I think someone really wanted to kill that guard."

"You mean specifically?"

"They didn't have to do that to her just to escape," Shantel answered, her voice dark.

"I assume you'll have it towed back to the office." We had a boneyard behind the sheriff's office where we could store vehicles that were evidence in major crimes.

"Yep. I got A-One Towing on standby." She looked back toward the barricade. "The folks from the coroner's office can get the body now."

I turned and waved to Linda, Dr. Darzi's assistant, who had been waiting eagerly for the all-clear. Then I put on a pair of latex gloves and peered through the back doors of the van that had been left open by someone after the crash.

"See the amount of damage to the head and face?"

Shantel pointed to where the body of the female guard lay curled in a defensive fetal position, pressed against the reinforced plexiglass barrier that separated the back of the van from the cab. On the left side of the van was a long bench, custom-made for transporting prisoners, where up to four could be seated and shackled to a bar running along the floor. On the right side was a jump seat for the guard.

I crawled in carefully, as the rear of the van was tilted up at a forty-five-degree angle. As I moved forward, I took note of the gash in the side of the van, and the many smears and pools of blood on the floor and walls.

"We took samples from all of it," Shantel said, anticipating my question.

Most of the blood had probably come from the guard, or the prisoners if they had been injured in the crash. Still, there was a possibility that the driver of the backhoe might have cut himself trying to help free the prisoners.

I noticed the empty shackles under the bench. They had been unlocked, not broken.

"Did you find any keys?" I asked.

"Bagged and tagged. They were in the lock in that set," Shantel said, pointing to one of the shackles.

Hunched over, I crept closer to the body. The woman was middle-aged, approximately two-hundred pounds and almost six feet tall. On the pale skin of her upper arm, I could see a series of aquatic tattoos featuring dolphins and sharks. Due to the number of blows she'd received, her face was unrecognizable. I could see a metal ring on her duty belt where the keys to the shackles had probably been attached.

"You want to let the professionals in?" Linda called from the door.

"I'll gladly let you take over." I had seen enough. "Any information you can give me on the order of the injuries would be helpful. For once, I don't think the time of death is going to be instrumental in bringing in a conviction."

"Yeah, I'd guess the prisoners aren't going to be able to claim an alibi for the murder." Linda stepped away from the van and let me climb out before taking her examination kit from a young man beside her and scrambling into the van. I assumed that her assistant, who looked like he'd graduated from high school just the week before, was one in a series of interns that rotated through the coroner's office.

"Someone was angry," Linda said, examining the face of the victim. Without looking away from the body, she introduced me to her help. "This is Ezra Reyes. Ezra, this is Sergeant Macklin."

Considering the gloves we both wore, I offered a wave instead of a handshake, then left Linda to her work and joined Shantel over at the backhoe. After donning a new pair of gloves, I climbed up the side to look into the cab.

"Julio took down the serial number," Shantel said.

The machine was a mess, all sooty from the fire and wet from the hoses. While the fire had done only superficial damage to the outside, the cab was a different story. The dash, wiring and the seat had all burned and melted into lumps of black plastic.

I stepped back down and looked at my gloves. "Did you find any evidence that stood out?"

Shantel chuckled. "You mean like a fresh cigarette with DNA written all over it in large letters? No. A few plastic bottles, food wrappers, but all of it looked like it had been out here for weeks, if not months. Of course, we collected a lot of personal items from the cab of the van."

"Probably all belonged to the guards," I said.

"We didn't find anything that I can point to and say that it likely came from the backhoe operator." Shantel looked around at the mud. "I hate working crime scenes when the firemen have been called in."

"Why didn't our bad guys torch the van?" I asked.

"Maybe they had some heart and didn't want to burn the driver to death."

"At least one of them was more than happy to beat the rear guard into a bloody pulp. Begs the question of why they killed her and not the driver."

"Maybe they thought he was dead too. Hondo said the driver was a mess."

Alejandro Cortez was one of the best EMTs in the county, and he was also skilled at observing and assessing a situation. If he said it, then I believed it.

A loud baying alerted us to the sound of the approaching bloodhounds. We stood back and watched as the handlers put the dogs to the scent, using a sheet from Neil Manning's jail cell.

I followed along as the four dogs snuffled their way to a spot a quarter of a mile up the road where a dirt hunting trail veered off to the west. There they stopped and began circling in apparent frustration.

"There are tire tracks and shoe prints!" one of the handlers shouted back to me.

They pulled the dogs back onto the paved road while I called Shantel, who immediately directed the guys from FDLE to come down and take 3D images and casts of the tracks.

"They don't want to follow the path any farther," the other handler told me when I got off the phone.

"I bet the backhoe driver parked his car here," I mused.

"Do you want us to try the other scents?"

"Absolutely," I told him.

This time the dogs were more willing to head into the underbrush and soon disappeared out of sight.

I headed back to the crash site where Linda and Ezra were placing the guard on a stretcher before wheeling the body back to the barricade.

"There's a deep gash on her right arm. I'd guess it was done when the backhoe tore into the side of the van," Linda told me as I walked with her. "Nothing else that you didn't see yourself."

I left Shantel in charge at the crime scene and drove back to Dad and the mounted posse.

"We'll be heading out in about half an hour," Dad told me when I arrived. "Mac is already saddled."

I thanked him and used the time I had left to sit in the car and read a few more reports. If a report was well written, it meant that I didn't have any questions about the event once I finished reading it. The one in front of me now wasn't even close to adequate. I felt myself grinding my teeth. It was the third subpar report in two days that I had received from Mick Klein, a veteran investigator who knew better.

I debated whether I wanted to talk to him now or wait. Knowing that it would eat at me if I didn't go ahead and confront him, I took out my phone and tapped on his name.

"Yeah," Mick answered grudgingly.

"We need to talk about the burglary report you just sent,"

I said.

"What? The jar of money and the watch?" he asked, knowing full well which report I meant.

"Yes," I snapped.

"Not exactly a federal case. The watch was a Timex worth about thirty dollars."

Clearly a phone call wasn't going to be the best way to handle this. "I want a sit-down with you before you leave today."

"Thought you were out scouring the woods looking for escaped prisoners."

"I'll make time to meet you."

"Thanks, boss," he said, each word dripping with condescension.

I thought of a thousand not-so-nice things I could say, but instead I just disconnected the call and ground my teeth for another minute before getting out of the car and shaking it off.

I walked up to Dad's horse trailer and rubbed my hand down Mac's bay neck, thinking how long it had been since I'd been on a horse. Mac and his brother, Finn, were both large, steady Quarter Horses, rare twins that my dad had owned for most of their nine years. Considering my lack of recent riding experience, I was glad that Dad was letting me ride Mac, as he was the more relaxed and lazy of the two brothers. I put my foot in the stirrup and hoisted myself on board.

Dad gave a quick briefing to the posse, explaining how the search would work. We would spread out in two groups, one led by Dad and the other by Bob Muller, working a rough U-formation through the forest.

I was assigned to Bob's group. Mac was perky and eager as we rode along a deer trail, obviously glad to be unhitched from the trailer.

"We're going to spread out and ride the area in as much of a line as we can maintain through the palmettos and pine trees," Bob told the group. "Watch out for tortoise burrows and rattlesnakes. If you find anything, and I mean *anything,* call out for Sergeant Macklin." He pointed to me. "He'll come take a look. Is that understood?"

There were nods and mumbled affirmatives from the riders as everyone urged their horses forward.

Florida boasts the most longleaf pine forests of any state in the country. The longleaf habit is almost as rich as a rainforest, with a tall upper story created by the pines and a thick, rich understory that supports many species of plants and wildlife unique to this area of the southern coastal plain. Due to the thick clumps of palmettos, we were reduced to following small animal trails. I watched as the riders picked their way carefully through the underbrush.

You could hide an army out here, I thought, squinting into the palmettos that reached almost to Mac's shoulder and spread out like a sea of green underneath the pines. If a person didn't mind taking their chances with the rattlesnakes, they could crawl into the palmettos and never be seen.

The riders found dozens of objects, mostly bits of trash that raccoons and other small animals had dragged off into the woods. There were several plastic Coke bottles and fast-food wrappers covered with tooth- and claw-marks. If they'd been out there long enough for an animal to gnaw on them, then they hadn't been left by our bad guys. The posse stuffed them into trash bags, just in case. If nothing else, we were doing a good job of cleaning up the forest.

"Sergeant!"

I'd been letting Mac pick his own path while I read a few text updates on my phone. I looked up to see the owner of the local feed store standing in the stirrups on the back of his tall chestnut gelding, waving excitedly at me.

When I joined him, I saw a piece of blue cloth stuffed under a palmetto. The material was liberally sprinkled with what looked like blood. I climbed off Mac to get a closer look.

"Good job," I told the man. "It's one of their shirts."

I called Shantel and told her what we'd found. "I'll stay

here until you come to collect it," I said, knowing that she wouldn't enjoy her trip deep into the woods. Then I climbed back on Mac and directed Bob to keep the rest of the posse moving.

My phone rang with a call from Julio while I was waiting for Shantel.

"What's up?" I asked.

"I've got a missing person. The manager of the First Bank of Calhoun. He didn't show up to work this morning. I got the report about an hour ago."

"Who called it in?"

"The assistant manager, Curtis Warner. He said that the manager, Roberto Cortez, is never late. Cortez isn't answering his calls and Warner even drove by Cortez's house before calling it in. I'm at the house now."

"And?"

"Locked up tight. No car in the driveway. Nothing in the garage. I've checked with the neighbors, but Cortez just bought the house six months ago, so they don't know much about him. One of them did say that his car is usually parked in the driveway."

"Any relatives you can call?"

"I'm waiting on Warner to get back to me. He said Cortez moved up here about a year ago from Tampa and, as far as he knows, Cortez doesn't have any family in this area."

"You think there's something to this?" I trusted Julio's instincts.

"I do," Julio said. "Warner says this is very out of character. Cortez isn't the type to just decide to take a personal day without letting anyone know. Still, nothing around the house looks out of place. I went over the driveway carefully, thinking that he might have been car-jacked as he was leaving this morning, but there weren't any scruff marks or evidence of a struggle."

"Seal the house," I suggested. "Put up notices on the doors with your name and number so no one enters, and Cortez will know to contact you if he returns."

"Will do. I'll also go back to the bank and try to find someone he was friends with."

"See if he went to a gym, a church, even any stores he frequented. Also, start a timeline of when people saw him last." Then a thought occurred to me. "Where is his house?" If I'd been in my car, I could have pulled Julio's dispatch notes up on my laptop, but so far no one had figured out a way to mount a laptop to a saddle.

"At the back of Green Fields."

Green Fields was a fairly new development on the other side of the county a long way from where we were searching. With two unusual events taking place at the same time, I couldn't blame myself for wondering if they were related, but it seemed highly unlikely that Cortez had been abducted by one of our escaped prisoners.

"10-4. Let me know what you find. Consider Cortez's case a priority for now." I didn't want us to fumble a major crime because we were focused on the escapees. I thought about whether I should let Phil Eccles know about the Cortez case, but decided it was too soon. Most missing people were just missing—not lost, dead or abducted.

I turned in the saddle when I heard a UTV coming up behind me. In the passenger seat was an uncomfortable-looking Shantel. The driver was able to get the vehicle within fifty yards of where the shirt had been found. Shantel stepped out cautiously and grabbed her bag out of the back. With her eyes sweeping along the deer trails, she slowly made her way over to me.

"I'm going to get you for this," she grumbled.

"What did I do?" I asked innocently.

"You found evidence out in this snake-infested maze." Shantel wasn't alone in her fear of snakes. I could name a dozen deputies who would squeal like kids if they saw one.

"Sorry. You can take it out on the prisoners when we catch them."

"Easy for you to take it lightly, sitting up there five feet off the ground."

"I'll get down and you can get on Mac," I offered.

Shantel glared at me. "I just want to collect the shirt and get out of here."

Feeling a little guilty about teasing her, I pointed toward the shirt. She took several photos, then placed the shirt in a paper bag instead of the usual plastic. With the humidity, and the shirt already damp from blood, putting it in plastic would increase the chance of mold that would destroy its value as evidence.

As Shantel hurried back to the UTV, Dad called and instructed me to have my half of the posse join up with his at a crossroad about two miles away.

"We caught up with the dogs. Looks like our bad guys found a car," Dad said with a grim edge to his voice.

"I don't suppose you have a description," I asked, knowing he'd enjoy pointing out the stupidity of my question.

"How the hell would I have a description of a car that isn't here? We're still out in the middle of the woods."

"See your point," I admitted.

"We're looking for any hikers or bikers who might have seen something, but it's a long shot."

"We're headed your way."

By the time we joined up with the rest of the posse, crime technicians from the FBI and FDLE were already swarming around a section of the dirt road.

"Stay clear!" Dad shouted to us. "We're trying to get prints of the tires."

I stood off with the rest of the posse. Mac caught sight of his brother, who was being held by another posse member while Dad coordinated with the techs on the ground, and let out a single whinny. Once Finn answered, Mac cocked his left rear leg and took a nap while we waited.

My butt was sore, and the deer flies were becoming intolerable. I was swatting at several on Mac's neck when my phone rang with another call from Julio.

"Just an update on Cortez. I've put out a BOLO on his

car, a Silver Mercedes G-Class SUV. I also talked with his ex-wife, who lives in Mobile. She confirmed everything that the neighbors and the employees at the bank told me. He isn't the type of person to disappear."

I still couldn't shake the feeling that this was too much of a coincidence. "Our escapees had help. We know that they stole a backhoe, and it's possible that they stole a car or two."

"Two?"

"The dogs have identified two last known positions, so they split up. It's possible they had more than one accomplice that stole vehicles to help them escape. I know it's a long shot, but go ahead and put a red flag on Cortez's SUV so, if it's spotted, everyone will know that it could have one or more of our escapees inside."

Promising to keep me updated, Julio hung up just as Dad joined us.

"Did you see my text to the department?" he asked as he stroked Mac's neck.

I nodded. "We're on round-the-clock twelve-hour shifts until the prisoners are recaptured and all requested leave is suspended." I knew this probably wasn't going over well with some members of the department who had requested leave months ago for the upcoming Memorial Day holiday.

"I want you to try to come up with anything that will help find these bastards," Dad growled.

"You know what I think of Manning," I responded, confirming my commitment. "Any word yet on the car?"

"No. The forestry service has promised to help find anyone that might have been hiking or biking in the area."

"Do you think they had a car waiting for them, or was it some unlucky bystander?"

He shrugged. "I hope it was waiting for them. Otherwise, someone else has probably been killed."

"If that's the case, then they were smart to take the body with them. If we had the owner of the car, then we'd know what kind of vehicle we're looking for."

"At this point, we need a little luck."

"If this was all planned, I say the finger points at Manning," I said.

"I agree, but we can't get tunnel vision on this one."

"How are you getting along with our friends from the government?" I nodded to where a group of U.S. Marshals and FBI agents had arrived.

"They're forming a joint task force. In theory, I'm a member." Dad frowned. "Unfortunately, this is their mess, so they get to take the lead."

"But they had to make the mess in our backyard," I sighed.

One of the dog handlers approached Dad. "We've circled the area a dozen times. I'm pretty sure your fugitives got into a vehicle and left the area. One or more acquired transportation here while one or more left from the first LKP we pinpointed."

I couldn't help wondering why they'd split up.

"That's what we figured," Dad told him. "I'm calling off the ground search. We'll get a helicopter to circle the area with their thermal image cameras tonight, just in case we're wrong and one of them is still out here somewhere." Dad looked over at the Feds. "Our part of the search will transition to patrol. We'll put out PSAs to the public and keep roadblocks on the roads out of the county."

The handler nodded. "We'll load up and get out of here, then. Give us a call if you get wind of your fugitives. My dogs would love to find them."

"The posse can call it a day," Dad said, sounding tired. He glanced at his watch. "There's a meeting of the task force in an hour."

"Have fun with that. I'll load up Finn and Mac and get them home for you."

"Thanks." He gave me a desultory wave as he headed over to the Feds.

CHAPTER FOUR

By the time I got Finn and Mac loaded in the trailer, I could smell the sweat and dirt that was caked to my clothes. I called my wife, Cara, as I drove toward Dad's place.

"All anyone is talking about is the escaped prisoners," Cara told me. The veterinary clinic where she worked was a hub for the local grapevine. "Is it true that Neil Manning was one of the prisoners?"

I filled her in on what we knew so far.

"If you let me know when you're coming home, I'll have some dinner waiting for you," she offered.

"Don't wait up. I should be home by nine, but anything could happen."

"Do you need anything?"

"I'm good. But what I *do* need is for you to be careful. With Manning loose, you need to be *very* careful. If someone could go home with you, that would be great."

"I'll be fine," she assured me.

"You could stay over at a friend's," I suggested.

"I need to get home and feed Ghost and Ivy."

I should have known that she'd be more worried about the animals. While our Pug, Alvin, spent most of his days with her at the vet as the clinic mascot, our two cats "starved" alone at home.

"Okay. Just remember to keep your car doors locked, and if there's *anything* odd or out of place at the gate or up at the house, stay in the car and call me or 911." I was glad that we'd finally spent the money to have an automatic gate installed. Getting out at the road to open the gate was one danger spot we'd eliminated.

"Don't worry. I'll be extra-super-special careful," she assured me, putting just the right amount of humor in her voice to let me know that I was being silly for telling her things she already knew. Of course, then she said, "*You* be careful. If Manning is loose…"

"Touché. We'll both be careful."

Once I got to Dad's, I unloaded the horses, fed them, brushed them down while they ate and put hay in their paddock before turning them out for the night. Then I begged a ride back to my car from Dad's wife, Genie, but not before she'd fed me a snack and insisted that I shower and change into some old clothes that I kept there.

It was past six by the time I was in my own car and headed for the office. I called Mick Klein and asked him to meet me as soon as I got there.

In my head, I played out all the possible ways my conversation with Mick could go. Mick was almost two decades my senior and had resented my promotion to sergeant. He and Lynn Lewis, another long-time investigator, had been demonstrating their passive resistance skills ever since I took over.

I hadn't been helped by Pete's absence. Originally, the plan had been that he would remain in CID for six months before moving over to our SWAT team, where he was taking over their sergeant's position. Now with his injuries, his future was up in the air, and I'd been without his help in settling in as the head of criminal investigations.

I was kicking myself for not yet having gone over Mick's personnel file. I had planned on reviewing the files for everyone in CID, just to bring myself up to speed, but I'd been sidetracked with other, more pressing issues. Part of the problem was that personnel files couldn't be removed from the human resources office. Five years earlier there had been a kerfuffle when private information from a deputy's records, specifically regarding treatment for depression, had been leaked to a defense attorney, who'd used it to undermine the deputy's testimony in a domestic battery trial. Since then, files weren't allowed to be transmitted electronically or to physically leave HR, meaning that if I wanted to go over the personnel files of the investigators I supervised, I had to set aside the time to read them in that office.

Water under the bridge now, I told myself as I pulled into the sheriff's office parking lot, which was almost full since we were running with all hands on deck.

Inside, I was surprised to find Pete working at his desk.

"I volunteered to come in while everyone is out hunting the prisoners," he said with a small smile. "If there are any reports you need me to work on, I'll be here."

"Good deal." I nodded. "I'll give you plenty of work."

As I opened my office door, I saw Mick Klein heading toward me. In his early fifties, he looked a little older. An extra twenty pounds had settled around his waist, but he still did well in the annual physical qualification tests required by the department. Hs clear brown eyes locked on mine as I waved him into the office.

I offered him one of the two chairs that faced my desk. The office was small, with only a few personal photos of Cara on the desk, but I still felt self-conscious about having a private office. I debated whether I should sit behind the desk or take the other chair next to Mick, but finally I chose to move behind the desk.

"What's this about?" Mick asked. His words were clipped and commanding, and I knew he was trying to take control of the situation. I was determined not to let him get away with it.

"That burglary report you submitted this morning. It's

not thorough enough. There were basic questions you left unanswered."

"I intend on following up."

"Then why submit the report now?"

Mick sighed and looked up at the ceiling. "Someone broke into the house and stole a jar with, according to the owner, less than fifty dollars in change and a cheap watch. No guns and nothing of real value was stolen. This is petty crime. I'll look into the case a little more and get back to you. If that's all?" He stood up.

"No, that's not all. This isn't the first report you've turned in that's been incomplete. I need you to do the work that I know you're capable of." As soon as the words left my mouth, I saw his face flush while he averted his eyes.

"You don't want to get into this now," he said menacingly.

"I just want you to do your job," I shot back, angry that *he* was angry.

I thought about the conference for frontline supervisors that I'd recently attended. The discussions of how to handle employees had made it sound easy. Not getting angry or escalating the situation was easy advice to give, but harder to follow when facing a recalcitrant subordinate.

"I do my job, for what little thanks I get. No one else is held to high standards around here," he mumbled.

"I don't see anyone slacking off." I was puzzled.

"What about your buddy out there?" He jabbed a finger toward the door.

"Pete?"

"If he'd done a better job executing a PIT Maneuver, he wouldn't be on light duty," Mick snapped.

I was caught off guard by this turn in the conversation. The Precision Immobilization Technique was taught to deputies as a way of stopping a target vehicle in a police chase.

"Come on. That's ridiculous," I said, keeping my voice low so that Pete wouldn't hear us. The last thing he needed was to think that people believed he'd failed in some way and caused his own injuries. "He couldn't get far enough ahead of her and time was running out. Besides, the PIT Maneuver isn't even recommended at speeds over thirty-five miles an hour. The review board cleared him of any wrongdoing."

"Was there ever a chance that the board *wouldn't* clear him?" Mick asked snidely.

"I'm not going to talk about Pete. This is about *your* work."

I saw him thinking about it and half expected him to quit right then and there. I was starting to think that his anger went deeper than resentment over my promotion.

Finally, he said, "I would put my work up against yours or your buddy's any day of the week." He took a deep breath before going on. "But you're the boss. I'll try and live up to your high standards."

I thought of a dozen snappy answers, but settled for a calm and measured, "Thank you."

Mick turned on his heel and left, closing the door only a little harder than necessary. Making time to sit down in human resources and read his personnel file moved way up my to-do list.

I had planned to put in some work reviewing reports and writing my own. Instead, after the confrontation with Mick, I decided that I should find Phil Eccles and bring him up to speed. I didn't want him to get blindsided if Mick filed a complaint against me or did something stupid because I'd called him out for his poor work performance. Phil was as new at being a lieutenant as I was at being a sergeant, but while I had zero experience as a supervisor, he'd been an acting sergeant many times before.

When I knocked on the door to Phil's office, I was greeted with a loud "Come in!"

"Wow!" I said, walking into the room and doing a double-take at the giant map of the county that he'd tacked up to the wall in his office.

"A friend of mine is a graphic artist, and he has a huge printer," Phil explained. "I got him to run this off and bring it by this afternoon when I got my assignment from the sheriff."

"What assignment? What do the numbers represent?" I asked, temporarily forgetting the reason for my visit as I looked at the dozen numbered pins stuck on the map.

"Your dad wanted me to check all the 911 calls and reports for the last twenty-four hours to look for anything that might point toward the fugitives." He gestured at the pins. "I found those years ago down in patrol. There were a couple of sets in different colors. Sergeant Kirby said that back in the day, they used the pins to track calls and patrol cars."

"And these are all the calls?" I asked, looking at a printout taped beside the map. Each event had a number beside it, which corresponded to a pin on the map. There were car thefts and burglaries, as well as calls about prowlers and trespassers.

"Yep. And so far, I haven't seen anything that jumps out at me or points to the escapees."

I told him about the missing persons case that Julio was working.

"Yep, I've got that one right here." He tapped some papers on his desk. "And I've marked his house with a yellow pin. Trouble is, we don't know where he disappeared from. That's why there's a yellow pin instead of a red one. Red's a priority incident." Phil went on to explain his whole system, then said, "Of course, the prisoners are probably long gone, or someone will just stumble onto them. Still, it's a good exercise."

We admired his work while he glanced from time to time at his computer monitor, which was showing a live feed of calls coming into our 911 dispatchers.

My phone buzzed with another update from Julio.

"Cortez is still missing. No one has had contact with him for at least twelve hours."

"Adults can go missing if they want," I said, not telling Julio anything he didn't already know. "We need a hook if we're going to get a warrant to enter his house or ping his phone."

"No one I've talked to knows anything about any health issues he might have. There are no signs of trouble around his house or at the bank. He's just not answering his phone and no one knows where he is, which everyone says is very unusual." Julio sounded frustrated.

"He wouldn't be the first guy to go off for a couple of days without telling anyone. Even people with responsible jobs and settled lives disappear occasionally for their own convoluted reasons." I was trying to convince myself as much as Julio. Not that our opinions mattered at this point. We had nothing a judge would consider probable cause.

"I've just got a feeling." Julio sounded like he expected me to give him some great words of wisdom, but I had none to give.

"If he still hasn't shown up in the morning, I'll meet up with you and we'll look into it some more."

"Sounds good."

I put the phone back into my pocket.

"I made sure that the watch commanders will hammer it home to patrol about all the vehicles with BOLOs out on them," Phil told me. "Our fugitives could be using any of them, including that of your missing person."

"For his sake, I hope he didn't run into them."

My phone went off again. This time it was a friend of mine with the Leon County Sheriff's Office who was one of their helicopter pilots.

"Weather looks like it will be good for us to go up and look around for your friends with our thermal imaging camera tonight. Want to come along?" Luke asked.

I should have told him I was busy, but I'd gone up with them a few times and every time it was a thrill.

"Give me forty-five minutes," I said, locking eyes with Phil, who nodded.

"You can help them focus on the best areas," Phil told me when I hung up. I didn't mention that, after they'd flown all over the area that morning, I doubted they needed my help.

"I almost forgot why I came down here. I want to talk to you about Mick." I didn't have a lot of time if I was going to get to the Tallahassee airport in forty-five minutes, but I needed to tell him what had happened.

"I noticed you were holding back his reports."

"Some have been… subpar. A burglary report this morning was the worst. When I called him on it, he got pretty steamed."

"Mick isn't an easy guy to get along with. I think he feels as though he's been passed over."

"I didn't even know he put in for the sergeant's position."

"I'm not sure he did," Phil said. "I think it's more general than that. He was a hotshot when he made CID after securing a major clue in a murder investigation. Now he's been sitting there doing burglary investigations for years."

"Normally he's great at it. His clearance rate is impressive."

"And that's probably what screwed him. He's been so effective in the position that no one wanted to move him up the ladder or give him more challenging tasks."

"So he's just dropping the ball?" I asked, frustrated.

"Maybe. Or, like all the rest of us, he's got a life away from the office. Could be problems at home or with his health. You're going to have to figure that out."

"Great." I turned to leave.

"One more thing. I've always gotten the feeling that Mick wasn't real happy when your father got elected sheriff. I know for a fact that when your dad was running the first time, Mick worked on the other guy's campaign."

"This just gets better and better." I shook my head. No one had told me any of this when I'd been encouraged to apply for the supervisor's job.

Before I got on the road to Tallahassee, I texted Cara to let her know about my evening plans, feeling only a little guilty for going off on what would basically be a joyride for me. Then I called Dad and asked him to text me any specific areas that we should concentrate on.

"More power to you. I hate flying in those things," Dad said emphatically. "One of them lost a rotor about a hundred feet off the ground and crashed near the Calhoun city limits. I was the first one to the wreckage."

"Thanks for that image," I said and hung up, though it didn't bother me. For some reason I'd always loved flying. Now the edge of a cliff was another matter. You couldn't pay me to walk to the edge of the Grand Canyon.

The weather at the airport was clear and warm as the helicopter drifted up off the skid they had used to transport it out of the hangar. As we flew, the trees hid many of the houses and streets, making Tallahassee look like a small town from the air. An orange-and-red sunset lit our way toward Adams County and the forest where the prisoners had escaped.

Sitting in the backseat and looking out the window, I felt lifted above all of my problems. Through the headphones, I only half listened to the chatter between Luke, who was piloting the craft, and an officer from the Tallahassee Police Department, who sat in the left-hand seat to work the camera.

"We have about an hour," Luke told me when we were over Adams County.

"Let's start from the site of the crash, then move out about a mile and do half circles covering the forest."

I could see the camera monitor from my position. The perspective took getting used to. The officer zoomed in and out on heat signatures with practiced ease and quickly dismissed objects before I even understood what I was looking at. Often his verdict was a small animal or a rotting log. The thermal images reminded me how many things give off a heat signature, including things that are rotting or going through any number of similar chemical processes.

The hour went by quickly, with only one moment when I thought we might be onto one of the fugitives. But it was only a black bear lumbering around a cypress pond.

Back at the airport, I thanked Luke for the flight and passed on his invitation to dinner. It was time to go home. I called Cara on the way.

"How's my flyboy?" she asked with a chuckle.

"I admit it was an indulgence on my part, but it was fun. Didn't find anything, though."

"Do you have to go back to the office?"

"No. My twelve hours are up, but I'm on call. That's going to be the case until these guys are caught. I checked in with Phil when we landed. No news yet."

"It's creepy knowing that there could be three crazy, desperate men wandering around the county."

"Particularly Neil Manning. With his grudge against me, you need to be extra careful."

"I'm looking at my gun as we speak," Cara assured me. She had made it a point to train regularly since I'd bought her the Glock 19.

"Glad to hear it. I wish I didn't have to leave you alone so much." The blackness beyond my headlights felt ominous tonight.

"I'm taking care of myself. You know, I worry about you as much as you worry about me."

"Convince Dad to buy a helicopter for the department and to pay for my flight training, then I'll be flying high above all the bad guys."

"I think that would come with its own set of concerns. I've seen you drive," Cara joked.

"I'd feel better if you could find someone to stay with you until Manning is caught. I'll be doing long hours and I don't like you being at home by yourself."

"I don't know who I could ask… Let me think about it,"

she promised.

When I got to the house, Cara met me at the door with a hug, then pointed toward the kitchen where a warm plate of red beans and rice with biscuits was waiting for me. I sat down at the table and tucked in eagerly.

"So I've had an idea who could stay with me," Cara said in a tone that made me nervous.

"Who?"

"Dad."

"*Just* your dad?"

"I think that's kind of the point. Dad sounded like he could use some time away from Mom."

"She's getting on *his* nerves?"

"I think Mom's feeling her age and over-compensating."

"Your mom does tend to run at red level most of the time," I said, savoring the rice and beans.

"She's doubled down on her charity work and... other things."

"Other things?"

"You don't want to know."

"Oh."

Anna Laursen sometimes fancied herself as a natural healer, somewhere between a Native American shaman and a Druid priest. The trouble was, she didn't care if some of her drugs were controlled substances or not. From what Cara had told me, they'd never lived in a house where there wasn't a pot plant or two within an easy stroll.

"Anyway, Dad thought a road trip would be good for him."

"You've already asked him?"

"No. We were talking last week and he asked about coming up for a couple of days. We just didn't talk about a date for the visit."

Henry Laursen was a little less Druid and a bit more Viking, over six feet tall and strong as an ox. I wouldn't mind knowing that he was there watching over Cara.

"Sounds good to me. If he's free."

Cara smiled. "I'll call him."

Henry was amendable and arrangements were made for him to come up from their home in Gainesville and be at our place by noon the next day.

CHAPTER FIVE

Much to my surprise, I managed to get several hours of uninterrupted sleep, but I still growled when the phone went off at six with its obnoxious wake-up noise. Cara gave me a push out of bed, then rolled over and went back to sleep as I headed for the bathroom.

After feeding all the animals, eating a bowl of microwave oatmeal and giving Cara a kiss as she pulled herself out of bed, I headed out to my car. Once there, I decided it was late enough to text Julio. The response came within a minute.

No word from Cortez. Do you want to meet at his house?

I can be there in twenty.

Roberto Cortez's house was nothing fancy, but it was so new that the landscaping had a just-planted look to it. Like most of the subdivisions in Adams County, of which there weren't many, this one was laid out with large lots of at least two or three acres between neighbors.

I parked at the curb just as Julio turned onto the street. By the time he parked, I'd looked in the mailbox and saw what appeared to be at least a day's worth of mail.

"Looks like one of the smaller homes in the subdivision," I said as Julio walked up to me.

"Still not cheap. Right now, in this neighborhood, maybe

three-ninety-five." Julio's wife was working on her real estate license, and he had a good handle on the current market.

I whistled. "And I thought this was a middle-class neighborhood."

"That *is* middle class."

"Now I know why I live in a trailer in the woods."

"You'd be surprised what you could get for your place," Julio said as I followed him up the driveway. "The house looks the same as it did yesterday."

"I guess no one gets the newspaper anymore," I said, looking at the empty lawn.

"All the doors and windows are secure." Julio waved toward the house as we walked up to the garage and around the corner of the house, where we found a window facing the lot next door. I peered inside. Two tracks of dirt on the pavement were the only signs that the garage had ever been used.

I slipped on a pair of gloves as we moved around the house, hoping that the act would magically produce some evidence for me to play with. It didn't work. The backyard was clean. No toys, no grill, not even a lawn chair.

"Our bank manager doesn't spend a lot of time in his yard," I observed.

"I spoke with that neighbor." Julio pointed to the house on the east side of Cortez's. "He told me that Cortez was a quiet guy. Came and went at regular hours. No noise at night or any parties on the weekend. Terrance, that's the neighbor, said he'd talked to Cortez a few times, mostly about hunting and fishing. Same thing his ex-wife told me. Those are his only hobbies."

"Nothing is in season around here. So maybe he went fishing."

"I called around to all the fish camps I could think of yesterday. I also alerted Fish and Wildlife to be on the lookout for his car in case it's parked at a boat ramp or on state property."

"More than one guy has gone fishing and failed to

return." I frowned. "Doesn't make a lot of sense in the middle of the week, though."

"Hiking after work, maybe?"

We had walked all the way around the house and hadn't seen anything out of the ordinary. In fact, we hadn't seen much at all. I could have been convinced that this was a model home for all the personal touches around it.

"I'd like to get inside," I mused, but we didn't have any more probable cause now than we'd had yesterday. Back at the front of the house, I looked up and down the street, wondering if any of the neighbors had a key.

"I'll canvas the neighbors and see if anyone has a key," Julio said, only slightly creeping me out.

"I don't know how much luck we'll have. He doesn't look like he's spent much time becoming friendly with the neighbors. Pick which side of the street you want."

"I did several of the houses on this side of the street. I know which ones I talked to and which ones weren't home," Julio said.

"Fair enough." I headed to the other side of the street. It was almost eight o'clock, so I figured most of the folks should be up and getting ready for work.

I knocked on ten doors and received more questions than answers. Everyone I talked to was concerned, not for Cortez, but for the safety of the neighborhood. To be fair, none of them had more than a passing acquaintance with him. Needless to say, no one had a key to his house or had heard or seen anything out of the ordinary in the past week.

Julio hadn't fared any better than I did.

"It's after nine. Let's go to the bank. I'd like to talk to his coworkers," I suggested, getting pulled into the case in spite of myself.

It was still quiet at the First Bank of Calhoun, with only a few cars in the lot and one or two more in the drive-thru. I parked and answered half a dozen texts before getting out of the car and joining Julio, who was standing by the door waiting for me.

"You might want to wrap something around your head to keep your jaw from hitting the floor," he said with a grin. "Just in case Catalina is here."

"Who?"

"Catalina Knight, the head teller. She looks like a movie star. Her name even sounds like one. She's... impressive."

I was surprised. Sure, we had deputies that commented on women, though these days most of the comments were respectful with only a hint of suggestiveness. However, Julio was happily married, and I'd never heard him make even a benign reference to an attractive woman.

"Keep your mind in the game," I said with a grin.

"You'll see." He waved me toward the door.

The lobby was neat and understated, a small-town bank projecting fiscal responsibility. I'd only been inside a dozen times, since Cara and I banked with the local credit union instead.

Julio walked over to one of the glassed-in offices. The man behind the desk stood up as soon as he saw us. Julio introduced me to Curtis Warner, the assistant manager. Well dressed in a tailored blazer and slacks, Warner looked less than ten years out of business school. His dark black hair was lightly gelled, and his eyes were friendly and open.

"Have you heard anything from Mr. Cortez?" Julio asked him.

Warner shook his head. "I was hoping you would have some news. This is very upsetting for all of us."

"Is there anyone here at the bank that he has a close relationship with?" I asked.

"Close? No. He's... aloof. No, that isn't the right word. I guess I'd just say that he's very business-like with all of us. Even when we go to lunch together, he talks about business, or sometimes hunting and fishing. I'm not much of an outdoorsy kind of guy, so we haven't really connected on a personal level." He shrugged apologetically.

I caught movement out of the corner of my eye and turned to see an absolutely stunning woman approach us.

Julio had been right about Catalina Knight. She was slender with bright blue eyes, flowing chestnut hair and the lithe movements of a dancer. Her smile was captivating, but it turned to a concerned frown as she approached us.

"I'm sorry, but I just had to come over and ask if you've found out anything about Mr. Cortez?"

"They haven't," Warner told her, and her frown deepened.

"I don't know him personally, but this is so unlike him that I'm sure something awful has happened."

"I've talked to his family and they agree with you." Julio leaned toward her like a moth to a flame. "But they all live out of town and couldn't help us locate anyone local who might know where he might be."

"Do *you* know of anyone at the bank that he may have connected with personally?" I asked Catalina.

She shook her head. "No. But I know he likes hunting."

"Who else at the bank hunts?" I asked.

"I guess a few people," Warner said. "Amy hunts with her husband. She always wants a couple of days off in the fall when deer season starts. And Bert, our head of security, does a lot of hunting."

"Can we talk with them?"

"Sure. Here, you can use this office. It's empty." He led us over to one of the glass cubicles, then hurried off.

A few minutes later, Warner brought over Amy Galvin and introduced her. Amy was close to fifty with short brown hair and a motherly appearance.

"Is it true that Mr. Cortez is missing?" she asked as soon as Warner had left.

"We haven't been able to locate him," Julio admitted. "When was the last time you saw him?"

"Day before yesterday. He was here all day. I was working loans."

"You're a loan officer?"

"I've been with the bank for fifteen years and have held several positions. I have a daughter who has... some problems. Occasionally, I need time off to take care of her and my granddaughter, so I just fill in where they need me. The bank has been very good to me."

"How well do you know Mr. Cortez?"

"He's my boss and he's only been here about a year… I mean…" She looked apologetic.

"You hunt?" Julio asked, causing her to look confused. "We just thought that you and Mr. Cortez might have… you know, bonded as friends over a shared hobby."

She smiled. "Honey, hunting isn't a hobby to my family. We eat a lot of venison. Mr. Cortez and I *have* talked about hunting a few times, but there's a world of difference between what we do and what he does."

"What do you mean?"

"To him, hunting is a sport. Almost like the TV shows. You know, an extreme this or extreme that. He goes out hunting during bow season with a recurve bow, and during regular hunting season he told me he's taken a deer at five hundred yards with his rifle. He's even shown me a picture of some of his rifles. Those things cost more than my car. Since he's been here, he's gone on a hunting trip to Alaska and another one to Canada. My family just walk out into our woods and climb a tree stand, or go two miles up the road to our hunt club."

"So the differences in your hunting styles haven't left you much to talk about," I said.

"Not that he's snooty about it. He's very nice and has seemed genuinely interested in where we hunt. He's always asked how I did when he's known that I'd been out."

"Has he ever talked about his friends?"

Amy looked thoughtful. "I get the feeling he likes to be alone. I've never heard him talk about hunting with friends. When he's talked about his trips, he's made it sound like it's just him and maybe a guide."

We went over the usual questions about how Cortez had been acting and if she had seen anyone strange hanging around the bank, but she had nothing else useful to tell us.

Next, we moved on to the security guard.

Bert Hodges looked like he was seventy even though in reality he wasn't yet sixty. His face was drawn and worn, and he couldn't have weighed more than a hundred and thirty pounds. When he walked, it looked like his knees were straining to carry even his light frame.

"I used to be with the Calhoun police," he explained. "Gettin' in and out of a patrol car all those years ruined my knees and back."

We told him to sit, and he groaned a little as he eased down into a chair.

"Mr. Warner told us you do some hunting," I said, wondering how he was able to get out in the woods.

"Yep, only thing I can still enjoy. Takes me a while, but there's nothin' that makes me feel better than bein' out in the woods on a cool day. What do you care about my huntin'?"

"We're looking for Mr. Cortez and everyone says he likes hunting," I answered. "We thought you might have talked to him about it."

"Can't figure him goin' missin'. He's one of those A-personality types. Always runnin' at a hundred and ten percent. Nice enough. At least he knows my name and has even asked my opinion about the security here at the bank."

"So you've talked?"

"Just small talk. He's into what I call adventure huntin'. Not like most of the folks around here. I saw you were talkin' to Amy. She and I just hunt for the pleasure of bein' outdoors and the food it provides. I've never shot a deer at more than seventy-five yards. Mr. Cortez showed me pictures of a couple of his high-end rifles. I shoot a .30-06 like most folks around here. But his rifles are fancy calibers. The rounds cost probably four or five dollars each!" He looked at us. "What's this have to do with him goin' missin'? Nothin's in season now. Only thing you might do this time of year is tend to your feed plot or set up game cams."

"We're just trying to find out if he has any friends. We need to get into his house," Julio explained.

"I see." Bert looked thoughtful. "No, I've never heard him talk about anyone outside of work, not even a woman. I heard he has an ex-wife, but he's never talked about her. A real serious guy. He's the type of boss that's not goin' to be your friend, but you can respect him. Which is fine with me."

"Do you have any suggestions on how we can find him?" I asked.

"Have you looked around his office?"

"Mr. Warner let me in there yesterday. I couldn't find anything useful," Julio said.

"Maybe we'll take another look," I suggested.

"Yeah, nothin' much in his office but travel pictures. If you want, I'll review the security footage for the last week. See if there's anythin'… odd."

"That would be helpful. If you could make a copy for us, we'd appreciate it. At the very least, save the data."

"No problem there. Not like the old days where they filmed over the footage every week. Now everything is uploaded to a central server or somethin'. They say they even have backups of the data offline."

"I noticed you work for Silver Security?" I said, nodding toward the patch on the sleeve of his shirt.

"Yeah. A couple years back, the bank contracted their security from Silver. Part of the deal was they would keep on us old-timers. Nice of the bank, and Silver Security has been good to me. Better insurance than I had. Plus they upgraded all the cameras, locks and security procedures."

"Let's take another look at Cortez's office," I said.

"Sure. I'll ask Mr. Warner, but if he let Deputy Ortiz in yesterday, then I don't think he'll have a problem with it."

We followed Bert out of the office and Warner came over to join us.

"They'd like to take a look at Mr. Cortez's office," Bert told him.

"Of course, not that anything has changed since yesterday."

"I'd just like to see it for myself. Different sets of eyes see different things," I told him.

"No problem." He turned to Bert. "I'll show it to them."

"I'll get that footage for you." Bert gave us a half salute and left us with Warner.

Cortez's office was twice the size of Warner's and those of the other bank officials. Along one wall there were three bookcases filled with various binders. Against the opposite wall stood a table and three chairs. His desk was of finely worked oak and a higher quality than the other furniture I'd seen in the bank. Behind it was a modern office chair that would have looked more at home on a spaceship than a bank manager's office. All of the pictures in the room were of Cortez doing various outdoor activities: hiking, hunting, fishing or horseback riding. About half of them had other people who looked to be guides. None of the pictures showed Cortez embracing or even standing next to another person.

I moved in and studied one of the pictures that looked recent. Cortez was holding a recurve bow and standing next to a ten-point buck. His eyes seemed to be looking through the lens of the camera and toward whatever his next adventure was going to be. His skin was a rich olive color and highlighted his strong, rugged features. Still youthful, his face was accented with lines around his eyes and across his forehead.

What's he doing at a bank in little old Calhoun? I wondered. He seemed better suited to being a world explorer.

Warner gave us permission to look through Cortez's desk with a warning that any bank records were off limits and would require a warrant if we wanted to look at them. The desk held nothing personal except an extensive store of vitamins and supplements in the bottom drawer.

"I'm sorry, but I can't help you search his computer. In theory, everything on it would be business-related. I can tell you that he carried a personal laptop with him when he came to work," Warner said.

Having found nothing of importance, we thanked the assistant manager as he walked us to the door. I caught sight of Catalina working behind the teller's window and thought of Roberto Cortez. If Adams County had ever held a competition for best-looking residents, they would have been shoo-ins for the top honors.

CHAPTER SIX

By the time I got back into my car, I had a dozen texts and a couple of voicemails waiting for me. I sighed and decided they could wait until I got to the office, which was only five blocks away. On the way, I listened closely to the calls over the radio to see who was doing what at the start of our second day of twelve-hour shifts. There were no hot leads on the fugitives.

At the office, everyone looked animated. Deputies like to be the good guys, and having some designated very bad guys running around the county had everyone focused. Most days we just dealt with the usual suspects, but this felt different. Adding to the sense of urgency was the fact that we all knew what a bad actor Neil Manning was.

Pete was hunched over a monitor when I entered CID. He looked happier than he'd been in weeks. The mental health benefits of working on a job he loved were obvious. He gave me a quick smile and a wave as I headed to my office to deal with all of my messages and waiting reports.

An hour later, with most of the overnight reports assigned and submitted reports read, I got up to check in with Phil Eccles. Like everyone else, I wanted to be on point in the hunt for the three fugitives. On the way to his office, I saw Jan Tennant, the head of our human resources department, walking down the hall.

"I need to come down and look at a file," I told her.

"Anytime," she said with a smile. "If I'm not there, Brad will be."

"Thanks. I'll be there as soon as I'm done talking to Phil."

Phil had heard my approach from the other side of his door and called out for me to come in. Apparently, someone else had heard me too. When I walked into the office, a black shadow the size of a mountain slammed into me. Only my hand on the doorknob kept me from hitting the floor. It was Mauser, my father's one-hundred-and-ninety-pound, four-year-old monster of a Great Dane.

The beast bounded out into the hall, scattering a few unwary passersby, then swung back for another pass at me. I managed to fend him off, receiving only minor damage to my ears when he let out a seismic woof. Then he settled on top of my feet, demanding ear rubs while I chastised him for almost killing me. Again.

"What are you doing here?" I asked the dog.

"Your dad asked me to keep an eye on him," Phil answered.

"I'm usually the one who gets saddled with babysitting duties."

"He'd convinced the Feds to come to his office for a meeting, but one of the guys was terrified at the site of Mauser. When the guy started to look like he was going to cry, your dad got worried that he might shoot Mauser, so he asked me to keep an eye on him. And just so your feelings won't be hurt, he did check to see if you were in the building before he asked me to do it."

I moved into the office and sat down as Mauser continued to slobber all over my clothes. "Better you than me."

Phil shrugged. "I like the big goof. Even more so now that I know he has the power to repel some of the Feds."

"How's the taskforce going?"

"As you'd expect. They share nothing with us and demand that we give them everything we have. One of them actually said that our deputies should report directly to him if they uncover any leads."

"I bet Dad took that well."

"He said… Let me see if I can get the exact quote… He appreciated their willingness to clean up their colossal screwup that allowed three dangerous men to run loose in his county, but that he doesn't trust them to find their own asses with both hands. He went on to say that if they want information from us, they'll have to share theirs. Finally, he told them that if they continue to disrespect his deputies, then he'll have no choice but to get the governor's office involved."

"That's my dad. They don't call him Mr. Diplomacy for nothing."

Phil chuckled. "Of course, it was all just a pissing match. After that, the tension meter remained in the red, but everyone settled down to business."

"Any updates?" I looked at the map on the wall where a dozen more pins had joined the ones from the day before

"Just tips. Lots of folks are keeping their eyes out for them, which is good, but it's running patrol ragged chasing all the leads. And the bad guys are probably already out of the area, if not the state."

"Guess that wouldn't break my heart except for the part where Manning gets away," I said honestly.

"I know. The Feds have been riding Rudy Manning hard. Anything he could use to communicate with his son—Wi-Fi, cell phone, land line, apps—everything is being monitored. Even your dad was impressed with their level of coverage on Manning. They've also scoped out the relatives of the other two fugitives and put bugs and tails on them."

"That's the kind of power we don't have."

"And why your dad didn't actually kick them out of his office," Phil said.

"And why he didn't defend your right to stay in his office," I told Mauser, who answered with a whiny sigh.

We talked for a few minutes, then, as I was getting up to leave, Phil reminded me, "Go down now and look over Mick's personnel file. You need to deal with that situation before it blows up into a bigger problem."

"That's next on my list," I assured him, then headed to human resources where I found Jan at her desk.

"What was it you needed?" she asked, turning away from her monitor.

"I need to see Mick Klein's file."

She pulled out a log and had me sign it, then said, "There's a paper file and an electronic one. You can sit at that desk over there." Then she turned to her assistant, Brad, who stood at a file cabinet, sorting through paperwork. "Would you go get Mick Klein's file while I pull up the electronic one for Sergeant Macklin?"

"No prob." Brad made me look old. I'd thought he was a high-school intern the first time I saw him in the office.

I settled down at the desk with the files and started to review them. With personnel files, it was important to read between the lines. While this was the first file I'd gone through in my role as a supervisor, as an investigator I'd looked at dozens of personnel files from various companies and organizations over the years, some for victims and some for suspects. If you knew what to look for, you could dig up some valuable information.

Mick's full name was Michael Hamelin Klein. He'd been born on May 10, 1968, in New Jersey, moved to Florida as a kid and went to high school in Cocoa Beach. He'd received a criminology degree from the University of South Florida in 1990 with a respectable GPA. From there he'd gone to the law enforcement academy. The file included letters of recommendation from three of his instructors at the academy, all glowing. He'd passed all of his courses without a hitch and finished in the upper ten percent of his class.

He'd been hired by the department straight out of the

academy in 1991. Dill Kirby had been his FTO. The only notes in the file from that time indicated that he was occasionally overzealous and reluctant to pass cases on to the investigators.

There was one other note after he'd finished his probation. A lieutenant had been upset that Mick had gone around him, and Mick had been given a one-day suspension, which wasn't much more than a slap on the wrist. Using my reading-between-the-lines skills, I decided that the suspension was mainly to appease the lieutenant's ego.

Almost all his evaluations were excellent, and he'd had an interesting transfer to CID. He'd been commended for his work on something referred to as "the Simmons murders" and, as a result, had been recommended for the next open investigator position, which he'd received. I couldn't remember Dad ever mentioning the Simmons case; though looking at the date, it would have occurred during my late teens when I wasn't paying much attention to him anyway. I made a note to look into it later, as much out of curiosity as anything, though it could give me more insight into Mick's behavior.

There was nothing else in his file of particular note. He had the normal amount of citizen complaints, but every deputy had a few. They had all been cleared by the internal affairs committee. Satisfied that I'd learned all I could from the files, I returned them to Jan with thanks.

On the way back to my office I thought of other avenues I could pursue in my quest to learn more about Mick. One was to talk to Lynn Lewis, our key investigator for sex crimes. Lynn and Mick were tight. Unfortunately, she didn't seem to respect me any more than Mick did. Having to deal with all of the office politics and personal feelings had been the main reason I hadn't been sure if I'd even wanted the promotion to sergeant. *I guess the next six months will tell if I'm cut out for the job*, I thought.

The other avenue I wanted to explore was to talk with someone outside the department who might know something about Mick. Local historian Albert Griffin maintained a physical archive of the county's history in the form of the morgue belonging to the now-defunct Calhoun paper, and he also possessed a sharp memory for all things Adams County. I'd stop by his place as soon as I had the chance.

When I got back to my office, Julio met me at the door.

"Any word on Cortez?" I asked.

"His sister called. She's going to drive up from Tampa. I asked her to go through all her texts with him since he moved here and to make a note of any names he might have mentioned."

"Good idea. Maybe he used a guide when he went hunting around here," I suggested.

"Who're you talking about?" Pete's ears had perked up at the mention of hunting and we filled him in on the missing man.

"Go talk to Hammer," Pete told us. "If your man is a big-time hunter then he's probably dropped in at Hammer's shop and used his services."

"I should have thought about that," I said, mentally kicking myself. Hammer was David Hamm, one of the owners of Fish and Game Sports Shop and the best gunsmith in the county. His partner Trey Carter covered the fishing part of the shop.

"Let's drive over there," I suggested to Julio, though I knew I was just trying to avoid dealing with, or even thinking about, the conflict with Mick.

Fish and Game Sports Shop was one of four storefronts in a small strip mall south of town, on the way to the largest lake and best bass fishing in the county. The interior of the shop smelled of oil and old wood. A few customers were milling about and looked up at me and Julio as the bell above the door announced our arrival.

Hammer, who was built like a bank vault, was eyeing a

double-barrel shotgun while a tall, lanky man stood on our side of the counter and watched him.

"Firing pin on the left side is broken. I'll tear it down, clean it and let you know if it needs anything else."

"Fix anything that's wrong," the customer said. "It's been sitting in my father's closet for twenty-five years."

They exchanged a few more pleasantries before the man left with a claim ticket in hand.

"What can I do for the law?" Hammer asked us with a smile.

"We're looking for this man." Julio stepped forward, holding out his phone with a picture of Cortez.

"I know him." Hammer sounded surprised. "Did he do something wrong?"

"No. He's missed work and his friends and family are worried about him," Julio explained.

"Yeah, not the kind of guy to just go missing," Hammer agreed.

"What can you tell us about him?" Julio asked.

"Sure, he's come in a dozen times or more. I'm building him a rifle. Nice guy. Likes expensive guns. Takes good care of them too. You'd be surprised how rare that is around here. Mostly we get the usual mix of hunters and shooters, nothing fancy, just functional. When we do get high-end guns, they're owned by folks who have more money than sense and don't take care of them."

"But not Cortez?"

"No. He has top-of-the-line hunting rifles and shotguns, knows how to use them and maintains them beautifully."

"Does some fishing too," added a voice from the back of the shop. Trey Carter came out of the workroom and stood beside Hammer. Trey was short and lean, making him look like a child next to Hammer's bulk. "You say he's missing?"

"Hasn't shown up for work since Monday," Julio said. The two men looked at each other. "You know where he might be?"

"We gave him a few places to scout when he stopped by

Monday afternoon." Hammer sounded concerned. "Nothing way, way out in the forest or anything. Just some rumors we'd heard about spots with good-size bucks and a couple of bears. He's hoping to get one of the bear tags this year."

"How was he acting on Monday?" Julio asked.

"Same as usual. Intense. He takes his hunting very seriously. I'll tell you the truth: it took him coming in here a few times before I warmed up to him."

"Because he's serious about hunting?" I asked, a little puzzled.

"Most of our customers are from around here. You know, downhome folks. But Cortez definitely wasn't," Hammer explained. "At first, I thought he was stuck up. We get customers who think they know everything. Usually, they're just YouTube experts who think that having the money to buy the most expensive guns makes them an authority. But after talking with Cortez for a while, I figured out that he wasn't faking it. He knows his guns and he knows more than most people about hunting."

"Knows a helluva lot about fishing too. Kind of nice to have a customer who's interested in more than having a fast bass boat and a cooler full of beer," Trey chimed in.

"Did he seem worried about anything the last time you saw him?" Julio asked.

"Nope," they said in unison.

"Did he mention taking any trips?"

"Oh, sure, he's always planning hunting and fishing trips. I think he's planning to go out to Idaho this summer."

"That's right, to do some trout fishing," Trey added.

"But nothing in the near future?"

"No, the trip to Idaho is August. That's when the best trout fishing is. He said he already has his guide lined up," Hammer said.

"Where are these places you told him to scout out for deer and bear?" I asked.

Hammer went over to a metal desk piled high with old paperwork, a monitor and keyboard, as well as assorted tools and parts. From the top of a pile, he grabbed a bound volume of geological survey maps. I could see dozens of Post-It Notes sticking out from the edges of maps.

He set the book of maps on the counter and flipped through four or five pages before stopping and tapping on a spot. Next to it was a note that a nine-point buck had been sighted in the spot a month earlier. It took a minute for me to find landmarks on the map that told me the site was ten miles outside of town.

Hammer flipped through the book, showing us a few more spots that he'd pointed out to Cortez. When he flipped to the fourth map, I recognized the area immediately. My blood grew cold as Hammer pointed to a spot on the map that couldn't have been more than a hundred yards from where the hounds had lost the second trail. Julio and I looked at each other.

"Thanks for your help. We've got what we need," I told Hammer.

"I've got one more," he said, sounding confused as we waved and headed for the door.

I assured him that we didn't need to see it and thanked him again for his time.

"Not good," I said to Julio once we were outside, pulling out my phone.

"Who are you calling?"

"Dad. Then he can call the FBI and the U.S. Marshals," I said.

Dad answered on the third ring, and I filled him in on what we knew.

"Good work. I'm afraid it doesn't bode well for Mr. Cortez." I heard the concern in his voice.

"Julio is texting you the information on Cortez's car now."

"I'll take it from here. Don't be surprised if you hear from the men in black."

CHAPTER SEVEN

Five minutes later my phone rang. It was Special Agent Redcliff instructing Julio and me to meet Agent Padilla at the FBI's command center sooner rather than later. I was surprised when he told me that they were at the city's police station.

The first thing I saw when I pulled in was Darlene Marks, Calhoun's chief of police and my former partner, leaning against the back of her police SUV and staring at the FBI's command RV that was taking up the majority of her small parking lot.

"What's up, Junior?" she greeted me with a half smile. "See what your pa has done to me? Had to get all up in their grill, so now they're squatting on my land." Her cowboy impression was quite good, except for one thing.

"Do cowboys really say 'all up in their grill?'" I asked.

Darlene rolled her eyes. "I'm sure they do these days. Look at that." She pointed to a black cable plugged into the RV and running up to an outlet on the outside of the police station. "How much is that going to cost me?"

Redcliff came around from the back of the command center, waving toward us.

"We're being summoned," I told her.

"What'd you do?"

"We might have a lead on the bad guys they let loose," I said over my shoulder, loud enough for Redcliff to hear.

"Good for you," Darlene said and gave me a small salute.

"Inside," Redcliff said like a goon working for the Mob. He nodded toward the door.

"We need everything you have on Roberto Cortez," Padilla said without preamble when she saw us.

"It's Julio's case," I said, gesturing for him to step in front of me.

A little nervously, Julio gave them all the details he'd gathered so far, ending with, "We will write up the request for the warrant to search his—"

"Done," Padilla said, cutting him off. "We should have the data from his cell phone shortly and are working on a warrant for his car if we find it."

The words were barely out of her mouth when Redcliff's phone buzzed.

"His carrier just sent us the pings for his phone," he told Padilla, doing his best to ignore us.

I couldn't help but be impressed at how quickly they'd gotten the information.

"Nelson is analyzing it now."

Redcliff moved over to a monitor. With a flick of the mouse, the FBI logo disappeared from the screen and a login page appeared. Soon, Redcliff was looking at a map and the image of the aforementioned Nelson in a chat box. After swapping several messages back and forth with Nelson, Redcliff became noticeably excited.

Padilla looked over his shoulder.

"Son of a bitch," she muttered. "Now we know where the phone is. Let's just hope it's wherever *they* are."

"How can you be so sure?" I asked. Most ping data provided only a general location for a phone.

"We got some data from one of the apps on Cortez's phone," Redcliff answered, making it clear that he thought I was a very dull student.

"There's no guarantee that Cortez was carjacked by the fugitives," I pointed out, receiving a frown from Padilla. "Why would they take him? If they stumbled on him in the forest, why wouldn't they just kill him and take the car?"

"If they left the body, then we would have known hours earlier what kind of car they were in," Padilla answered, making me feel like an idiot when I remembered that I'd made the same argument to Dad only yesterday. Then she added, sounding almost complimentary, "If it wasn't for you all tracking down Cortez's last known location, it might have worked for them."

"Where are the U.S. Marshals?" I asked.

"They're tracking a lead we got earlier," Padilla said, dismissing their absence. Then she snapped at Redcliff, "We need a team."

He already had his phone out. "I've got Randel on standby."

"So where *is* the phone?" I asked innocently.

Padilla looked reluctant to tell me, but I could see the wheels turning in her head. She didn't want us involved, but on the other hand, she needed local intel.

"Your father's an ass," she finally said.

"He has his moments." I smiled.

Padilla took out her phone and showed me a map. "You can follow us out there on one condition."

"Which is?"

"This is an FBI operation."

"Understood. My main concerns are rescuing Cortez if he's still alive and recapturing Manning."

"We'll take into consideration any hostages being held by the fugitives when we move in." Padilla started strapping on body armor. "I guess there's no way you aren't going to tell your dad."

"Nope."

"Redcliff, inform the sheriff's office where we'll be and tell them to stand off. If they give you any grief, tell them that Sergeant Macklin is with us and... What's your name?"

she asked Julio.

"Deputy Ortiz," he answered.

"Got that?" she asked Redcliff, who was already calling our watch commander.

My phone rang before we were out the door. It was Dad and he wasn't happy.

"There's not much you can do," I reminded him and received a growl in return. "You've been spending too much time with Mauser."

"If Cortez has been murdered, it's our case," Dad said emphatically.

"I'll tell Padilla. Maybe it won't come to that."

"Maybe. If he was carjacked by these men, then he'll need prayer and lots of it."

"I've got to go," I said, watching Julio as he rooted for gear in the back of his car.

"Keep your head down and keep me informed," Dad said and hung up. I knew he wanted to come out to the scene, but he wouldn't give Padilla the satisfaction of ordering him around. In the end, they would both just say things they'd regret later.

"Get your plates," I told Julio as I dug around in the truck of my own car. "We don't know what kind of firepower these guys have." Kevlar was fine against nine-millimeter handguns and knives, but it wouldn't stop a high-velocity rifle round. For that, you needed a solid steel plate which was heavy, but effective.

Cortez's phone was reported to be in an old house on a dirt road at the edge of a wildlife management area. We parked a mile down the road from the house and the FBI's tactical squad arrived within minutes.

"We're going to fly our drone close to the house and assess the situation," Agent Randel, commander of the squad, told Padilla.

Images from the drone showed Cortez's SUV partially hidden under some rusted pieces of tin roofing, a ripped blue tarp and several pieces of pine-tree deadfall. All appeared quiet and still outside the mold-green, concrete block structure. My guess was that the house had been meant for farmworkers, cheaply built and poorly maintained.

"I don't want to do anything that will alert them," Randel said, barking his words like a drill sergeant on the parade ground.

"Everyone should remember that Mr. Cortez could be alive and being held hostage," I said, and received deadeye stares from the assembled agents.

"We're aware of the situation," Randel snapped.

"Macklin's right. Care should be taken to protect any bystanders," Padilla said, surprising me.

"The civilian," Randel growled, holding up a picture of Cortez on his phone and showing it to the members of his squad. He flipped through some other images and held the phone up again. "Neil Manning, bad guy." He swiped the phone again. "Lester Stevens, bad guy." Then one more swipe. "Doyle Waugh, bad guy. I've sent you all the photos. Don't shoot the good guy."

Randel glared at me like it was unreasonable for me to ask them to not shoot the hostage, then continued, "My team is going in first. I'll signal when we have secured and cleared the location. Then, and *only* then, is anyone else authorized to approach the scene. Is that understood?" Not only did he look at Julio and me, but his eyes swung over to Redcliff and Padilla, who answered with curt nods.

Randel's squad consisted of eight men with enough firepower to take on a German Panzer division. They moved off at a trot down the dirt road and we were left with an ariel view supplied by the drone.

"He's a charmer," I said, nodding at the monitor where Randel could be seen gesturing for the squad to slow down as they got closer to the house.

"Randel knows his job." Padilla kept her eyes on the monitor. Just when I thought she wasn't going to say more, she added, "He's a prick, but he runs a tight squad."

A second monitor suddenly lit up with multiple images.

"Cameras are on." Randel's voice came from the monitor where most of his squad were streaming their bodycams.

"Roger that. Cameras are working," said the tech sitting in front of the monitors.

We watched as the squad took its time approaching the block house. The dusty and cobweb-covered windows were all intact. The men hunkered down when they each had a clear view of a different part of the structure, with about fifty feet of open ground all around it.

Randel waited for an all-clear from each of his team before signaling them to move forward. One of the men had to walk past where Cortez's SUV was partially concealed, and he cleared it as he moved toward the house. From what I could see, the vehicle wasn't damaged and there were no signs that it had been involved in anything violent. I said a little prayer for Cortez.

Once all of the agents were crouched next to the building there was another pause. We heard Randel ask each of his team if they detected any movement or sound from inside. All of the responses were negative.

Randel counted down before giving the signal to breach the doors. There was a wild flurry of movement that was impossible to follow on the monitors. I cursed when we heard shots ring out—first a blast that sounded like a shotgun and then half a dozen sharp bangs from the FBI rifles.

Ten minutes later, Randel gave the all-clear.

"Area is secure. We have two dead in the house. Lester Stevens was DOA. Doyle Waugh posed a threat which was neutralized, resulting in the fugitive's death. Agent Marcos has been shot, but not seriously. And I'm sorry to report that a third body was discovered in the rear of the stolen SUV. It appears to be that of Roberto Cortez."

As the FBI began to deal with the aftermath, I called Dad and filled him in on what had happened, including the fact that Neil Manning was still on the loose.

"You have my support to assert our jurisdiction over Mr.

Cortez's murder." He took a deep breath. "Of course, I won't let any squabbling compromise the murder investigation. I just think we're the best office to do the job."

"I don't think they're going to fight us over it. They're going to be focused on the agent-involved shooting and looking for any clues that might lead to Manning and whoever helped with the escape."

"Keep me informed. If I need to be on scene, let me know."

It was another half hour before Julio and I were allowed to drive up to the house, along with Padilla and the rest of her team. No one looked happy. The FBI could count. Two dead fugitives left one still on the loose.

Once we were parked outside the house, we were told to wait again while the FBI brought in their crime-scene techs. The shooting of and by their agents added another layer to an already complicated web of multijurisdictional investigations.

"Looks like trouble in paradise," Julio said, nudging me as we leaned against the hood of my car. A contingent of U.S. Marshals had arrived and a pair of them were taking turns arguing with Padilla and Randel.

Finally, we were told that we could don our PPE gear and survey the scene. The heat and humidity made this a miserable experience, but it would only get worse. In another month, heat exhaustion would become a concern for everyone at a crime scene.

Julio and I stuck close to Padilla as Randel escorted us over to Cortez's SUV. A crime scene tech was taking pictures while another shot video. I wished that Shantel and Marcus were doing the work, but there were a number of reasons why that wouldn't work. First, Padilla would never allow it. While a murder in our county was our jurisdiction, the federal loophole was that Cortez had likely been kidnapped by the escaped prisoners. Kidnappings were the FBI's jurisdiction. Second, it was never a good idea to divide a crime scene into multiple jurisdictions. That was a perfect recipe for things to get lost and screwed up. Since the inside of the house was clearly a matter for the FBI, with two of their agents involved in a shooting with an escaped federal prisoner, it made sense to let them collect all the evidence in and around the house.

What I *was* going to insist upon was that Dr. Darzi should do the autopsy on Cortez. If the FBI insisted on doing their own, then I wanted Darzi to perform a second one.

"We'll have a 3D image of the full crime scene taken before anything is moved," Padilla told Randel. "Where are the men who were involved in the shooting?"

"I've sent them back to the command center to be debriefed. We've secured their body cams and equipment. Marcos had a few minor injuries from shotgun pellets, so we'll send him on to the hospital to be cleaned up and checked out."

"Good."

Staying out of the way of the techs, we took a look at Cortez's body folded into the rear of his Mercedes.

"It looks like someone shot him with a shotgun while he was in the vehicle," I said.

"Not a bad way of preventing blood and evidence from being scattered," Padilla said. "Shoot the suspect inside and most of the mess stays in the car, which would be tainted anyway. We've seen this with professional hits."

"Our fugitives weren't smart, but they were experienced criminals," Randel said. "Waugh used a shotgun today, could be the same one. Ballistics won't be much good, but we can analyze the shotgun pellets and any shells we find to see if the ammo is similar."

"I'd like our coroner to do the autopsy," I said, and Padilla and Randel stared at me.

Finally, Randel said, "Cortez, yes. Not Waugh or Stevens."

I wasn't surprised that they would insist on overseeing the Waugh autopsy since one of their men had shot him.

"That's all I'm asking." I held up my phone. "I'd like to bring them in now to see the body *in situ*."

I thought Padilla was going to balk, but she nodded. "The only condition is that our techs are present when the body is taken out of the vehicle in order to document the scene and any evidence that's found."

I called the coroner's office and asked for Dr. Darzi. After I explained the situation, he agreed to send a team out to collect the body.

"You always have the most interesting situations," he said, and I could practically hear his bemused smile over the phone.

CHAPTER EIGHT

Next, we headed for the house. Outside the door were boxes containing hazmat suits.

"Only one of you can come into the house," Padilla told us. "We found drugs. Meth for sure, and possibly mixed with fentanyl. Anyone entering has to put on full hazmat gear."

This sort of thing was becoming more common. Dad had brought in experts to train all our deputies on what to look for when entering a structure. If there were any warning signs of fentanyl, we were to exit immediately and call in a hazmat team to check things out. Even transfer contact with fentanyl could be dangerous.

"That's fine. I'll let Julio go in." I nodded to Julio, who looked less than thrilled about this particular tour.

I stood outside the house and watched as the techs worked. I couldn't complain about their thoroughness, and I knew they had many more resources to draw upon than our department. Still, I wanted to be the one sifting through the evidence. Somewhere could be a clue to Manning's whereabouts, and the sooner we found him, the better.

Following a safe trail marked out by the techs, I retraced my steps to Cortez's SUV. I couldn't touch anything until Darzi's folks arrived, but I wanted to look over the scene again.

Who killed Cortez? Was it one of the two fugitives who were dead in the house? Was it Neil Manning? Or was it whoever was helping Manning? And did this sort of violence rule out Rudy Manning as an accomplice for his son? I couldn't see him as a cold-blooded killer, but then again, I didn't believe that he'd been hands-on in his son's escape either. Rudy Manning ran a large trucking business that worked in half a dozen southern states. He could find muscle if he needed it.

"Shouldn't think this one is going to take much of your Sherlockian deductive powers."

I turned to see Linda from the coroner's office standing behind me.

"You're here already?" I knew it was at least forty minutes from the hospital to where we were standing.

"We were on the interstate near the Calhoun exit when Dr. Darzi told us you had a body. I already got the scoop from one of the FBI agents. Sounds like the bad guys are dead too."

"I don't think this is as cut-and-dried as our friends from Washington do," I said, nodding toward a couple of FBI agents walking the grounds and looking professionally bored as they went about collecting evidence.

"I'm surprised they're letting us do the autopsy," Linda said.

"It's only because they're convinced that one of the two dead men in the house killed Cortez and stole his car." I looked around with a frown. "Which seems a reasonable conclusion. It might satisfy me if we had the other fugitive and whoever is helping them."

"You had a run-in with the other guy, didn't you?" Linda narrowed her eyes. "I remember that. It was when your father was stabbed. Manning sounds like a total creep. I don't like weirdos and especially not ones that manipulate innocent people."

"Me neither. Let's see if poor Mr. Cortez can help us

recapture Manning."

"We'll need a few minutes before we'll be ready to move the body." With gloved hands, she gently touched one of Cortez's fingers and it moved slightly. "The body has lost most of its rigidity. Dead at least twenty-four hours. That's good news for us. It'll make him easier to move."

Behind Linda, I could see Ezra carrying equipment from the coroner's van. Linda never took her eyes off of Cortez's body. She gave it all of her concentration as she gently probed and peered at his clothes and features. I'd seen her work around a number of bodies and the odor never bothered her, though Cortez was far from the worst corpse I'd come across in my career. That honor went to a body that had been stewing in a hot tub. Still, the odor around the SUV was pungent.

"I'll let y'all work," I said when I saw Julio step out of the house and strip off his hazmat suit.

Linda nodded. "We'll call you when we're ready to take the body out."

I headed over to intercept Julio.

"They got here quick," Julio remarked.

I explained the miracle to him, then asked, "What's the inside look like?"

"I..." He seemed hesitant. "Look, there's something hinky about this." He glanced over his shoulder as though he expected an FBI agent to run up and start arguing with him.

"What in particular?"

"The one guy, Stevens, has been dead almost as long as Cortez. Overdose from the looks of it."

"Where'd he get the drugs?"

"Good question. I'd guess there was about two-hundred-dollars worth in the house, based on current street prices. Not sure if it was laced with fentanyl or not. I got some pictures of it."

"I want to see the lab report on the drugs. That could point us to who the dealer was." Different sources used different methods and combinations for the drugs that they sold. Our vice squad might be able to identify if it had been made locally.

"Padilla said she'd send us the report. But who brought it to them?"

"Did they find Cortez's phone?"

"Not yet. There was a burner phone in the house that looked new. Padilla said they hadn't touched it yet. They've got their IT tech standing by to clone it as soon as crime scene is done."

"They're as anxious as we are to look at the information on that phone, since it could lead to Manning or his accomplice. I just wish we could get our hands on it first."

"I think they've got us outnumbered." Julio smiled.

"Dad should have played nicer with them."

"Do you really think that would make any difference?"

"No," I said honestly. The FBI were great to have on your side, but they came with an attitude that made it clear who they thought was best, and they were stingy with information if they wanted to bulldog a suspect.

I walked back over to the SUV. Linda and Ezra were in the process of taking measurements and scrapings off the body.

"Do you have Cortez's cell phone number?" I asked Julio.

"Yep." He took out his phone and pulled it up. "I called it a couple of times yesterday and this morning. Not that I thought he'd answer."

"Dial it now."

Julio tapped his phone. We listened, trying to hear it ring over the sounds of all the agents collecting evidence. Nothing.

"Worth a try," I said.

"Battery could be dead, or it's turned off."

"I don't think the FBI could have located the body without it being turned on," I said, wondering how closely they could pinpoint the location of the phone and if they had tried. "Let's not say anything to the FBI. Maybe we can find it first."

I felt a little silly for wanting to get my hands on the phone first. I understood why the FBI wasn't making it a priority. They had the records for the phone, so they knew that no calls had been made since Cortez had disappeared. Since it was unlikely that he'd been involved in the escape, any information on the phone prior to his unfortunate meeting with the fugitives had no value in finding Manning.

"With a dozen agents and crime-scene techs hunting for evidence, someone will find it," Julio said.

"Macklin, Ortiz." Linda waved us over to the car.

"What's up?"

"The victim's hand," she said, reaching out and pulling up Cortez's right hand. "See, he's got what looks like coins clutched in his fist." She was able to separate his fingers a little.

"Looks like a dime, a couple of pennies and some more silver coins I can't make out," Julio said, peering between Cortez's fingers.

"Reflex?" I asked. "Though his hands weren't in his pockets when we found the body."

Linda looked thoughtful. "Yeah, maybe. I could see him clenching his fist when he was shot and trapping some coins in his fingers."

"But this looks deliberate, like he meant to hold onto them," I said.

"Maybe he grabbed them from one of his killers. He might have thought there would be DNA on them," Ezra offered.

"And there might be," Linda said. "We'll remove them during the autopsy. I just wanted you to see them before I bagged up his hands."

"Thanks," I told her.

We stepped back and let them continue prepping the body for its transfer from the rear of the SUV to a body bag, all under the watchful eyes of two FBI techs. While we waited, I called Phil Eccles and filled him in on current events.

"What are you thinking?" he asked.

"I wish the murder weapon had been a rifle or a pistol so we'd have some solid ballistics. As it is, we won't know for sure if the shotgun in the house is the one used to kill Cortez."

"Based on the tracks the dogs followed, it looks like Manning may have left from the wreck site while the other two fugitives headed out in the direction of where Cortez's car was likely parked, implying that your two dead bodies were the ones responsible for carjacking and killing Cortez."

"That's what the FBI is going with," I agreed.

"You think differently?" Phil asked.

"I don't think anything right now. I'm just looking at the evidence."

"I've got your back. Do what you need to. All I ask is that you continue to cover your regular duties while you're mudwrestling with the FBI."

"Roger that."

I hung up and saw a text from Cara. Her dad was in town, and I breathed a sigh of relief that she wouldn't spend another night alone before we found Neil Manning.

I looked up to see Linda and her assistant manhandling Cortez's body out of the SUV and onto a stretcher. When they were done, she wiped sweat from her cheeks and said, "Unofficially, I'd say he died more than twenty-four hours ago and probably less than forty-eight hours. We might be able to do a better job after the autopsy."

"That fits with what we know," I said.

"We've got half a dozen autopsies before this gentleman."

"There's no rush. I really can't think what you could find that would help us at this point. I think it's safe to say the shotgun blast to the chest killed him."

"From the looks of the wound, that's a safe bet. He was certainly alive when he was shot."

They took the body back to the van while Julio and I

took a closer look at the back of the SUV.

The cargo compartment was a mess. The blast of the shotgun had slung blood and flesh all over the interior. Inside was a gym bag with a change of clothes and a duffle bag filled with game cameras, bird calls, a field notebook filled with notes on animal sightings and tracks, and other hunting supplies. Pushed behind this bag was Cortez's cell phone.

"It's on." I stated the obvious when Julio picked it up and the lock screen lit up. He slipped it into an evidence bag.

"I'll make sure it's his." Julio called Cortez's number and the phone lit up. "Someone's turned off the sound and vibration feature."

"Cortez was scouting for game. Makes sense he might have turned off any sound alerts. Even the vibration makes a little noise." I thought about it. "But why put it behind the bag if he'd turned the sound off? Besides, I'd think he would have wanted to have it along for its GPS app."

"His notebook has coordinates next to the entries. Maybe he hid the phone in the back hoping the fugitives wouldn't find it," Julio suggested.

"I don't know. Would he have had time? And if he saw them coming, wouldn't it make more sense to dial 911?"

"And if our bad hombres had found the phone, they would have just destroyed it or tossed it out," Julio mused.

"We'll take it straight to Lionel," I said. "There's a chance there's a tracking app or something else that might give us clue as to what exactly happened when he was killed."

After that, we made a careful inventory of everything else we found in the car.

"Okay," was all Padilla said when I showed her the list so she could take a picture of it with her phone. "We'll want access to everything you take and any analysis from the evidence."

"How are your agents who were involved in the shooting?" I asked in an effort to show we were all on the same team.

"Marcos suffered only minor injuries. Randel says he should be able to handle the stress of the shooting. Solid family relationships, a network of friends inside the bureau and out. The other agent is ex-military and, according to everyone, is tough as nails."

"Good to hear. People underestimate the trauma for the person acting in good faith."

"Yeah. Just because the shooting is justified doesn't mean it doesn't affect you." Padilla sounded like she had personal knowledge of the subject. I made a note to myself to look into it. Not just because I was nosy, but because knowing her better might make her a little easier to deal with. Maybe.

"Speaking of trauma." She paused, as though uncertain if she should go on. "Your father was hurt pretty bad when that woman stabbed him."

"It was the head injury he got when he fell that was the worst part," I said cautiously, wondering where she was going with this.

"It's just that he seems to be… touchier." She saw the frown on my face. "And I'm the same bitch I've always been so…"

"I don't know if it's his injury or if he's just getting to a point in his career where he doesn't want to…"

"You can say it." She smiled.

"Take a lot of shit."

"It happens. My father was a mechanic, owned his own shop just outside Cincinnati. Always had a couple of guys working for him until he hit sixty. Then he told me he didn't have the patience to deal with employees anymore. He ran the shop for another fifteen years by himself. If he didn't like a customer, he just told them to go somewhere else."

"There's another reason Dad might be a little more sensitive. Manning being one of the three escaped prisoners makes it a wee bit personal."

"For you too," she said, lifting the corner of her mouth in a lopsided smile.

"Guaranteed. It's not just what he did to my dad. He

brutalized that woman."

"I've read the report." Padilla nodded. "I get it. Just remember that I have a job to do, and I won't tolerate any cowboy moves."

"All I want is to see him back in jail."

"Manning has a good lawyer. If we do anything over the line, Thorne will make the little snot look like the victim."

I nodded. She was right. Manning hadn't even been convicted of anything yet. If we gave his lawyer an opening, Manning could be walking the streets again.

CHAPTER NINE

It was evening when I got back to the office. I still had reports to review and my own reports to write.

"Don't worry, Dad's here," Cara told me when I called to check on her.

"I'm very glad about that. Y'all have dinner without me. I'll be there when I can."

"Be careful."

"No, I'm going to run down the middle of the street holding a pair of scissors," I joked.

"I know, I know. But it's like a talisman or a ritual or something. If I don't say it, then I'd worry more."

"I'm teasing you. I can't stop myself from saying it either."

The silly conversation with Cara kept me smiling through the first several reports that I read. Then I remembered Mick Klein and his burglary report and the smile left my face. He still hadn't sent it to me yet.

I started to chew on it. What was he trying to prove? Was this a power game? Was he so burned out that he couldn't even do his job at the simplest level? This last question seemed negated by the fact that he'd followed up on four or five other investigations assigned to him in the last couple of days and they'd all seemed competently done. It was maddening.

When I left the office two hours later, I was still irritated that I was going to have to confront Mick Klein again over a stupid burglary investigation. Then I remembered the Simmons case that had gotten him promoted. I would need to request copies of the case files from our records department since it had happened so long ago, but it wasn't too late to stop by Albert Griffin's. He had always touted himself as a nightbird and it wasn't yet nine.

I pulled into his driveway and saw that lights still burned brightly inside the house. I went to the back door which was closest to his study. The interior door was open, letting the cool evening breeze come in through the screen door. I tapped on the door and shouted "Hello!" into the house. A minute later Mr. Griffin, dressed in slacks and a polo shirt, came into the hallway and his face lit up when he saw me.

"Larry! Don't you have a home to go to?" He unlatched the screen door and pushed it open.

"You shouldn't leave your door open like that," I chastised him.

"I fastened the latch on the screen door," he said, waving away my concerns.

"An exhausted squirrel could push his way though that screen door."

"And if one did, I'm sure I could handle him. Now, what can I get you to drink?"

We settled down at the kitchen table with a couple of glasses of iced tea.

"I'm betting you didn't come by just to chat," Mr. Griffin said knowingly, "but I don't see how I can help you find Neil Manning."

"I wish. No, this has to do with an old case."

He smiled. "My favorite kind. Which one?"

"The Simmons case. The murders happened back in 2002."

"I remember it well. Husband and wife. It happened two

blocks over, in a very nice Greek Revival house. I think that was what really sparked interest in the case—I mean, beyond Adams County—the fact that the house gave it a Southern Gothic feel for the news media. You add a creepy daughter and I'm surprised no one has written a book about it yet."

"Creepy daughter?"

"Maybe *I* should write the book." Mr. Griffin raised his eyebrows.

"So what happened?"

"Your father would know better than most. I know he was mentioned in several of the articles about the case." He sighed and stood up. "I've got a good memory, but not a perfect one. Let's go back to the morgue."

When the local paper had gone under, the library didn't have room to store the paper's back issues, so Mr. Griffin had carted thousands of pounds of newspapers to his house.

"How's Eddie?" I asked. Eddie Thompson had been my best confidential informant before he'd gotten clean and moved into Mr. Griffin's garage apartment.

"He seems very happy working at the library. The only drama in his life is his off and on love affair with Jessie."

"*Is* it a love affair?" I asked as I followed him through the house. Out of the corner of my eye, I caught his black cat, Brutus, watching me from under a table. One of several cats in the house, Brutus was clearly the alpha and he guarded the house like a Doberman.

"Who knows. They run hot and cold. Of course, she's busy with her courses at the academy. Just when I think they've entered a cooling-off period, then he's helping her study or she's hanging out with him at the library." He threw up his hands in a hopeless gesture.

Jessie Gilmore had dealt with a troubled past, but had come out on the other side and was now attending the law enforcement academy. Over the last year, she and Eddie had developed a close friendship that occasionally seemed to veer into something more. Mr. Griffin and I were both witnesses to the highs and lows.

We entered the room where he had the old newspapers assembled in boxes on a dozen metal racks.

"Eddie's gone through and relabeled the boxes."

"Nice." I admired all the neatly printed content labels.

Mr. Griffin scanned the shelves until he found several boxes labeled "2002." He pulled one off the shelf, then nodded to a second one. "Bring that one too."

I took the box and followed him to a small desk and two chairs by the door. A metal lamp sat on the desk. Mr. Griffin set his box down, flipped a switch on the lamp and started rummaging through the boxes. Thirty minutes later, the boxes were on the floor and a small stack of papers was in front of us.

"We're in luck! Kathrine Bass covered the story. Kathy was the best reporter the paper ever had." He arranged the papers in chronological order and picked up the first one. "I thought so. Your father was the responding deputy. Ummm, let's see… 'Deputy Macklin responded to 478 Finnegan Street in order to perform a welfare check on Mr. and Mrs. Charles Simmons, who had not been seen for at least twenty-four hours. Finding all the doors locked, Deputy Macklin secured a key from a neighbor. Upon entering the house, Deputy Macklin discovered Mr. and Mrs. Simmons dead in their second-floor bedroom.'" He stopped reading. "I remember hearing that the bodies were a mess. She'd been stabbed a dozen times and his wrists were cut."

"That sounds like a murder-suicide," I said.

"That was the assumption."

"But I guess it wasn't that easy. You mentioned a crazy daughter."

"The Simmonses had two children. A boy that they'd had when they were first married and a daughter, Riley, who was born fifteen years later when Mrs. Simmons was in her mid-thirties."

"How old were the Simmonses when they were killed?"

"They were both in their mid-fifties. The daughter was twenty."

"And she killed them?"

"Yep. She was attending classes at the University of South Florida. At first, she appeared to have an alibi, but it turned out that she'd driven up here, killed them and then drove back to Tampa in under ten hours. Did it for the inheritance."

I whistled. "Sounds like a psychopath."

"That's what her brother called her during the sentencing phase of the trial."

"How many years did she get?"

"Two life sentences. I assume she's still serving her time."

"Probably down at Lowell." Lowell Correctional Institution was located south of Gainesville. The Lowell Annex was where some of the most dangerous women in Florida were housed. "Do any of the articles mention Mick Klein?"

"Yes." Mr. Griffin thumbed through a couple of issues. "Here, according to this article, he was the first one to suspect that it was a double homicide. He found a receipt for an oil change that led to questions about some unexplained mileage on her car. Blah, blah, he helped find additional evidence, blah blah."

"No wonder he got moved into CID," I said.

"Nice when someone is rewarded for doing a good job." Mr. Griffin paused and looked at me. "What does all this have to do with the escaped prisoners?"

"Nothing."

"Playing your cards close to your vest." He wagged his finger at me.

I grinned. "Okay, you got me. I'm just trying to get a little insight into Mick's motivations."

"It's not easy supervising people. Guess it can be even harder in a stressful job like law enforcement. The few times I've met the man, he's always seemed nice, smart."

"I…" Though it was tempting to confide in the older man, I decided I should keep the details to myself. "I'm just trying to find out everything I can about the folks I'm working with."

"Very wise." He stood up. "Let me know if I can give you any more help. Where do you think Neil Manning is?" he asked as we started for the back door.

"Part of me thinks he's here in the county and another part believes that he's long gone."

"His father probably has money socked away somewhere. Wouldn't be hard to sneak him out of the country in a boat or truck."

"Yep, they own a trucking business. Manning could ride clear across the country or into Canada or Mexico."

"Or hitch a ride on a boat to the Bahamas. Money opens a lot of doors," Mr. Griffin said knowingly.

"I didn't even like it when he was out on bail and wearing an ankle monitor. He's always been a flight risk."

"Why was he back in jail?"

"Federal charges kicked in. They had set bail at a million dollars and his father was still thinking about it."

"Maybe his father decided to break him out. Better to do it before you've put up bail."

I'd been thinking the same thing.

We said our goodbyes and I glanced up at the garage apartment as I got into my car. There were no lights and no sign of Eddie. Wondering if he was out with Jessie, I smiled and shook my head. Love was a crazy thing.

I called to let Cara know I was on my way home.

"We're outside," she told me. "Dad built a fire."

"Isn't it a little warm for a fire?"

"Never too warm for a campfire," I heard her father say with a booming laugh.

When I pulled up to our house, I saw Henry and Cara sitting around a small but glowing campfire. As I got out of the car, a dark shadow raced toward me.

"What are *you* doing here?" I shouted at Mauser, whose black coat blended into the dark shadows cast by the fire. As he ran away from me only to circle back for another gleeful charge, I felt like a diver being hounded, pun intended, by a shark.

Once I'd calmed the Black Hellhound of Adams County, I walked over to the fire and leaned down to give Cara a kiss. Before I could stand all the way back up, Henry embraced me in a bearhug.

"Great to see you!" he said, patting me hard on the back.

"I'm glad to see you too, Henry." I paused, then asked, "So why is Mauser here?"

The dog was sitting at Henry's feet, looking up at the big man like he was a god.

"I stopped in at the sheriff's office when I got to town. You weren't there, so I visited with your dad and Mauser. You know how I love this big bruiser, and I thought if Cara needed protection, what could be better than me staying here? Me and this guy." He was bending over, ruffling Mauser's ears and rubbing his chest. The dog was eating it up.

"I do appreciate you coming up, and I guess I can put up with Mauser."

In answer, the behemoth leaned into me and slobbered on my clothes.

"You want a steak?" Henry asked, sitting down and pointing at a cooler beside his chair.

"Steak?" I was surprised because Cara's mother was an on-again, off-again vegetarian, though she'd never gone fully vegan. She was too fond of all the products made from cow's and goat's milk. She was an old-school earth mother.

"I know what you're thinking. Anna approves of these. They're from a friend of ours who raises cows on this beautiful ranch in Ocala. The cows have a wonderful life."

"I'd love a steak." I hadn't realized how hungry I was.

"Potato?" He picked one up out of a sack beside his chair.

"Enjoy your meal." Cara gave me a kiss. "I've got some work to do. Are you going to stay out here with the men or come in with me?"

The question was aimed at Mauser, who looked from Cara to Henry and back again, torn between two of his favorite people. Novelty won out and he gave a little whine, leaning up against Henry and almost knocking his chair over. Henry just laughed.

The steak was wonderfully tender while the flavor of the potato was enhanced by the smell of wood smoke and the light of the stars over our heads.

"That was great." Feeling full and mellow, I set my plate down for Mauser to lick. "I appreciate you keeping an eye on Cara while we try to find this monster."

"Glad I was able to come up and help out."

"How's Anna?"

"She's doing fine. It's the rest of us that are going crazy." He chuckled. "Having to go to the hospital and have… you know. It made her feel… a little old and, I guess, a little helpless. Now she's trying to make up for it by taking on too much. She's got at least a dozen charity projects she's working on as well as all the usual drama at our co-op." He looked across the fire at me and smiled. "It's the pleasure of growing old with someone. You get to experience the ups and downs of two lives."

"I guess that's something to look forward to," I said with a gentle smile.

"I've got a little something for you to try." Henry leaned over and pulled a mason jar out of the same bag that had held the potato. In the glow of the fire, I could see the crystal-clear liquid in the jar. Henry twisted off the lid and took a swallow. "You know, we lived on a commune in Tennessee for a while. Well, I still have some friends up in the hills who know how to make the good ol' mountain dew." He stood up and handed me the jar.

I looked at it with a suspicious eye. I had run afoul of Anna and her magic mushrooms once before, so I'd learned to be cautious when it came to Cara's parents.

"Go ahead. You won't go blind," he promised.

Feeling like a thirteen-year-old who'd been handed a beer

by a mischievous uncle, I put the jar to my lips and took a small sip. There was a sweet little burning sensation down my throat. I took a larger swallow and felt my sinuses open up. Still, it didn't hit like whiskey.

"Smooth, right?"

I nodded and handed the jar back to Henry.

"What proof is it?"

"Clayton has a range. Some are as low as forty while another batch will be as high as a *hundred*-and-forty. This is eighty proof. I think it's the sweet spot."

We talked for another hour until I felt my eyelids droop. I'd had two more swallows from the mason jar and wobbled a little when I got up from my chair.

"This was great. But with Manning on the loose, you probably shouldn't stay out by the campfire at night," I mumbled to Henry.

"Ha! You asked me up here to protect Cara. Before the sun went down, I strung wires out in the woods with alarms on them. I judged the visibility for a shot at night at thirty yards in these woods, so the alarms are out to forty yards."

"I guess we brought in the right guy," I said, surprised. Though I shouldn't have been.

"Spend enough time with moonshiners and pot-growers, you learn a few tricks. Mauser and I'll sit out a little longer." Mauser had been snoring for the last half hour.

Inside, Cara looked up from the kitchen table when I walked by.

"You didn't drink anything out of that jar, did you?" she asked, looking at me closely with a smile on her face.

"A couple of drinks is all."

"You'll have a headache in the morning."

"I'll be fine."

I took a shower and when my head hit the pillow, that was all she wrote.

CHAPTER TEN

The alarm on my phone woke me from a dead sleep. I groaned as I fumbled it to silence.

"You were still snoring when I got up," Cara called from the bathroom.

"You could have woken me gently with a kiss," I grumbled.

"Not with your morning breath."

"Yeah, yeah." I stood up and my brain throbbed. "I might be feeling that moonshine."

"You always were a cheap date."

Glad that the twelve-hour shifts had been called off once Stevens and Waugh had been found, I revived myself with a bowl of cereal and a cup of sugar with a little coffee in it, at least enough to drive to work. At the top of my to-do list was talking to Mick, again. I tried to come up with a nonconfrontationally confrontational way to do it, but nothing came to mind. The one hope I had that the report might be waiting in my inbox when I got to the office was quickly dashed. Finally, I decided to just have it out with him.

I saw Julio walk by my door and called him in.

"Did you get Cortez's phone to Lionel?"

"He cloned it after Shantel finished with it. I went through the data last night. There wasn't anything related to the prisoners. Honestly, there wasn't anything related to much of anything except hunting. A little bit of back and forth with his sister and even less with his ex-wife."

"Parents?"

"Both dead. Natural causes."

"Friends?"

"A few hunting buddies, but I got the sense they weren't friends. More like guys who belong to the same club."

"We didn't expect there to be any ties to the fugitives." I shrugged. "What about the geo location information on the phone?"

"Lionel said he'd analyze it today."

"Let me know when the autopsy is scheduled."

I went through the night's reports and assigned cases to each of the investigators under me. Normally, I'd take a couple of the cases myself, but I wanted to keep on top of the search for Neil Manning. Pete had a doctor's appointment that day, but he offered to take a couple of the routine reports that could be followed up with phone calls.

I couldn't get Manning out of my head, so I got up and went to Phil's office to see if there was any new information.

"It's been harder to get the FBI and U.S. Marshals to share their leads since your dad had his dust-up with them." Phil sighed and leaned back in his chair. "Is there anything you can add to your report from yesterday?"

"I'm still hung up on where they got the drugs from."

"Yeah, I got that. You think there's something else going on?"

"Maybe whoever broke Manning out figured they'd set those two up as patsies. But what gets me is why not encourage them to leave the area? The farther they fled and the longer it took us to catch them, then the better for Manning. Now with them dead, we can focus all of our attention on him."

"Maybe it's just a fluke that they got ahold of drugs and

hunkered down at that house."

I shook my head. "Julio didn't think the drugs were already in the house, and they certainly didn't get them from our victim. Cortez makes Mr. Clean look dirty. Though it's possible they got the shotgun from him. He was an avid hunter. But even that doesn't ring true. Julio said the gun was a Remington 870, nothing fancy, with gouges out of the wood stock and pitting on the barrel. Our victim went for premium guns. But who knows, maybe he kept this one in his car for emergencies."

"The FBI will follow up on that. They'll want a full history on the gun since it was used in an officer-involved shooting."

"Finding some of Cortez's blood on the shotgun would certainly help pin the murder onto our dead guys." I'm sure my voice reflected how unenthusiastic I was about that idea.

"You can't push the evidence," Phil told me. "If the evidence points to the dead guys, then that's where you have to go with it. I know how much you hate Neil Manning, and I'm telling you, you have to rein those feelings in."

"On the other hand, we can't just close the case because it's the easy thing to do," I argued.

"Nobody is saying that. Our priority is catching Manning. Can we agree on that?"

"Absolutely." I nodded.

"I've logged a dozen more suspicious incidents that could be tied to him." Phil pointed to his map.

"I want to interview his father," I said, ignoring the map. If Phil had any incidents that were strong evidence that Manning was in the area, then we'd have already been on them.

"What reason do you have for talking to Manning's father? Or maybe I should say, what excuse are you going to use?" Phil asked skeptically.

"He has to be involved. Directly or indirectly, and I'd put my money on directly." I'd been running hot and cold on Rudy Manning's involvement, but right now I was hot.

"And you don't think that the FBI hasn't looked into his activities over the last month?" Phil challenged.

"I know they have, but they don't know the Mannings like I do. Besides our original investigation last winter, I've spent the last couple of months putting together a full report and briefing for the State Attorney. I know the Mannings."

"And Rudy Manning knows you. He doesn't like you any more than you like him. So why would he agree to come in for an interview?"

"I haven't figured that out," I admitted.

"I think you're grasping at straws. Even if he knows where his son is, Manning isn't going to tell us. We're going to have to find him on our own. Or the FBI is going to have to find him."

"Any reason that I can't snoop around Manning's properties?"

"Other than the risk of being accused of harassing him?"

"I'll go easy," I promised. "But putting a little pressure on him can't hurt, and maybe I'll see or hear something useful."

"Do you really think one of the Mannings killed Cortez?"

"We can't rule it out." I sighed. "I'll admit the odds are that one of the other fugitives killed him. Still, if Manning helped orchestrate his son's escape, then he's still *responsible* for Cortez's murder, not to mention that of the guard."

"*If* he was involved," Phil pointed out.

"Those two murders are our hook into this investigation. Even so, the Feds are working hard to keep us out of the hunt."

"I'm not going to stand in your way. The mood that your dad's in, I don't think he'll stop you from being a thorn in the FBI's side."

We spent the next half hour going over the new incidents Phil had logged on the map. There were a few interesting break-ins a mile or so from the house where the fugitives had hidden. Nothing much was stolen, just some food, clothes and a bit of money. They were more likely the result of local kids on a dare than anything our suspects had done.

When we'd exhausted the possibilities on the map, I left his office and headed down to the records department to see if I could pull the reports on the Simmons murders.

There was a large group of people gathered around a table where Beth Miller, the head of the department, had placed her latest culinary creations. She was known for making the best baked goods in the county, and they were coveted by everyone who worked at the sheriff's office. It was rumored that some deputies planned their shifts around Beth's baking schedule.

Today, Captain Roy Grant, who oversaw our patrol division and also served as one of our five watch commanders, was entertaining a couple of the dispatchers, who were picking up treats to take back to their hard-working colleagues. Grant was an effusive mountain of a man, known for his sense of humor and respected for his meticulous professionalism. He was a deacon at the largest black church in Adams County and often took to the pulpit when the regular minster was out of town.

I enjoyed a bit of office gossip, then grabbled a cookie before asking Beth to pull the records for the Simmons murders. There were two boxes of reports and photographs. I selected one of them and carried it back to my office, reluctantly setting it in the corner. As much as I wanted to get lost in the old case and to see what it might reveal about Mick Klein, it would have to wait.

I tackled a mound of paperwork and other reports before deciding to take a ride and see what sort of trouble I could get into. I had decided that Phil had given me free rein to, if not actually *harass* Rudy Manning, then at least investigate him. While I knew that the FBI and the U.S. Marshals had already dug into his alibi, finances and business dealings, I still couldn't stop the urge to look into things myself.

As I walked out of the office, I saw Lynn Lewis walking around the corner of the building toward a stone picnic table near the back door. The table was the designated smoking area for the office. It was shaded by a large live oak tree, which made it a pleasant retreat, even this time of year.

I debated whether to go and speak with her. She had been almost as snarky as Mick when I was promoted, but I hadn't seen any issues with her work, and she had been mostly civil toward me. If anyone knew of a personal issue that could have been affecting Mick's work, it would be Lynn. I followed her to the picnic table.

Lynn eyed me as she took out a pack of cigarettes. She held it out toward me with a smirk on her face. "Want one?"

"No, thanks."

"You know, there are only three of us left. There are five others who vape, but that doesn't count." She rolled her eyes as she stuck a cigarette into her mouth and pulled out a Bic lighter with a personalized silver cover. She took a deep drag on the cigarette, then asked, "Did you come over to tell me that I shouldn't smoke?"

"No." I was feeling awkward and second-guessing my decision to talk to her.

"I get that crap all the time. A week ago, I was sitting at the taco truck, not bothering anyone. I'd finished my tacos, made sure I was downwind from everyone and lit one up. A guy, I swear he was five hundred pounds, comes over to me and tells me how I'm killing myself by smoking. I gently suggested that he might want to cut back on the sour cream." She smiled and held up one finger. "But wait! The best was last year when I was at the liquor store next to the Fast Mart. It was my day off and I stopped at the store for lotto and cigarettes. I'd been wanting a smoke all day, so I opened the pack and lit up as soon as I was out of the store. That's when a young couple comes out of the liquor store. Girl takes one look at me and starts telling me how I'm polluting their world with my cigarettes. I could smell the booze on her breath, and his unfocused eyes told me he was drunker than a skunk. I just stared at her. Finally, she shot me the bird and they both stumbled to their Nissan."

"I can see what's coming," I said, shaking my head and unable to resist an evil grin.

"I got in my pickup and pulled out so I was blocking them in. I didn't want the little snots to try driving away. The look on their faces when I pulled out my star was priceless. Some days it's good to be a deputy. After I handcuffed both of them and handed 'em over to patrol, I went into the store and arrested the clerk for selling them alcohol in their condition and not calling 911 when he saw them getting into a car." She paused and took another draw from her cigarette. "Sorry, but you kind of triggered one of my pet peeves when you came over here. Nonsmokers avoid this area like the plague. You'd think we're contagious."

"I'd like to talk to you about Mick," I said, and I watched as her eyes narrowed.

"What can I tell you about Mick?" Her voice was flat and cold.

"Y'all have made it pretty clear you didn't want me as your supervisor. No one has to like me. All I'm asking is for the work to get done." I felt exasperated with the pair of them.

"You really are clueless, aren't you?" she shot back, taking me by surprise.

"What?" I asked defensively.

"Mick and I figured you were going to force us out of CID." She flicked the ash off her cigarette.

"Why would I do that?"

"Are you serious?"

"I don't have any idea what you're talking about." I was beyond confused.

"How long have you been in CID? About four years now? Mick and I were there years before you ever showed up."

"And maybe one of you should have gotten the promotion—" I started to argue.

"That's not it! No." She dropped the cigarette in a planter filled with sand. "The whole time you've been in CID getting some meaty cases, working with Pete and Darlene, not once, not ever, did you ask for Mick's or my thoughts on a case.

Were we ever invited in on a strategy session?"

I was stunned. "I…" I started, but I didn't know what to say.

"Exactly. Sure, you occasionally asked us for information. Wanted to know about cases we were working that might link up with your murders, but you never really asked for our help or wanted to know what we thought." Lynn held up her hand. "Look, I understand why you wouldn't think about me. I'm used to it. If you work sex crimes, and particularly ones dealing with minors, you get used to the fact that even cops don't want to hear about your cases. Everyone avoids me 'cause they think I'll start talking about all the horrible things I have to deal with day in and day out."

"Hey, we've all seen bad things," I protested without much conviction.

"Do you want to hear about the Ruttledge case?" she asked with a pugnacious expression on her face.

"No!" I said quickly. I had heard enough details when the arrests were being made that I'd almost vomited. "Okay, you have a point."

"Like I said, I understand everyone avoiding me. What I don't get it why you all didn't want Mick's help. The guy is smart."

"I… It just… He seemed like he was happy working his burglaries and…" I shrugged, mentally kicking myself for being an idiot.

"People like to be asked."

Chastened, I said, "You have a very good point. I shouldn't have assumed you were busy with your own cases. I need to think about this and see how we can better pool our resources."

"Communication is a two-way street. You made the effort to come over and talk to me, so I'll clue you in on something. There is no one working here that has more experience with the FBI than I do. I'd say seventy percent of my cases involve other jurisdictions, and many are interstate cases where I work with the FBI. Most of the predators these days use the internet to find and contact their victims. The human trafficking networks often stretch from one end of the country to the other. Texas, California, New York, you name it. I've worked with several of the agents that work for Padilla. A couple of times, she's been directly involved with an operation. I'm usually just a small piece of the puzzle, but… I know how to work with them."

I rocked back on my heels and really looked at Lynn. She had a solid no-frills appearance. Her hips pushed her sidearm out almost defiantly. Everything about her said that she meant business. I'd never heard anyone complain about her performance or willingness to back up another officer. And I knew that she excelled in her marksmanship. Of all of us in CID, Pete was the most likely to strike up a conversation with her, and he'd mentioned how well she handled firearms.

"I'm going out to… check on Rudy Manning. Want to come along?" I asked.

"Are you humoring me?" she asked suspiciously, but with a small smile.

"No. I'm trying to make up for being a dumbass. If anyone needs help negotiating with Special Agent Padilla, it's me."

"I'd like to put Neil Manning back in jail. Locking up creeps isn't just what I do for a living, it's what I do for fun." She stood up eagerly.

"We'll take my car."

CHAPTER ELEVEN

I brought her up to speed on the recovery of the bodies of the two fugitives, Lester Stevens and Doyle Waugh, and what we knew about the murder victims, Roberto Cortez and Florence Murray.

"And you don't think Stevens or Waugh killed Cortez?" Lynn asked, reading between the lines of what I'd told her.

"Right now, I just don't know. They're the most likely suspects, but there's still Neil Manning and whoever helped them escape."

"Padilla is going to want to wrap it all up in a neat package. She's good at her job, but she's even better at the politics that go along with it. I've worked on a couple of investigations where she was quick to pick the ripe fruit and move on when there were loose ends I thought needed tying up. To be fair, she gets pressure from above to keep things quick and neat."

"And the Feds already don't look good having let these guys get loose in the first place."

"Exactly. She's been sent in to clean up the mess. That's not the kind of case she likes to work. Padilla prefers cases that she's developed from the ground up," Lynn said.

"So she doesn't have to share the glory." I nodded.

"That… and she likes the control."

"How's that play out when you bring them a case?" I asked, curious.

"No problem for her. She takes anything a small fry like me brings to the table and makes it her own. Luckily, I don't have an ego where cases are concerned. As long as the creep is locked up for a good long time, then I'm happy. Which is a plus in Padilla's column. She works well with prosecutors. A few times prosecutors have tried to work a plea bargain with some scumbag and Padilla raised hell until the prosecutor agreed to play hardball."

"I'm going to cruise by Rudy Manning's house, see if he's around. Maybe check out Neil's house and then go visit Darlene at the police station if I haven't attracted the attention of the FBI by then."

"I heard the FBI has been camped out at her place," Lynn said noncommittally.

"You and Darlene didn't seem to hit it off when she was working in CID," I said in an equally neutral tone.

"What? We should get along because we're both *girls*?" She put more sarcasm into the word than I would have thought possible.

"No. I… Well, yeah, maybe… I don't know." I hated it when I got trapped dancing around awkward subjects.

"Darlene's okay. We're just different." I thought Lynn was going to leave it at that, but she went on. "She's got that Pollyanna attitude. Underneath it all, she really thinks the world is a good place and the people in it are good."

"And you don't?"

"I was born cynical. My mother said that when I was a child, I always assumed the worst would happen. I never grew out of that."

"That's dark."

She shrugged. "It serves me well working the cases I do. If I'd come into this job thinking people were decent, I would have changed my mind after the first month… or dove so deep into a bottle no one would have ever found me."

"I can see that."

"You know why I'm good at working sex crimes? First, I've got the guts to look at these crimes head-on. Second, I have the discipline not to rip the throats out of the monsters that perpetrate them."

I wanted to change the subject and ask about her family, friends or hobbies, but the tone of the conversation had become so grim that I couldn't think of a natural way to turn it around.

Finally, Lynn sighed and let me off the hook. "Look, I'm not all doom and gloom. I've got a big extended family and I even like most of them." She sounded surprised at the admission.

"Where're you from?" I jumped at the conversational lifeline she'd thrown me.

"Born in Live Oak. Most of my family is still around there. We're farmers." She gave a short, harsh laugh. "Maybe that's where all the cynicism comes from. A farm lives and dies at the whim of God."

"Who said that?"

"My grandfather after every drought, every infestation and every flood."

"You don't *have* to be a pessimist to be a farmer," I pointed out.

"You're right. In fact, most farmers are optimists. Or at least gamblers. Always betting that they can get away with planting a little later than everyone else, or that this crop or that crop will go sky-high this year. My family are more the slow-and-steady type of farmers. The investors that have a diversified portfolio. Never making a bunch of money, but never losing everything either."

I had a thought. "You know what? I think I'll drive out to AmMex Trucking first, see if Rudy is out there."

"Bold move. You think we can take on a bunch of truckers?"

"I guess we'll see." I thought about calling Phil Eccles,

but decided against it. He'd already sort of given me the go-ahead to do what I thought was right. "This is only one of their shipping hubs."

"Neil Manning ran that one, right?"

"Yeah. All he had to do was not run it into the ground. Mostly he used it as a front for his obsessions."

AmMex was a hive of activity, with semis coming and going out of the driveway. I didn't see any expensive cars parked in the lot, so I figured Rudy Manning probably wasn't there. Still, I decided to go in and look around. Maybe if I could get Rudy annoyed enough, he'd seek me out himself.

"Ready?" I asked Lynn.

"Why not?" I saw her adjust the gun on her hip as she stepped out of the car.

I had no idea what type of reception I would get inside. Shortly after the wreck that had led to Neil's arrest, we'd taken statements from most of the employees. At the time, they were still in shock. Now, after almost six months of Rudy defending his son to them, who knew how they would feel toward me.

A woman I didn't recognize was stationed at the reception desk. She smiled politely when I walked up.

"Is Rudy Manning in?" I asked nonchalantly.

"No. He normally works out of his home office. We don't see him too much. Barry is the manager. Would you like to talk to him?"

"Sure," I said obligingly.

"You are?" She'd picked up the phone and was waiting to press Barry's number.

I pulled out my bifold and showed her my star and ID.

She didn't even raise an eyebrow as she pressed the button on the phone. "Sergeant Macklin is here to see you."

"Another FBI agent?" I heard a man ask.

"I don't think so. He's got a star or something." She hung up the phone and pointed us toward the office behind the counter.

The door was open and a middle-aged man with grey

hair, stooped shoulders and a good-natured smile greeted us as we walked in.

"Barry Hillar." He stuck out his hand to me and nodded to Lynn as we introduced ourselves. "How can I help you? We've already talked to the FBI a couple of times. Like I told them, none of us are going to protect Mr. Manning's son."

"I'm glad to hear you say that," I said.

"When Mr. Manning hired me, I told him that anyone who had helped his son had to go." Barry shook his head sadly. "I'm not a fool. I know we've probably got some guys that might do something that's not exactly legal. It's the same everywhere. But what that guy did was… sickening. I know that he's lucky some of his drivers didn't find out what he'd done and got ahold of him before the law did."

"What did Rudy Manning say about cooperating with law enforcement?" I asked.

"I called him as soon as the FBI showed up. That was the morning his son escaped. Mr. Manning told me to answer any of their questions and to let them go anywhere they wanted, look at anything they needed to. Of course, if he'd said anything different then he'd have been looking for a new manager. I've got one of the best reputations in the business and I mean to keep it. When I took the job, there were a dozen truckers who came to work for us 'cause they respect me and what I do."

"We appreciate that. Are there any of the older employees we could talk to?"

"Talk to anyone you'd like," he offered. "I'll get Stew to show you around."

I recognized Stewart Wilson from an interview after we'd arrested Neil Manning.

"I can't believe that Neil's escaped. It's crazy. Like a movie or something." Stew was wiry and shorter than me or Lynn. Even though he was probably as old as Barry Hillar, there was a boyish quality about him that made him look younger.

"Can you think of anywhere around here that Neil might

hide?" I asked.

"Here? No. And he doesn't have any friends here either." Stew set his jaw and narrowed his eyes. "Most of us felt betrayed by what he did. That fact that he was working here and… well, torturing that girl. It's horrible."

"Neil Manning had supporters when we first confronted him," I pointed out.

"Nobody knew that he was a monster. Also, we respected his dad. Still do."

"Are there people here who would do a favor for Rudy Manning?"

"Of course… Now, wait. If you're suggesting we'd help Neil because Rudy asked us to, you're wrong. I like Mr. Manning a lot. He's a great employer, but I'm not going to help a sadist and a kidnapper just 'cause I like my boss." Stew looked genuinely appalled at the idea.

"Is there anyone here who might?" I pushed.

Stew paused and looked thoughtful. "I don't think so. There are a couple of people who are… I guess you would say particularly loyal to Mr. Manning." He shook his head. "I still can't see it. What Neil Manning did was… repulsive. If he'd robbed a bank, or maybe even if he'd accidently killed someone in a hit-and-run or something like that, then I could see it. But not what he did. These are good people I'm talking about."

"Okay, just show us around and let us talk to some of the folks."

I noticed that Lynn stayed quiet and calm while I talked with Stew. She would turn her head and stare at people or objects as we passed, as though putting them through some private evaluation process.

We wandered through the trucking company's main building, including the loading docks and maintenance bays. There were plenty of places a person could hide from law enforcement, but almost nowhere they could hide from the people who worked there. Everyone we met seemed concerned and supportive of our efforts to get Neil Manning back under lock and key.

"So what do you think?" I asked Lynn when we were back in the car.

"I think Stew is mighty naïve. I'd bet you there are people there who'd hide Manning if the boss asked them to. Especially if he incentivized the request with a bit of cash."

"You're a suspicious sort."

"I've seen a lot. Met a lot of good truckers and people who work in the industry. But I've also met my share of scumbags who were willing to pack people like sardines in the back of a truck and drive them across the country in the middle of summer to make a little money. Half of them were described as good people right up to the point that the back doors swung open and the odor wafted out."

"Good point," I admitted. "Let's drive by Neil Manning's house."

I started the car and we headed for the house that Rudy had bought for his son.

"It must be nice to have a dad with money," Lynn commented when we neared Manning's house, then she pointed to a driveway across the street. "We aren't alone."

There was a white van with the logo of an air conditioning repair company out of Tallahassee painted on the side.

"You think it's FBI?" I asked and got an eyeroll from Lynn as I parked in Manning's driveway.

"Bet you a hundred bucks."

"No deal. Should we go say hi?"

"Nah. They'll know that we know that they're there. No harm in a wave though," she said as she got out of the car and gave a casual salute in their direction. "Shows they don't really think he's dumb enough to come back here."

"How's that?"

"If they really thought he was coming back here, they would have gotten one of the neighbors to let them set up a stakeout nest *inside* a house. They know that Manning's not an idiot and he'd probably check his house out a time or two before coming back to it. If he saw a van parked down the street all day long, he'd be suspicious."

Crime-scene tape and a notice on FBI letterhead were on the front door.

"I see what you mean. They aren't exactly keeping a low profile."

Then my phone rang, and a quick glance told me it was Padilla. "Yes?" I answered cheerily.

"Don't give me that crap. What the hell are you doing at Neil Manning's house?"

"Same thing your guys are." I gave the van a wave of my own. "I'm guessing you all did a thorough job searching his house."

"They're going to have to do a lot of redecorating before they can sell it," she said bluntly.

"You know, if you kept me briefed on your efforts to find Manning, then I wouldn't have to waste my time coming up behind you."

"It would be easier to liaison with the sheriff's office if the sheriff hadn't kicked us out of his parking lot."

"Touché." I decided to push my luck. "I want to talk to Rudy Manning."

"So talk to him."

"What has he said to you?"

"What he's going to say to you. That he didn't have anything to do with his son's escape and he doesn't know who did. We've searched his house, his businesses *and* Neil Manning's house. We're still doing a forensic deep-dive on his electronics, but so far everything comes up nada. Of course, Manning's lawyer is playing interference, but he hasn't shut us out completely. Like I said, feel free to ask him anything you want."

"Where is he?"

"At his house right now. He's spent a lot of time hovering around us, which could mean he's guilty and trying to find out what we know, or that he's being honest and is worried about his son's wellbeing." Padilla paused, then added, "For what it's worth, he seemed upset and worried when he learned of the deaths of the other two fugitives."

"Interesting. Thanks."

"Let me know if you find out anything."

From the sound of her voice, I got the feeling she was running out of leads. How long would the FBI maintain a presence in the county before they scaled back to a passive national search?

"Let's go see if we can talk to Rudy Manning," I told Lynn.

CHAPTER TWELVE

Rudy Manning lived in a large brick house on several acres on the edge of Calhoun. When we pulled up to the gate, I pressed the buzzer on the intercom.

"What?" His answer was surly.

"It's Sergeant Larry Macklin. A colleague and I would like to talk to you." I made it sound as friendly as I could, considering our history, though talking into the speaker made me feel like a peasant asking permission to speak to the lord of the manor.

"I don't have anything to say to you."

I'd been expecting this sort of response. What could I lay on the table that might get him to grant me an audience? I could think of only one thing, but I'd have to be careful.

"I was there when the other fugitives were killed."

There was a long silence. Just when I thought he wasn't going to answer, the gate began to swing inward.

As I drove up to the house, Lynn whistled. "I can only dream of living like this."

I was surprised when Rudy himself answered the door. It was silly, but I'd sort of been expecting a butler.

"Come in," he said with a gesture toward the foyer. "We can go into the den."

We followed him to the right and into a room that looked like a set from *Downton Abbey*. He waved us to a sofa on one side of a fireplace that was big enough to sleep in.

"If it isn't the naked detective," said a derisive voice from a corner of the room near a window. I hadn't noticed David Thorne when we'd come into the room.

"Thorne, I want to talk to Macklin and…"

"Deputy Lewis," Lynn said without smiling or extending her hand.

"I've advised you against talking to them," Thorne said flatly, making it clear that his advice wasn't to be taken lightly.

"I'll remind you that you're Neil's lawyer, not mine," Manning snapped. I was amazed that they weren't presenting a united front.

"When was the last time you talked to your son?" I asked him.

"Four days ago. He called because he wanted me to put up his bail."

"And you refused?"

"I thought it would be best to wait until the different jurisdictions were done charging him."

"Did you agree?" I asked Thorne.

"I'm certainly not going to answer your questions," he responded.

I ignored him and returned to Manning. "I assume Neil was upset?"

"Yes. He told me he would sell his house if he had to. He has some other assets too."

"What did you think of that?"

"I didn't have a problem with him putting up his own bail. Actually, I thought it was a good idea." He paused. "I've come to the realization that I've spoiled him. Though I guess that 'spoiled' isn't a strong enough word considering what he's done."

"Rudy, do I need to remind you that you're speaking to law enforcement officers?" Thorne was clearly incensed.

"I'm well aware of who I'm speaking to. Since you aren't my lawyer, I suggest you leave." Manning turned toward Thorne and glared at him.

Thorne held his ground for a few seconds before turning toward the door with a final sneer for us.

"You know how to reach me," he said on his way out.

"If he wasn't a great lawyer, I wouldn't tolerate the man. He may be my son's attorney, but I'm paying the bills." Manning shook his head. "I know. I won't pay Neil's bail, but I'll pay that ass a fortune to represent him."

"So he can go free?" Lynn asked.

"Honestly, no. I think it would be best if he was somewhere safe."

"You mean where other people would be safe from him?" Lynn persisted.

"As you say. I… It breaks my heart." Manning fell into a chair and put his head in his hands. I'd never seen him show any signs of remorse for what his son had done. Was it just an act?

"We need to catch your son. If you have any information that can help us, you need to speak now. You're required by law to help us," I told him.

"I mean it when I say that I want him locked up. You can't know how I feel. I hate what he's done and fear for what he might do. Still, he's my son. I don't want him hurt."

"He won't be hurt unless he wants to be," I promised. "Now what can you tell us?"

"Nothing I haven't already told the FBI." He paused and looked thoughtful for a minute. "I think he knew that the escape might happen."

"What makes you say that?" Lynn asked, watching him intently.

"You'd have to know him. He likes to think of himself as cleverer than everyone else. When he knows something that he thinks you don't, he gets this taunting tone to his voice. When I talked to him two days before the transfer, I heard it in his voice. I told him I'd come visit him as soon as he was at the correctional facility in Tallahassee, and he said sure. Just that, *sure*. But he said it in that stupid way he has. I knew he was holding something back. I guess I should have told someone, but it was just… a feeling."

"Who among his friends would help him escape?" I pressed.

Manning gave a short laugh and looked at me. "You went through his complete background, his phone, his computer. Did you find any friends that would help him? I doubt he has anyone who would loan him a dollar. The only people who pretended to be his friends were people who wanted to be part of my inner circle."

"Your son was much better at alienating people than making friends," I agreed. "If it wasn't friendship, then why would someone break him out of jail?"

"I've been trying to figure that out. Maybe he blackmailed someone into helping him."

"That's plausible," I said, wondering why I hadn't thought of the possibility. It would certainly fit Neil Manning's character.

"But that's bad." Manning leaned forward with a worried look on his face. "If he was blackmailing them, then wouldn't they just kill him once they had the chance?"

"Maybe not if he claimed to have evidence stashed somewhere," Lynn suggested.

"Would that really be any better?" Manning asked. "Wouldn't they just torture him until they found it?"

Lynn and I were silent, which answered his question.

"I wish that Neil could have taken his punishment like an adult." He gave a short, ironic huff. "Funny, Thorne's son, the one who videoed you and the other officer soaking wet in your boxers, reminds me of Neil when he was young. Smart. Maybe too smart for his own good." He shook his head. "I should have seen what he was becoming. Maybe I just didn't want to admit it. When he was in high school, there were signs… I just didn't know what I could do about it at that age."

"It's never too late for a spanking," Lynn said in a dead-serious tone. We both looked at her. "Hey, don't mind me. I'm a confirmed Neanderthal." She leaned in close to Manning. "You can even smell the cigarette smoke."

Manning looked temporarily stunned, then regained his composure. "There's a reason I let you in. I want to know what you found at the house... where the other prisoners were found."

"There's not much I can tell you. There was another victim found at the house."

"Roberto Cortez, the manager of the First Bank of Calhoun. I knew him." There was more sadness in his voice. This was a side of him I'd never seen. "With a murder to investigate, you can't give a bunch of details. Fine. I just want to know if... I guess I want your opinion. Do you think they might have harmed Neil?"

"No. I don't think they hurt him unless it was done at the time of the escape."

"So there wasn't any sign of Neil at the house?"

"I can't say. Even if I knew, I wouldn't tell you. I can't help you to find your son. You have to help *me* find him. Understand?"

"Don't talk to me like I'm a child!" As his anger flared, I saw the Rudy Manning I knew. He cursed, but as quickly as his temper had boiled over, it was gone. "I just want to know my son is alive."

"Tell us about that last phone call you had with him," Lynn said.

"Nothing to tell. Ever since he was sent back to jail, the calls have consisted of him asking me to get bail set and post it so he could get out. There was less of that in this phone call. I thought it was because of the transfer. He knew that once they moved him over to Tallahassee, there would be another hearing, and Thorne had assured him that bail would be set. You don't have to trust me on any of this. Special Agent in Charge Padilla had a transcript of the conversation on her phone. She read sections of it back to me."

"Did your son talk about anything he wanted to do when he got out of jail?" I asked.

"He took your capture of him personally."

"I took the fact that he manipulated a woman into attacking my father personally," I responded with more heat than was necessary. "Are you saying he might try and seek some type of revenge against me?"

"Neil said some… harsh words about you and your family."

"Do you think he would stay in the area?"

"The FBI pushed hard on that. I couldn't tell them anything more than I can tell you. Sure, he talked about other countries—South America, Thailand—but in my mind it was all just talk. Neil likes to control his environment. He's never liked to travel. Now, with the law hunting him down, would he try and escape to another country? Sure, I guess."

"Where would he get money?" Lynn asked.

Manning got quiet and I didn't think he was going to answer the question, but Lynn and I let the silence grow until he did. "I think he had some money salted away. My guess would be in cryptocurrency. He was always talking about it."

"That takes like passwords or something, right?" I didn't fully understand what the cryptocurrency thing was all about.

"Passwords only, and you can't use the old forgot-your-password button to reset it. The password *is* the money. Crypto is used regularly for illegal activities. Think about it. If you're the buyer, it's untraceable. And if you're the seller, you don't have to launder the money. It's all just sitting there waiting for you to use it for whatever dark purpose you want… or to buy a pizza. Of course, it's all just ones and zeros. If confidence is lost, it can all go away in a minute." Manning frowned.

"Great. So he could have access to an unknown amount of resources." I didn't like the feeling that, if Neil Manning managed to stay hidden, I'd always need to be looking over my shoulder.

Rudy Manning shrugged and stood up. "If I knew where he was or how to get ahold of him, I would beg him to surrender. I would."

Lynn and I asked a dozen more questions, but none of the answers were helpful.

"What do you think?" I asked her when we were back in the car.

"I think he believes what he's saying, but if he had the chance to help his son escape…" She held her hand out and wobbled it back and forth. "Maybe he would and maybe he wouldn't."

"What he's really scared of is Neil being gunned down," I said.

"I don't think Neil Manning trusts his father," Lynn said, surprising me.

"Why do you say that?"

"I've seen it with other creeps. They want their family to believe they're the little angels they pretend to be. When they get exposed, they become defensive. In the dark recesses of their souls, they've always believed that their family would hate them if they knew about their disgusting secrets, so when the family *does* know, the perp assumes that they're now the enemy. Most of the time it's true."

"That makes sense. So Neil thinks his father might turn him in if he knew where he was hiding."

"Exactly. Which means Neil will stay away from him if he can."

"How does that help us?"

"It doesn't much. But I think someone else helped orchestrate the escape."

I sighed. "I guess it saves me wasting time focusing on Rudy Manning. If Neil was desperate for money or help, I think he'd contact his father regardless of whether he trusted him or not. But if he has someone else, then there's no reason for him to contact his father. In fact, there's every reason not to."

I headed for the police station in downtown Calhoun. I

could see half a dozen suits standing around the FBI's command center as I pulled into the lot. Darlene's SUV was parked in her spot and every other space was full. I finally had to pull back out of the lot and park on the street.

We walked over to the command center, where Lynn was greeted by several of the agents. Unlike Lynn, I didn't recognize any of them and they didn't recognize me. I was about to step up to the door of the RV when Padilla came out. Behind her were a couple of older men who, judging from their age and the cut of their suits, were clearly higher up the food chain than Padilla.

"We'll complete our investigation this week," the taller of the two men said.

"I'd like to get my agents back in the field as soon as possible," Padilla said.

"We'll keep you in the loop," the man said, while the shorter man beside him nodded along. They were doing a very good impression of Will Smith and Tommy Lee Jones.

Padilla waved as they walked on past her with several of the other suits in their wake. Then she turned to me. "What do you want?"

"I want to discuss your current strategy for catching Neil Manning."

"Hi, Lynn," Padilla said, seeming to notice Lynn for the first time. She had walked up beside me after chatting with the other agents.

"Elaine. It's always a pleasure."

Elaine? I realized that this was the first time I'd ever heard anyone use Padilla's first name.

"You with him?" She pointed a finger at me.

"He's my boss," Lynn said, and Padilla raised her eyebrows.

"Come in." Looking reluctant and tired, she nodded toward the command center and gestured us inside.

"Unless we get on his trail soon, our operation is going to be scaled back," Padilla told us before I could ask any questions. "The brass and his entourage were here for two reasons. They're reviewing the agent-involved shooting, and they want to know if we can get out of this situation without losing too much face. The good news is that they're almost certainly going to put their blessing on the shooting. The bad news is, they've decided they can blame the escape on the U.S. Marshals and leave a token effort on the ground looking for Neil Manning. The hunt will move to a mostly passive phase, with Manning taking a prominent position on the Most Wanted list."

"Just declare yourselves winners having caught two out of three and head home," I accused, feeling my blood rising.

"It's politics. To be fair, Manning is most likely outside of your county, maybe the state."

"You don't want to add country?" Lynn asked.

"Our profile says he's not likely to flee the country. Besides, it's not that easy to do. You need money."

"Is there a chance he has access to cryptocurrency?" I asked as if I'd just come up with the idea.

Padilla looked at me for a minute as though reevaluating her opinion of me. "We've considered that possibility. We've ordered more thorough forensics on the electronics that were seized when he was originally arrested. Even if he had currency to draw from, he doesn't appear to have the type of connections that would help him go to another country and set up a new life. Besides, if he wanted to do that then he'd have to choose a country like Thailand or Columbia. Not his style."

"I can't disagree with you there." I thought of the evil spoiled brat we were talking about. Neil wouldn't do well in a country where the locals played hardball.

"Anything you can do to help us would be helping you." Padilla looked earnest. I knew she didn't like to fail, and now she was apparently willing to humble herself a little if it would help find her quarry. "I can share some of the evidence we've gathered if it will help bring in Neil Manning."

"How long are they going to give you?"

"This is Memorial Day weekend. They'll probably pull the plug Tuesday."

"You know that Manning has a motive for revenge against me?" I didn't want to go down this path, but I was willing to meet her halfway along the road to cooperation.

"We've been doing secondary surveillance on you and your wife," Padilla admitted.

"Secondary?"

"No wiretaps or bugs. We haven't been watching you 24/7. We *have* been cruising by your property and monitoring the comings and going at your wife's clinic. We took notice of your father-in-law's presence."

"Great." I looked down and bit back any irritation I felt that they hadn't told me about this already. "Look, I appreciate you looking out for us… or using us as bait, whatever. I've got a few questions. First, have you vetted the driver of the van, Willie Mathis?"

"Short answer, yes. His background is clean. Current finances are good. Stable home life. Absolutely no connections to the three prisoners or their families. We were able to interview him in the hospital yesterday and he remembers very little about the crash. Not surprising considering his head injury."

"What about Florence Murray, the guard?"

"By all accounts she was competent and gregarious. Well liked by her colleagues and bosses. Like Mathis, there's nothing in her history that would suggest that she was involved in the escape. I'll authorize the agent in charge of the backgrounds to release the information to your department."

"I appreciate the resources you have at your fingertips."

"I only have those resources for as long as my bosses let me use them. Is Lewis available to help?" Padilla nodded toward Lynn.

"Almost any of our assets will be available through the holiday weekend. A lot of our deputies were already scheduled to be on duty to cover joint traffic operations with the highway patrol."

"Are you speaking for the sheriff?"

I nodded. "Look. The only reason Dad got so irritated with your… operation was because he feels so strongly about Neil Manning. I'll update him on the situation, and if he doesn't agree with anything I've said, he'll let both of us know. You can count on it."

CHAPTER THIRTEEN

When we came out of the command center, I saw Darlene standing by her SUV talking to one of her officers. She waved us over as the officer walked away.

"Look who the cat dragged in," she said.

"Chief," I said with a smile.

"Don't try to butter my biscuits with that 'Chief' crap. Lynn, what are you doing riding around with this troublemaker?"

"He's my boss," Lynn deadpanned.

"You still bucking for Little Miss Sunshine?" Darlene asked, causing me to wonder if this was going to get ugly.

"If I was, I'd come to you for lessons, Polly-freakin'-anna." This time Lynn allowed the corners of her lips to curl up just a little.

"Don't mind us. Opposites don't always attract," Darlene told me as Lynn gave her a friendly finger.

"Yeah. Larry asked why we didn't work together more when you were with the sheriff's office."

"Different styles." Darlene smiled. "Both effective, just different. Now you and I..." She pointed at me. "...were Batman and Robin, the Green Hornet and Kato, Holmes and Watson, Mulder and Scully. You, of course, being Robin, Kato, Watson and… Mulder, I think."

"Thanks, Batman."

Darlene nodded toward the command center. "What's going on with our MIB? Or should I say WIB?"

"Manning is still on the loose and the brass is getting bored."

"Of course they are. The media picked up the story of them finding two of the fugitives and has moved on. Without the media breathing life into the case, it's easy to sweep Neil Manning under the rug."

"Oh, they *are* going to put him on the Most Wanted list," I told her. "Fourth or possibly even third on the list."

"I'll be glad to have them out of my parking lot. Still, I'd feel a lot better if they'd take Manning with them." Darlene looked as frustrated as I felt. "I've been in touch with Phil Eccles and have kept the information front and center with my officers."

"Appreciate it. We're going to try one more grand push over the next four or five days to find him."

"We?" Darlene raised her eyebrows.

"Padilla says she's willing to share all her information and resources with us if we'll reciprocate."

"She's desperate. Well, count me in. Though my officers are going to be spending most of the holiday weekend working to keep local parties under control and drunk drivers off the street."

Lynn and I headed back to the office. It was lunchtime and I offered to stop at the taco stand on the way.

"Not today. My mother's in town and I'm meeting her at the Palmetto for lunch." Lynn took out her phone. "I told her I'd text her."

We parted ways in the parking lot, and I headed straight inside to Dad's office. His assistant's desk was empty, so I knocked on the door and heard both a loud bark and a curt "Come in!"… presumably not from the same set of vocal cords.

Mauser met me as soon as I opened the door.

"I think he knows your knock," Dad said.

"I thought Henry was watching him."

"I met with a group of kids at the middle school this morning." Dad always took Mauser along for community meet-and-greets, especially if there were going to be kids around.

Mauser's greeting was short and slobbery. After getting some ear rubs, he went over to the twin mattress beside the desk and flopped down, exhausted from all the attention he'd received that day.

"Any news on Manning?" Dad cut to the chase.

"That's why I came to talk to you. The FBI is about to change focus. Scaling back the local search and moving to a national search."

"Making Manning one of their Most Wanted?" Dad asked skeptically.

"Exactly. The brass has given Padilla until Tuesday to show results. She's asking for our cooperation."

"Meaning she doesn't have anything to hang her hat on."

"We don't either," I reminded him.

"By placing Manning on the Most Wanted list, it makes it look like they're still focused on him. From the FBI's perspective, getting out of Dodge is the smart move. The two murders can be chalked up to the dead fugitives."

"Which is why the FBI is going with that theory. And that's probably the reality. What we need to worry about is, if Manning is still here in Adams County, then he's staying here for a reason."

"And that reason is revenge?" Dad frowned. "Still seems unlikely. Wouldn't he have made a move already? And what about the person who helped him? What's their motivation? Assuming it is anyone other than his father."

"I don't think it's Rudy Manning," I admitted.

"You've had a change of heart?"

"We talked to him today and... I don't know. He seems different, more subdued, more repentant."

"Who's we?"

"Lynn Lewis. I hadn't thought about her relationship with the FBI and her knowledge of internet crimes until now. So I took her along when I went to talk to Manning and Padilla."

"Smart to get a different set of eyes and ears on the case. I've found she comes at problems from a different angle than most. Glad you're working with your whole team." From Dad, this was high praise.

"I'm still trying to get an angle on Mick Klein."

"I don't think he's ever been happy with me being sheriff. You might be getting some reflected scorn."

"What's he got against you?"

"I've never figured that out." Dad shrugged. "Hell, it was my own ineptitude on a case that got him into CID."

"So what happened with the Simmons case? I talked with Mr. Griffin about it, but I haven't had time to dig into the case files."

A shadow seemed to pass over Dad's green eyes, then he sighed. "You want the truth?"

I nodded.

"I screwed up. Simple as that. I arrived at the scene as the responding officer. It was a welfare check, so I circled the house knocking on doors and checking windows. Nothing looked out of place. Looked around the yard and saw a car through the garage window. I could have walked away at that point, but I didn't. I've always taken welfare checks seriously. I remember calling in a few on your grandparents when I couldn't get ahold of them back in the day."

"I didn't realize they'd ever needed looking after."

"You were young. This was just after he'd fallen and broken a hip and her eyesight wasn't very good. Anyway, I talked to the neighbors until I found someone with a key. Inside, I found the bodies on the bed in the master bedroom on the second floor. Lots of blood. One of the bloodiest scenes I'd experienced so far in my career. Of course, I called for backup and an investigator.

"His name was Archie Huff. He was competent, but he didn't have much insight. He asked me to go over what I knew, so I told him what I'd heard from the neighbors. Most had mentioned two things. They'd heard arguing from the house on a couple of occasions, and the Simmonses hadn't seemed themselves for the last month."

"And the doors were locked."

Dad sighed. "Yes, and the doors were locked. The bodies looked like they hadn't been moved. Mrs. Simmons had the most wounds. Mr. Simmons's throat had been slit, as well as his wrists. The knife was on the floor beneath his outstretched hand. Both victims had bled out on the bed. Anyway, I made the mistake of voicing my opinion that it was a murder-suicide."

"And Huff agreed with you?"

"He loved to close cases on the same day he got them. He had to wait for the autopsy and a more thorough questioning of friends, coworkers and neighbors, but, yeah, he was glad to stamp it a murder-suicide. All wrapped up in a neat package."

"Where did Mick come in?"

"He was the first deputy who showed up when I called for backup. He helped with crowd control and then, when the coroner showed up without any help, Mick volunteered. While he was helping the coroner with the bodies, he spotted a few things I'd missed and pointed them out to Huff. He took notes, but he wasn't really invested in the idea that it was a double homicide."

"So who went to bat for the idea?" I asked.

"Mick kept dropping hints until he found someone who'd listen. Turned out that the assistant sheriff at the time, James Rickert, attended the same church as the victims. He knew Mr. Simmons and didn't think the man could commit murder, let alone murder and then suicide. So Rickert started riding Huff until he actually went to work. It didn't take long for the evidence to point to someone else."

"The daughter."

Dad nodded. "The arguing that the neighbors had heard in the days prior to the murders had been between the parents and their daughter over the phone. And sometimes it had been the parents fighting over what to do with their daughter. But apparently she decided that if her parents were dead, then she'd have half their money and be free of their nagging."

"She did it by herself?"

"Like a pro. She dressed up in a raincoat and snuck into their room. The first thing she did was slit her father's throat."

"Didn't her mother wake up?"

"Riley knew that her mother always took a sleeping pill. After slitting her father's throat, she moved to the other side of the bed and went full Lizzie Borden on her mother. Seems there was more anger there than with her father."

I felt a shiver go down my spine. "What was the evidence against her?"

"When they looked more closely at the blood evidence, it became apparent that the father had died first. If he died first, then he couldn't have killed the wife. And the wife had too many stab wounds for hers to have been self-inflicted."

"I guess once they established it was a double homicide, then they looked at who had a motive."

"Which led them straight to Riley. Her alibi was weak at best. She claimed she was at her apartment in Tampa watching TV when it happened. I remember that she had gone to a lot of trouble to memorize the plot of the movie she claimed to have watched. She must have thought she was in a *Columbo* episode or something. It was Mick again who broke the alibi. He'd found out where she'd had an oil change the week before and got the mileage. She couldn't account for all the extra miles on her car. The irony was, she got the oil change because her father always told her to do that before she took a road trip.

"Once the alibi was broken, they looked closer and found some of her blood on the scene. She'd cut herself during the attack. Confronted with the evidence, she confessed, receiving two life sentences as part of a plea bargain."

"And Mick got moved into CID."

Dad nodded. "The way I heard it, Assistant Sheriff Rickert asked Mick what he wanted: either a promotion to sergeant or to be moved to CID. Mick chose CID."

"Interesting," I said, thinking that I might have just learned a lot about Mick.

That's when both our phones started ringing and exploding with text alerts. Dad's phone was on his desk, and he looked at it before I could get to mine, then leaped to his feet.

"There's a 911 call from the vet clinic." He was already moving toward the door with the phone to his ear. "Talk to me."

My heart dropped into my stomach when the source of the call sank in.

"An assault at the clinic. Two men!" Dad shouted to me as we both ran down the hall.

I felt only a little relief hearing that the call was about two men. Emergency calls weren't always accurate. Adrenaline-fueled witnesses were notoriously bad at giving dispatchers exact details.

I followed Dad to his truck since it was closer than my car, and I knew Dad would drive it like he stole it. We heard several other sirens in the distance, and Dad flipped his on as he wheeled out of the parking lot.

The clinic where Cara worked was only a few blocks away, but my mind still had time to envision all sorts of traumatic scenarios. I heard dispatch and deputies exchanging words over the radio, but none of it was penetrating the internal alarm that screamed for me to get to Cara's side.

Dad pulled into the clinic's parking lot, where a patrol car and a black sedan that looked suspiciously like it belonged to the FBI were already parked. I was out of the truck and heading for the front door when I noticed a group of people gathered around the side of the building.

"Dad, are you all right?"

I heard Cara's voice and realized that Henry was standing in the center of the group of a dozen spectators, along with Deputy Matti Sanderson and an FBI agent. Knowing that Cara was okay, my body immediately relaxed, and I paused as Dad jogged up beside me. Looking more closely at the FBI agent, I saw that he had a bloody nose, a tear in his jacket and a snarl on his face that made it clear he was ready for round two.

"Turn around!" he shouted at Henry, who was a good six inches taller and standing his ground.

"I didn't know who you were," Henry explained, irritation evident in his voice.

I saw the man reach back toward his gun and Sanderson stepped between the two men.

"I really don't think that's the right approach," I heard her say.

"I'm with the FBI," the agent said through clenched teeth.

"We've established that," Sanderson said calmly. "What we need to know is what happened here."

I heard more cars enter the parking lot as I walked over to Cara and put my hand on her shoulder. "What happened?" I asked as she turned toward me.

"Dad saw this guy lurking around the clinic. I guess he thought he looked suspicious, so Dad... well, he kind of jumped him."

The rest of the group was a mix of clinic staff, clients and passersby. They seemed enthralled with the drama playing out in front of them. I pushed through the group until I was face to face with Henry.

"What happened?"

"You need to keep your nose out of this," the agent told me in a menacing tone.

I flipped out my bifold and showed him my identification.

"Thought you looked familiar," he huffed. "I'm agent Terrance Cash and this man assaulted me."

"I was sitting in my car when I saw this guy creeping through the parking lot, looking in cars," Henry said, ignoring the agent. "I came up behind him and said…" Henry looked a little embarrassed. "Boo!"

There was a titter of laughter from the crowd.

"You snuck up behind me and screamed in my ear!" Cash growled.

"The guy turned and was going to hit me, so I thumped him in the chest. I blocked his swing and… might have hit him in the face," Henry admitted sheepishly.

"He's under arrest for assaulting a federal officer," the agent insisted.

"Cash!" shouted a voice from behind us. I turned to see Padilla pushing her way through the crowd.

"Ma'am," Cash said in a softer tone.

"Did you identify yourself as an FBI agent?" Padilla asked.

"I didn't have time!"

"Was there a badge or anything visible that identified you as an agent?"

Cash bit his lip and looked down at the ground.

"Did you raise your hand to this man?" Padilla continued.

"I heard… He shouted… I thought I needed to defend myself," Cash finished lamely.

Padilla turned to Henry and me. "I think we're finished here."

"What are you talking about? He assaulted me!" Cash puffed up again.

Padilla whirled around with fire in her eyes. "What do you expect when someone's worried about an escaped convict who's made specific threats about their family, and they see some guy peering in car windows like a stalker?" Her words were fast and furious. "Write up a report and I'll submit it with mine." The implication that the two reports had better be compatible was obvious. "Now go do something that isn't counterproductive."

Cash brushed himself off and walked away, along with the dissipating crowd.

Padilla turned back and apologized to Henry, Cara, Dad and me.

"He's overzealous. Sorry, Mr. Laursen." I don't know why I was surprised that she knew his name.

"I just wondered who the hell he was. If he was a bad guy, I wanted to be close enough to nab him." Henry sounded like a character out of a 1950s Western.

"Leave the nabbing to law enforcement," Padilla told him with a smile.

"I appreciate your… response," Dad said, clearly holding an olive branch out to Padilla.

"Did Larry tell you that we have five days to find Manning?"

"I'll walk you back to your car."

"That looks encouraging," Cara commented as they walked away together.

"We're all in the same leaky boat," I told her.

"Sorry about hitting the guy," Henry told me.

"I just wish I'd seen it."

"You two are going to get in trouble," Cara said. "It wouldn't be the first time."

"One of those times got you out of a sticky situation," I reminded her. I saw Julio pull into the lot. "I need to go."

"And I need to get back to work," Cara said, giving me a quick kiss and her father a hug.

"I'll stay out here and try not to get into any more trouble," Henry said and headed for his truck.

"Everything all right?" Julio asked me as he got out of his car.

"Fine. Henry hit an FBI agent who was skulking around the parking lot. Padilla was cool about it and quashed any repercussions."

Julio looked like he was trying to decide if I was kidding

or not. I went ahead and filled him in on our new timeline for catching Neil Manning before we lost the assets of the Feds.

"I know they're annoying, but they can get things done in a fraction of the time we can," I said. "When Lynn and I were talking to Padilla, she showed us the geofencing data they'd gotten from Google for the day of the escape. Not only had they collected in a few days what might have taken us weeks, but they'd already analyzed it. Of course, it didn't help. Whoever was working that backhoe either didn't have their cell phone with them, had it turned off or had at least disabled all of the location-sharing options. Speaking of the backhoe, she said they turned that information over to you."

Julio nodded. "They did. Most of it I already knew. It was stolen from a construction site just on our side of the county line. It was a site that had been temporarily shut down because of permitting issues. Agent Redcliff is running backgrounds on the employees and former employees of the construction company."

"The upside is that their ability to analyze any DNA evidence is way beyond ours and Dad won't mind that the Feds are picking up the tab for the testing."

"Do you think Manning is still here in the county?" Julio asked.

"That's the current Final Jeopardy question," I said with a shrug. "I want us to go back to basics with the Cortez murder. Let's act like we just found his body in the back of his car."

"How will that help us find Manning?" Julio asked.

"If there's more to Cortez's murder than meets the eye, then that connection or motive or whatever you want to call it could help us to find the person who coordinated the escape. In my mind, that's the key to finding Manning. Who's helping him?"

"Cortez's sister is going to be here tomorrow."

"Good. She's one person who might give us some insight into who our victim is."

"I'll check her alibi," Julio said. I looked at him to see if he was kidding, then decided he was right. If we were going to look at his murder like any other, then even close relatives couldn't be ruled out.

"And look for any motive she might have had. I also want to talk to his coworkers again. What are you doing this afternoon?"

"I've got interviews for a domestic abuse case from Monday. I'll be busy all afternoon. I don't mind if you go talk to folks at the bank without me. Just take good notes." Julio smiled.

"Thanks, boss," I joked. "I don't want to intrude on your case."

"As soon as the Cortez case got mixed up with the escaped fugitives, it became a group effort."

"I'll talk to them and see if we need to bring any of them in for a formal interview. At some point we'll need to get formal statements."

Dad was talking on the radio as I walked back to his truck. Padilla was nowhere in sight.

"You make nice?" I asked him.

He just muttered under his breath.

"She's not that bad," I told him as I climbed inside the truck.

"It's all about the attitude. Some of that's gone now that she's facing a deadline with a slim chance of meeting it." He slipped on his seatbelt and pulled out of the parking lot. "There's another thing I want to talk to you about." His tone changed to concern. "How's Pete doing?"

"I doubt I know more than you do," I hedged. "He had a doctor's appointment today. They're getting a second opinion on his leg. I know this new doctor had him do another MRI."

"It's his attitude that's worrying me." Dad looked over at me with a grim expression. "You remember Sally Waterson?"

"Yeah." I felt a cold chill settle over me. I'd only met

Deputy Waterson a couple of times. She'd taken her life when I'd been at the academy.

"I'd only been in office a couple of months, and I never saw it coming. That's one of my deepest regrets. She had a few issues—didn't get along with one of the other deputies; had recently broken up with the father of her son. But nothing that most other deputies don't go through at some point in their careers. I talked to her family afterward and they were all shocked by what happened." He took a deep breath. "I don't want to get blindsided by something like that again. I've never seen Pete moody the way he is now. Not that he doesn't have good reason. Still, I want to get on top of this."

"I… You're right." A wave of guilt washed over me. I'd been so caught up in my life and career that, while I'd noticed Pete was having a tough time, I hadn't taken it as seriously as I should have. "I'll talk to him this evening and maybe talk to Sarah. But I've got to be careful talking to Sarah. I don't want Pete to think I'm going behind his back."

"Better for him to think there's a conspiratorial circle of friends trying to help him than for him to feel like he's all alone," Dad said as he parked at the sheriff's office.

"I'll talk to him tonight."

"You were right to get him involved in some cases. I'm open to anything you suggest if it helps him and his family."

"I'll let you know."

CHAPTER FOURTEEN

I went to my office and closed the door so I could get some work done. If I was going to spend part of the afternoon talking to the people at the bank, I needed to clear my inbox first. It was three o'clock before I was ready to leave.

The bank was busy when I arrived. Above the door was a black wreath and a picture of Roberto Cortez with a placard that read: *Missed by all.*

Curtis Warner, the assistant manager, was talking with a client so I took a seat in the lobby to wait. After only a few minutes, he walked up to me with his hand outstretched and a grim expression on his face.

"Sergeant Macklin, right? I can't tell you how devastated we were when Deputy Ortiz informed us that Mr. Cortez had been murdered. It's simply awful."

"I'm sorry for your loss. Now that we know what happened to him, I need to ask some additional questions," I said sympathetically.

"This way," he said, leading me back to his office.

"What can I do to help?" Warner asked once we were seated.

"Can you think of anyone who has had an argument with or held a grudge against Mr. Cortez?"

Warner shrugged. "Bankers make people angry all the time. Goes with the business. But it's not like he was the loan officer. That's the hotseat. Cecilia Foster handles most of our loans. Let me think…." He frowned. "Truly, I can't think of any problems he had with anyone. He was all business and very polite and considerate with everyone."

"What about someone who was angry with the bank? Maybe an employee who was fired?"

He looked thoughtful for a moment before saying, "No one has been fired in the last year. And I can't think of any customers who had more than a disagreement with a teller or a bank officer. Nothing out of the ordinary."

"When Mr. Cortez went missing, did you think anyone in the bank acted odd? Maybe they didn't seem very concerned… or they seemed overly concerned."

"Everyone wondered where he was, but I wouldn't say anyone was acting… abnormally."

"Was anyone absent from work around that time?"

"Now that you mention it, Cecilia was out the day we reported him missing, but I don't think there's anything nefarious about it. She called in saying she had to take her three-year-old to the doctor. I forget what the issue was."

"Is she here today?"

"Oh, yes. Do you want me to get her?" Warner offered.

"I'll talk to her after we're done. I assume that you will take Mr. Cortez's position as manager?" I tried to ask the question without putting any inflection on the words, but from the look in his eyes it was clear he understood my intent.

"Really! You think I… That's silly… Anyway, I'm just filling in until a replacement is appointed by the board. I can think of at least three other people here who are equally qualified."

"I'd like you to write down their names for me."

Warner scowled. "Now it's one thing to ask me questions, but it's quite another to ask me to give you the names of colleagues who might feel like I'm fingering them for… a… a murder that seems like an open-and-shut case." He was clearly flustered.

"I get it. I'm not going to go around accusing them of killing Mr. Cortez. When I speak to them, I'll let them know that the sheriff's office wants to be thorough in investigating the murder of one of their colleagues. Don't you think they would want that?" I asked.

He settled back in his chair and looked mollified. "I suppose."

"I won't tell them that I got the names from you. Probably any number of employees could tell me who's likely to fill the manager position."

"That's true." He took out a pen and began writing names on a pad of paper.

"Does Rudy Manning bank here?" I asked.

Warner looked surprised at the question. "Yes, of course. I saw him yesterday. He was making a deposit."

"When was the last time you saw him talking to Mr. Cortez?"

Warner sat back and raised his eyebrows. "I'd have to think about that. Maybe two or three days before he went missing."

"Did you notice anything off about their last meeting?"

"I really didn't pay much attention. They always seemed cordial."

"Do you remember Mr. Cortez ever talking about Manning's son, Neil?"

"Yes, we all talked about it. I don't remember anything specific he said. Mostly he felt sorry for Manning's victims… and for Rudy Manning."

"Would Mr. Cortez recognize Neil Manning?"

"I think he would. I know he met him a couple of times when Neil was running AmMex for his dad. Plus, there was plenty of media coverage after his arrest. Do you think Manning had something to do with his death?"

"We're looking at all the possibilities. What about the rest of the bank employees? Were any of them friendly with Neil

Manning?"

"Depends on your definition of friendly. We train our staff to be courteous to all our customers. Remember that Rudy Manning is one of our largest business accounts. Now, having said that, Neil Manning was an odd duck. I can't say that he made many friends here. He liked to be the big fish and would talk about how rich his father was, that sort of thing." Warner paused and looked uneasy. "There's one more thing I should mention. He made our female employees uncomfortable. In light of his crimes, I can see there was good reason for that."

"Did they ever mention this to you before he was arrested?"

Warner shook his head. "Not really. It was mainly bank gossip. None of them made a formal complaint. They would just say he was a creep or a jerk, that sort of thing." He sighed. "I'm not proud of my response. I reminded them that his father is an important customer and that they shouldn't talk about Neil like that. I should have taken it all more seriously."

"Did Neil ever do anything overt?"

"No. That's just it. They would say it was a look in his eye or the way he smiled at them. The occasional compliment about their hair or clothes. Nothing that wouldn't have sounded fine coming from someone else."

A dozen more questions didn't get me any more usable information.

"I'll see the loan officer now." I stood up and Warner escorted me back into the lobby.

"You'll need to wait. She's with a client." He stepped over to a glassed-in office and leaned through the door. I couldn't hear what they said, but the woman nodded, and Warner came back to tell me that it would only be a few minutes.

In less than five minutes, the customer exited the office and Cecilia Foster came out to greet me. She was in her late twenties, barely five feet tall with fine features, but her eyes seemed older than her years.

"Mr. Warner said you wanted to speak to me?" Her voice was light and musical. Something about her seemed familiar, but I couldn't think of where I'd seen her before.

"I wanted to ask a few questions about Mr. Cortez."

She waved me toward her office.

"I remember you from our church. You came with your father just before the last election," she said, and I finally remembered seeing her as a soloist in the choir at the First Methodist Church.

"You have a beautiful voice," I said.

"You said that at the dinner on the grounds." Her smile let me know she was teasing me. "You know, you and your dad can come to church any Sunday, not just the ones before elections."

"I… we… will," I stuttered, caught completely off guard.

"Let's make a date for your dad to bring Mauser to Sunday school the second week of June." She was enjoying this. "Some of our kids had met him at school and were disappointed that you all didn't bring him last time."

"I'll talk to Dad and see if he can do that." I loved the idea of making plans for Dad instead of the other way around.

Cecilia turned serious. "I'm sorry. I know you came here to talk about Mr. Cortez. I've been trying not to think about what happened. I liked Mr. Cortez a lot. He was not… I don't know… Always all about the office and business. I don't mean he didn't take it seriously. You don't run a bank unless you take the work seriously. But I sensed that he could just turn it off, if you know what I mean?"

"I'm not sure."

"I guess it's just that he didn't get all uptight about little things around the bank." She snapped her fingers. "That's it! He knew how to prioritize what was important and what wasn't. He would never tolerate any mistakes in the paperwork, but if I needed to take a day off for my boy, he understood the priority of family. A month ago, I got called by the daycare because Galen fell down and cut his forehead. Mr. Cortez was like, 'Go, I'll cover for you.' And that's what he did. I came back three hours later, and Mr. Cortez was reviewing a loan application with two more people waiting to talk to him. He was just a nice guy. It's awful what happened to him." She stopped and gave me a sad little smile.

"I know it can be hard to accept. I'm here to do some background on Mr. Cortez to see if it might turn up anything that could have led to his kidnapping and murder. I'll be asking a lot of questions that might not seem important considering how Mr. Cortez died, but we want to be thorough. Let's start with the obvious question. Did Mr. Cortez have any enemies?"

Cecilia shook her head quickly. "No. No one. I've had several jobs since I graduated, and he's the first boss I've had that no one disliked. He just knew how to manage people."

"Is there anyone here that he was particularly close to?"

"No. See, that's part of it. He didn't get personal with anyone, so there weren't any feelings of jealousy or, you know, thinking someone is getting special favors. Everyone equal, but different."

"You sound like you admired him?"

"I saw him as a model for the type of leader I want to be some day." She wiped a tear from the corner of her eye.

"You were out the day he was reported missing?" I asked.

"Galen had a headache in the morning. This was the third time he's complained about his head hurting since he had the cut on his forehead. I got a little scared and worked up, thinking he might have gotten a more severe injury than they thought, so I took him to the doctor again."

"When did you find out that Mr. Cortez was missing?"

"I got a text from Catalina, the head teller, asking me if I knew where Mr. Cortez was. It weirded me out a bit. I was already worried about Galen, and then someone was asking me where Mr. Cortez was." She looked like she was reliving the anxiety she had felt that morning.

"Did anyone say anything else to you about Mr. Cortez being missing?"

"When I was finally done at the doctor's I texted a couple of people to see if he'd ever shown up to work, but no one had seen him. If I hadn't been so tired from dealing with Galen, it would have really freaked me out."

"What time did you get home?"

"Around three. Momma came over and helped with Galen while I made dinner."

"Do you know Rudy Manning?" I asked, changing the topic.

"Oh, yes. Everyone at the bank does. Though I've never worked with him directly on anything. If he needed help, he went straight to Mr. Cortez."

"What about Neil Manning?"

She looked upset at the mention of his name. "I saw him when he would come into the bank sometimes. That's all."

"Did you ever talk to him?" I pressed.

She didn't answer and I let the silence draw out.

"I didn't like him," she finally said.

"Did he do something to make you dislike him?" I knew from her face that there was more to her story.

"I don't want to talk about it."

"What did he do to you?" She was looking more and more upset, so I held up my hand. "If it will help, I can get one of our victim's advocates to come talk to you. Or, if you'd like, I can refer you to a counselor who can talk you through whatever happened."

Cecilia took a deep breath and placed her hands flat on the top of her desk. They were shaking slightly.

"No, I'm okay. It… There's a hallway at the back of the lobby where the restrooms are. I came out of the women's room one day and… and… he was there. I thought he was going into the men's room, but he stopped right in front of me. I felt like he was blocking me in. For a second I thought it was just one of those moments where you sort of dance back and forth awkwardly with someone. You know, you go right, they go left, then you go left and they go right? But just when I was going to smile and make a joke of it, he looked at me. I mean his eyes looked *into* me. I... froze. If I hadn't just gone to the bathroom, I think I would have peed myself."

"Neil Manning can be very intimidating," I said gently.

"I was going to step around him when his hand came up and he reached for me, almost like he couldn't help himself. When I saw that hand coming towards me, I almost screamed. Instead, I ran back into the bathroom. I stayed in there for thirty minutes, trying to convince myself that I was all worked up about nothing. Finally, I went back to my desk, but I couldn't work. I thought about telling someone, but what would I tell them? The son of one of our biggest depositors looked at me weird? It was a couple of days before I could shake it off. Even then, I kept worrying about what would happen the next time he entered the bank."

"When was this?"

"About a week before he was arrested. When I heard about what he'd done to that woman, I almost passed out. It was like I'd seen that darkness in his eyes. I can still see it." Silent tears ran down her cheeks.

"I can't imagine what you must have felt like."

"When I heard he'd escaped... I've just been holding it together these last couple of days."

"We'll catch him," I assured her. I thought about how happy she'd seemed when we started talking and I realized how often people hide what they're really feeling.

"I've been praying for it."

"I'd still like to put you in touch with our victim's advocate," I offered.

"I'll be okay. I think I can talk to my mama about it now."

We talked for a few more minutes, but I didn't ask any more questions. I just wanted to see her relax a little before I left.

"Now don't forget about bringing Mauser to Sunday school," she reminded me as I stood up to leave. She was smiling again as I assured her that Dad would do his best to come visit their church in the near future.

Feeling drained from her emotional revelations, I stopped at the water fountain and looked toward the bathroom hallway. It was just narrow enough that a person could block another person from getting by if they wanted.

When I turned back to the main lobby, I saw Bert Hodges, the security guard. He waved at me.

"I saw you come in," he said as he rested his hands on his duty belt. "It's awful about Mr. Cortez. Good man. Glad those bastards that killed him are dead."

"The murder is still under investigation," I told him.

"You don't say? I heard it was open-and-shut." Since he'd worked for the police department for years, I wasn't surprised that he had his sources.

"Would you mind if I asked you a few questions?"

"Sure thing. Ask whatever you want."

"Is there anyone here who didn't like Mr. Cortez?"

"Nah, he was a real nice guy. There was a little grumblin' about schedules and that sort of thing, but nothin' in particular."

"Did you notice anything odd about him?"

Bert gave a little laugh. "He didn't look at the head teller as much as most of the guys. That was a little surprisin'." He leaned in close to me. "Not to get myself in trouble with HR, but I'm just sayin', she's a real looker. If I was twenty… well, maybe thirty years younger, I'd be doggin' her close."

I pondered that for a minute. "But Mr. Cortez didn't watch her. Do you think it was an effort to hide a relationship?"

"Like they didn't want anyone knowin' they were havin' an affair? No. He was just one of those guys who always does the right thing. The kind of guy you respect, but you're not goin' to invite to your bachelor party, if you know what I mean."

"Did you notice anyone in the bank who was friends with Neil Manning?" As soon as I said the name, Bert's face darkened.

"That… Man, I never liked that guy. You know, I was jokin' about lookin' at a pretty woman. Most guys just kid around and admire a woman. He was different. I saw guys like him a few times when I was workin' for the police department. Soulless is what my mother would have called it. Nothin' behind the eyes. Nowadays they call them psychopaths. Most of them try to hide it, but not him. Maybe because his father had his back, he didn't think he needed to hide it." Bert paused. "What was your question?"

"Was anyone in the bank chatty with him? Maybe even friendly?"

"Nope. Once in a while we'd get a new teller who knew his family was rich and at first they'd be a little flirty with him. Never lasted long. He just gave off this chill that would spook anyone with a sense of self-preservation."

"Gives," I corrected him. "He's still alive and he's loose."

"Don't think I've forgotten. I might get a little lazy working in here, but not since I heard he was on the loose. I went out to the range yesterday and emptied a couple boxes of ammunition. I could see that weasel comin' in here and trying to get money." Unconsciously, his hand slid back toward the gun at his hip.

"Make sure of your target and what's beyond it," I said, only half joking.

He looked at me for a minute as if trying to decide if I was being a smartass. "I never had to shoot anyone when I was a cop. That doesn't mean I haven't thought about it every day that I've worn a gun on my hip."

"I wasn't making fun of you. Sometimes we're called on to make tough decisions and adrenaline can cloud your vision."

"If I ever pull the trigger, it will be spot-on and done right," Bert assured me.

"How often did you see Mr. Cortez interact with Neil Manning?"

"Not too many times, between Mr. Cortez comin' to

work at the bank and Neil goin' to jail. Maybe half a dozen times. Mr. Cortez treated him like any other customer. Maybe a little more personal treatment because of the amount of business Rudy Manning does with the bank, but nothing surprising."

After a few more questions, I left him to speak with Catalina Knight, the head teller. Bert winked at me as I walked away. She was talking with another teller on the far end of the counter and smiled widely as soon as she saw me heading her way.

"Can I ask you a few questions?" I asked.

"I'll come around." She turned and headed for the door that led out into the lobby. "We can use Mr. Cortez's office, if you'd like?" she suggested, extending her hand toward the door like Vanna White. "It's sad being in here and knowing what happened," she said as we sat down in a pair of chairs facing his desk.

I looked again at the pictures of Roberto Cortez in his hunting poses. Even in those pictures, he looked like everyone had said: professional and focused.

"Tell me about Mr. Cortez's interactions with the bank's staff," I said, giving her an opening to create her own narrative. Sometimes this approach could give a suspect or a witness just enough rope to hang themselves or someone else, but not in this case. Catalina painted the same picture of a man who had been the epitome of a good manager. Then I asked her about Neil Manning.

"That creep!" She laughed. "He always struck me as a weirdo. I made it a point to warn all of the tellers, female *and* male, to deal with him but not to *engage* with him, if you get my drift."

"Do you know if he ever had any inappropriate interactions with bank employees?"

"He never touched anyone with his hands. His eyes were a different matter." She sighed. "Okay, I know I'm an attractive woman. So getting *that* look from people is normal. Most of the time it's a compliment and I take it that way. But every once in a while it's more of a threat, and I've had to show more than one guy that I have claws. But Neil is in a whole different category of creepy. His look is a promise. A promise of the bad things he'd do to you if he had the chance."

"Did you show *him* your claws?" I asked.

"It wouldn't have done any good. A monster like that would take it as a challenge. He's like a rabid grizzly bear. If you can't kill it, then avoid it at all costs."

I couldn't disagree with her assessment.

"Where do you think Neil Manning is right now?" I asked, throwing her a curveball.

She blinked for a minute as though trying to understand the question or trying to come up with a good answer. "I hope far away or dead," she finally said without any hint of humor. "What's with all questions anyway? Didn't the other two prisoners kill Mr. Cortez?"

"We aren't going to assume anything. I want to make sure we have the right man in the murder of Roberto Cortez."

"The FBI agents seemed sure it was one of the two men that are dead."

"They're concentrating on the search for Manning. The sheriff's office is handling the investigation of the murder. Actually, I should say *murders*. One of the guards was killed in the escape. While it would be almost impossible at this point to prove exactly which of the prisoners killed her, whenever Neil Manning is arrested along with whoever helped them escape, they'll both be tried for felony murder."

"What's that?"

"Anyone involved in committing certain felonies—escape from custody being one of them—that result in the death of someone else can be charged with felony murder."

"I see." She looked thoughtful. "I guess that makes it easier in that case."

"Much. It also allows us to bring down the hammer on the person who helped them escape. Or persons. There could have been more than one person involved in planning and executing their escape."

"Like Neil's father?" she suggested.

"Possibly."

"And he could be charged with felony murder? I mean, if he helped them?"

"Yes."

"Wow." Her eyes grew big, "I hope he wasn't involved. As much as I hate Neil, Rudy seems like a nice guy."

"And now you know why we have to ask so many questions." I stood up. We were getting into the tall weeds, and I didn't think she had anything else to tell me.

I talked to a few more people, including Cortez's other possible replacements, but I didn't learn anything new. I was finally back in my car when I got a phone call from Deputy Randy Spears.

"I've got an unattended death," he told me. "Mid-seventies, in bed, no signs of trauma. The house was locked."

"I'll get someone or come myself. Rope off the house, go ahead and call the coroner's office, but don't let them in. Gather some intel while you're waiting for us."

"Not my first day on the job, boss." Spears was good-natured and one of our most dependable deputies.

"I've got to preach to someone," I joked.

I called around. Julio was still doing interviews and I didn't want to send Mick or Lynn, so the buck stopped with me. After informing dispatch, I headed to the address Spears had sent to me.

CHAPTER FIFTEEN

The house was in an older neighborhood less than a mile from the sheriff's office. The homes were a mix of mid-century block-and-stucco and long brick ranch houses. Most lots were at least half an acre or larger, and all the homes were set a minimum of a hundred feet off the street. The landscaping was standard Old Florida, with lots of live oaks, azaleas, magnolias and the occasional palm tree.

Spears's patrol car was parked in the driveway. As I pulled in beside it, I spotted him talking with an older woman in front of the home next door. He closed his notebook and walked toward me. The air was warm but surprisingly dry as I stood in the shade of an ancient oak.

"That's the neighbor who called in the welfare check." Spears flipped open his notebook. "Her name is Frances Newton. The deceased is Nicholas Archway. Approximately seventy-five years old."

"What made her call it in?" I asked as we walked up to the front door.

"He didn't come out and get his mail yesterday or today."

"She knows when he goes out to the mailbox?" I looked back at the white wooden mailbox. It was impossible to tell if there was anything in it without opening it.

"That's what she says. Claims he was like clockwork. At five every day, he walked out and checked the mail."

"And she watches for him?"

"She said that she and her husband are planning a trip to see their new grandbaby. I had to look at ten pictures of the kid. Anyway, she wanted to let Nick, that's what she calls him, know that they're going to be gone and ask him to keep an eye on their house and take in their mail. She thought she'd just catch him when he came out to check *his* mail, but he never did so she got worried."

"Let me guess. He never goes anywhere without letting her know."

"Exactly."

"Got to love neighborhoods like this."

We both put on gloves and Spears opened the door.

"Did the neighbor provide the key?" I asked, knowing the answer.

"Yep," he said as we walked through the living room toward a hallway in the back of the house.

To say that the house was neat wouldn't quite cover it. I suspected that Mr. Archway had been a little obsessive-compulsive. All of the books were lined up neatly on the shelves, magazines were squared to the edge of an end table, nothing seemed out of place and there wasn't a speck of dust anywhere. It would be almost impossible to murder someone in a house like this without leaving a few traces.

The hallway was dark and cool, lit only by the natural light coming from the living room and the open door to the master bedroom on the other end. When we got to the bedroom everything inside seemed orderly and immaculately maintained, just like the rest of the house.

Under the covers on the bed was the body of an elderly man. His thin grey hair was cut close, and the skin of his face had the bloodless pallor of death. If it weren't for that, and the odor of recent death, I could have been convinced that he was asleep.

I stepped up to the side of the bed and leaned over. The

man's mouth was partly open and clear of any obvious obstructions. His eyes were glazed and dry but showed no signs of trauma. I pulled out my phone and took a few pictures before gently moving the sheet and coverlet from his upper body. He wore a T-shirt and boxers.

"I can't see anything that would point to suicide or homicide," Spears said.

I nodded. "This looks like a natural death, and not even a very traumatic one. Probably heart failure, an aneurism, blood clot, that sort of thing."

Out of habit, I continued to look around the bed. On the floor between the nightstand and the bed I spotted a piece of plastic the size of a penny. It was a little thicker than Saran wrap, like it might have come from the plastic packaging of underwear or socks. The only reason I even noticed it was because everything else was so tidy.

"Go get an evidence bag," I said to Spears.

"What'd you find?"

"Probably nothing. It's a small piece of plastic I want to preserve, just in case."

He headed out to the car to get a bag while I took a picture. When I stood back up, I took another look around the room and thought about the murder case that had gotten Mick moved into CID. Was I being overly cautious about a random piece of plastic at the scene of an apparently natural death because I'd just learned about a case where my father had let his own assumptions lead him in the wrong direction? I didn't know and frankly decided it didn't matter. Better to be careful than be careless. I'd had an instructor at the academy who'd tossed that saying around like he was throwing beads off a Mardi Gras float.

Spears returned with the bag, and I placed the piece of plastic inside and sealed it.

Next, we looked at the bathroom that adjoined the master bedroom. Again, nothing was out of place. I put on a new pair of gloves and opened the medicine cabinet, using my phone to take pictures of the prescription bottles inside.

Mr. Archway had made it easy to take the pictures. Each bottle was carefully turned so the label faced the front. I recognized most of them, including a cholesterol medicine, a non-opioid painkiller and a mild sleep aide. None of the bottles were empty. The painkiller and the sleep aide had roughly the right amount of pills to be expected, based on the date the prescription had been filled.

"Let's walk through the rest of the house," I told Spears. "I want you to take video and I'll do the same. At this point, I can't see calling in Shantel."

When we finished with the inside of the house, we went out to the garage. A 2015 Nissan Altima was parked squarely in the middle of the space. A tennis ball hung from the ceiling and just touched the spot on the windshield where the rearview mirror was attached. Not a speck of dirt or oil marked the floor of the garage, while tools were neatly hung on pegboards around the walls.

"This is how my wife expects our garage to look." Spears shook his head. "When I tell her I don't have time to be this neat, she tries to tell me I'd save time if I organized everything."

"I doubt I spend more than fifty hours a month hunting for tools I've misplaced," I agreed.

We had just finished going through the small laundry room when Spears received a text message. "The coroner's folks are here."

Outside, we met with two attendants that I only vaguely recognized.

"We were told this was an unattended death?" an Asian man in his twenties asked.

"Yes, but treat it as suspicious," I said.

"Really?" the woman with him asked. I remembered that she had worked for years as an EMT. Her name was Millie or Minnie... or something like that.

"You're working for the coroner now?"

"Pay's better, and working with the dead is easier than the living."

"Amen, sister," her partner chimed in. "We'll take all the vitals and write it up," he told me.

"Thanks."

"You want us to wait for your crime-scene team?"

"I can't justify calling them out. Just take pictures and touch as little as possible."

"Always," he assured me.

I watched them suit up and enter the house, carrying their equipment. When I turned back to the street, I was surprised to see Albert Griffin walking quickly toward the house. I went to meet him.

"What are you doing over here?" I asked. We were almost half a mile from his house.

"Larry." He shook his head and I could tell he was upset.

"What's wrong?"

"Nick. I just heard about Nick." He was breathing heavily, and I couldn't tell if it was the walk or his emotions that had him out of breath.

"You knew him?"

"Good friends. Many years."

"Come over here and sit down." I directed him toward a wrought-iron bench near the front door of the house. "Do you want me to get you some water?"

"I'll be fine. Just let me rest for a minute." He wiped the sweat from his brow.

I stood beside him and looked out at the tree-lined street as he struggled to get his wind back. A dozen people walked by as I watched. They tried to look like they weren't gawking at the coroner's van, the patrol car and my unmarked car parked in front of their neighbor's house.

Spears went to his patrol car and came back with a bottle of water.

"Not very cold, but it's wet." He held it out to Mr. Griffin, who took it gratefully. Spears turned to me. "Do you need me anymore?"

"No. Just send a copy of your report to me. Thanks, Randy."

"What happened to Nick?" Mr. Griffin asked me as we watched Spears head off to another call.

"Looks like he died of natural causes. Y'all were friends?"

"We lived close to each other growing up, but he was a few years older so he was ahead of me in school. We didn't become close friends until he taught chemistry at the high school for a couple of years. Nick was one of the smartest men I ever knew."

"When was the last time you saw him?"

"Last week. He's a regular at historical society meetings."

"How's his health been?"

"What you would expect for a seventy-five-year-old. He had the normal amount of complaints. When he was in his sixties, he had a run-in with prostate cancer. Came through that okay with chemotherapy. Let me think." He was quiet for a moment. "I'm trying to think how he looked last week. Far as I can remember, he was fine."

"How did you hear about his death?"

"Mutual friend who lives right over there." Mr. Griffin pointed to a mid-century home across the street. "Harold's not in very good shape. I'll walk over and talk to him before I head home."

"I'm sorry about your friend," I said, patting him on the back.

"I am too. He had a great sense of humor and still had an eye for the ladies. Wow, I'm going to miss him." I saw his eyes tear up. "I've lost a lot of my friends. You'd think you'd get used to it, but you don't."

"I'll drive you home."

"I got to go talk to Harold first," he told me.

"I'll walk over there with you."

"Thanks, Larry." He struggled to stand, but I knew better than to try and help him.

When we got up to his friend's door, I let Mr. Griffin push the doorbell. A minute or two later, the door was opened by a stooped man using a walker.

"Albert," the man said and scooted back from the door.

"Harold Powers, this is Sergeant Larry Macklin."

"Like the sheriff?" Harold was shuffling away from us.

"He's Ted's son."

"I like your dad," Harold said over his shoulder. "Excuse me. I got to sit down." He led us into the living room, which was as untidy as his neighbor's house had been neat. He dropped down into an overstuffed chair that had conformed to his backside, letting out a woof of air. "That's better. Did we really lose Nick?"

Mr. Griffin, who was standing beside Harold's chair, reached out and put his hand on his shoulder.

"Not going to be any of us left at this rate," Harold muttered. "Was it peaceful?"

"Yes. It looks like he died in his sleep," I said.

"Good. Guess there wasn't a woman with him? The old rogue always said that would be his death of choice." Harold and Mr. Griffin both chuckled at the memory of their friend.

"Don't get us wrong," Mr. Griffin said when he saw my bemused look. "Nick was the perfect gentleman. His idea of making a pass was buying a woman gifts and giving her amusing greeting cards."

"Glad you cleared that up. I had a picture in my head of him going around pinching women's behinds."

They both shook their heads and smiled.

"Not Nick. He was a dandy. In both dress and manners," Harold said, then pointed toward a small but well-appointed bar in the corner of the room. "Get me a glass of bourbon."

Mr. Griffin found the bottle of Kentucky bourbon under the bar and poured a couple of fingers into a shot glass before handing it to Harold.

"Pour yourself one and another for your friend here."

"I'm on duty." I waved away the offer.

With their drinks in hand, Mr. Griffin and Harold clinked their glasses together.

"To an old and dear friend." Harold downed the rich, maple-colored liquid in a single swallow. "Warms the heart." He looked at the glass as though he were wishing it would magically refill. At last, he set it down on the table next to his chair.

"How has Nick's health been recently?" I asked Harold after a minute or two.

"Ha! A hell of a lot better than mine!" He looked down and shook his head. "You don't expect miracles at our age. He had his problems. Nothing serious."

"Would he have told you if anything *was* serious?"

"He came over and we had breakfast together three or four times a week. When you've been friends as long as we have, you might as well be an old married couple. We complained to each other about every ache and pain. Feels better to have someone to complain to. Doesn't do any good, but you let someone else know. A pain shared is cut in half. Think I heard that somewhere." He discreetly wiped away a tear. Mr. Griffin reached out and patted his hand.

"Do you know who his doctor is?" I asked.

"Sure, it's… Sorry, I'll remember it later." Harold looked upset with himself. "His doctor's in Tallahassee."

"You can get the name to me when you remember," I told him. "Did he have any problems with anyone lately?"

Harold looked shocked at the suggestion. "No. Nick got along with everyone he met."

"No problems with neighbors?"

"No. Luckily our neighborhood is too old to have one of those homeowners associations. My sister has been fighting with hers forever. Every time she paints the house or puts up a new mailbox. I wouldn't put up with that."

"Did he have any problems that you know of? Like money problems?"

Harold stared at me like I'd grown another head.

"We never talked about money." He shook his head as though I was crazy to think that they would.

I wasn't sure if it was a Southern thing, a country thing or maybe just an old-guy thing. But this wasn't the first time I'd seen men of a certain age in Adams County acting appalled at the thought of talking about money. They never complained about being broke or bragged about being rich. There were farmers in the county who were worth millions who drove old rusty trucks and wore clothes that Goodwill wouldn't have given to a homeless man.

"Can you think of anything else that has been different about Mr. Archway in the last month or so?"

"What's this all about?" He looked at Mr. Griffin. "You're asking questions like this was a murder or something."

"He's just doing his job," Mr. Griffin assured him. "You wouldn't want the sheriff's office to just assume it's natural causes, would you? Only way to investigate a death is to ask questions."

"We investigate all deaths where the deceased passed away without an attending physician present or hospice assisting," I explained.

Harold nodded. I could tell he was getting tired. Mr. Griffin and I exchanged looks.

"Just one more question before we leave. Did he have any relatives?"

Harold shook his head. "No. He had a nephew he liked a bunch. Nice kid. Died about eight or ten years ago. I say kid. He was in his forties and died in car accident a month before his birthday. Nick took it real hard."

"No one else?"

"Not that I know of." Harold looked at Mr. Griffin, who nodded.

I stood up and shook his hand. "I'm sorry I had to bring you the news of your friend's passing."

"Is Sharon coming by this evening?" Mr. Griffin asked.

"As soon as she gets done at work," Harold said.

Mr. Griffin made sure Harold had everything he needed before we left. "I'll call his daughter and let her know what's happened," he told me as I drove him back to his house.

Having similar thoughts about Mr. Griffin, I called Eddie to let him know that his landlord had lost an old friend.

"Jessie's coming over to study for an exam. I'll tell Albert she needs me out of the apartment and I'll go spend the evening with him," Eddie promised.

"You're a good man," I told him.

CHAPTER SIXTEEN

It was well after five by the time I got back to the office. Before going home, I wanted to quickly go over any reports that had been submitted to me. I'd write my own about Archway's death later at the dining room table.

Though I probably shouldn't have been, I was astounded to see that Mick still hadn't resubmitted his burglary report. Frustrated and now a bit confused, I vowed to have a knock-down drag-out fight with Mick before the end of the weekend, if that's what it took. As part of my commitment, I looked through the box of reports from the Simmons murders and picked out the primary ones to read. With my work set for the night, I headed for the door.

I called Pete as I walked out to my car.

"Hi," he answered. For anyone else, this would have been a normal response, but from Pete it was less than enthusiastic.

"I was thinking about swinging by on my way home," I told him.

"Been at the doctor's all day. I'm pretty beat."

"Just for a minute. I want to run a few things by you," I lied.

"Sure."

I pulled up at Pete's place and his wife, Sarah, met me at the door. Her smile was wide and genuine as she gave me a hug.

"How's the big guy?" I asked, trying to keep my voice low enough that he wouldn't be able to hear from inside.

"It was a long day."

"He said you all had been at the doctor's."

"Come in and talk about me where I can hear you!" Pete shouted from the living room.

"How anyone who spends as much time as you do at the gun range can have such good hearing is beyond me," I shouted back as Sarah led me into the house.

"It's self-preservation at this point," he grumbled. "You said you had something for me to look at?"

I went over the Archway death with him.

"I know you think there's a murderer around every corner, but I can't see it," he said after looking at all the photos and video.

"I think it's the Simmons double murder that has me looking for things that aren't there," I admitted.

"I remember those murders," Pete said. "I went to school with the killer. She was one of the reasons I studied criminology in college."

"How well did you know her?"

"Ha! Not well. She was the popular cheerleader type and two years behind me in high school. She lived down the street from me, and I'll admit that I had a small crush on her. All the guys did. When I heard what she'd done, I had two images in my head. One was of her as the smiling cheerleader, urging our football team on to victory, and the other was of her creeping into her parents' room and stabbing them to death. What freaked me out was that both images seemed… right.

"I couldn't figure out why I could see her as a vicious killer until I remembered a look I'd seen her give this other girl one day at school. The girl had told her that her hair looked bad. It was totally a catty move designed to get

Riley's goat, and it worked. Riley told the girl to go to hell, then the girl turned away with a flip of her hair. That's when I saw a look on Riley's face that was so… hateful, so… disdainful. I don't quite know how to describe it. But I quit having lustful thoughts about her right then and there. From that moment on, every time I saw her, I felt my testicles draw up. Not a good sign."

"I'm proud of you for not being attracted to psychos," Sarah laughed as she came back into the living room with a tray of cookies.

I took one, but Pete waved the tray away. "I need to lose some more weight."

"How'd the visit with the doctor go?" I asked.

"We reviewed the results of the latest MRI and this new orthopedic surgeon talked trash about the guy who pinned my leg back together. He said he can make it right, but that'll be another operation."

I didn't know what to say.

"More time and pain," Pete mumbled.

"Still, if it gets it done right," Sarah said encouragingly.

"I know." He was clearly exasperated and changed the subject. "How's the search for Manning going?"

I told him about Cara's father hitting the FBI agent, which brought the first real smile to his face since I'd been there. I went on to outline what had been found at the house in the woods and my investigation into the murder of Roberto Cortez.

"You're really working at ignoring the Occam's Razor answers." Pete shook his head. "You have a natural death you want to make into a murder, and a murder with two obvious suspects that you want to turn into an Agatha-Christie-style mystery of the week."

"I bang my head against the wall because it feels so good when I quit," I said with a grin. "And sometimes I'm right."

"Have you worked things out with Mick?"

"Still trying to figure out what makes him tick."

"He just doesn't like you being sergeant."

I told him what Lynn had said about us excluding them from our more interesting and complex cases.

"We all have our own work to do. She never discusses her cases with us. Which I'm grateful for, considering the type of cases she investigates," Pete said a little defensively.

"I think she has a point. When I get the chance, I'm going to talk to Mick about it. Maybe that will bridge some of the gaps in our relationship."

"Relationship? I'm a little worried hearing you use words like that," Pete said, a little of his old humor returning.

"I've always been the sensitive type," I quipped, then put on my serious face. Sarah had disappeared into the back of the house, leaving us alone. "I'm not going to let you get away with blowing off my concerns for you. I want to hear what's going on inside that head of yours."

"How the hell do you think I'm doing?" He took a long, deep breath, holding it in before letting it out as a long sigh. "I'm scared, Larry. I love being a deputy. Everything about it. I know I've made a bunch of mistakes during my career, but did I deserve this?" He thumped his damaged leg.

"You know it doesn't work like that. There are any number of positions you can fill in the department if you aren't able to be on the street." I knew he didn't want to hear it, but I couldn't think of anything else to say.

"I told you before that what really drives me crazy is the timing. I was so close to reaching a personal goal. One that would have helped me on both a personal and professional level." He paused and gritted his teeth in frustration. "I just find it maddening."

The way this rolled off his tongue told me he'd been running the same words over and over in his mind. "Morbid thoughts" was the phrase an instructor at the academy had used for them. Once they began playing over and over in your mind, it became nearly impossible to turn them off.

"I know there's nothing I can say to make this better," I told him. "But we all put on a uniform knowing that awful things can happen to us. You got dealt a bad hand here. All you can do is stay in the game until the cards get better."

"Really? A poker analogy?" he asked with the tiniest hint of a smile.

"Best I could come up with. And you didn't let me finish. You're surrounded by friends and family that care about you. Don't let this define you."

"The surgeon we talked to really does think he can help me," he admitted. "And, yes, I know no one wants to listen to me feeling sorry for myself."

"That's not what I'm saying. If that's how you're feeling, I *do* want to hear it. What I'm telling you is that you can't let this defeat you. If you can't deal with it yourself, talk to someone. No shame there."

"I got this." His voice was soft and unsure.

"I need you." I gave his arm a gentle punch.

Pete looked up at me and nodded. "I know you would be lost without me."

"I've got to get home. Are you coming into the office tomorrow?" I asked and saw the doubt in his eyes.

"I'll think about." He gave me a forced grin, which was really more of a grimace. "See, I'm better."

"That's what I'm talking about," I joked and received a genuine smile in return.

I left the house and was halfway to my car when Sarah scared the hell out of me by running out from the back of the house.

"Jeezus, don't do that!" I laughed, holding my hand over my chest.

"Sorry! But I wanted to catch you before you left." She stepped in close. "What do you think?"

"About what?"

"His state of mind. His emotions. His fear. I don't know." She was close to tears.

"Sarah, it's going to be okay." I reached out and put my hand on her shoulder.

"The girls are getting frustrated with him. He doesn't talk to them the way he used to. I'm scared he's… I don't know… getting lost in his depression."

"We're all worried about him, Dad included. You know if there's anything we can do, all you have to do is ask."

"Everyone at the sheriff's office has been great. Major Parks and Jan in HR have helped us with the health insurance claims. I'm afraid his… I know this sounds melodramatic, but it's like his spirit is broken. He won't go to church with us anymore since I asked Reverend Thomas to talk to him. Part of the problem is, every time I reach out for help, it upsets him more."

"What about the doctor? He said this new surgeon is confident that he can help."

"Which just worries me. What if we get our hopes up and we're right back here again in six months? I think that's what's worrying Pete too."

"How can I help?" I asked, fighting back my own frustration and fears over the situation.

"I don't know if anyone can. Pete has gotten pulled into this vicious cycle of self-pity, followed by self-loathing, followed by self-pity again. Everything I do to try and pull him out of it just irritates him. I know he'd be angry if he knew I was out here talking to you." She paused. "Work helps. The more you can give him to do, the better. Nothing is really going to help until he has some vision for his future that he can hold on to."

"Would you like Dad to get him to go talk to a professional?"

She fidgeted. "I don't know. I don't want him to withdraw from y'all too."

"Dad can make him see a mental health counselor. Anytime there's an officer-involved shooting, it's a requirement. But he's done it for other reasons. I've seen one before. It's not fun, but it might help."

"I'll think about it." She glanced back at the house. "I better get back inside."

"Call or text me anytime," I said, adding Sarah and her daughters to my list of people to worry about.

When I got home, Cara and her dad were eating dinner in front of the TV and watching *The Great Outdoors*. I knew that John Candy was one of Henry's favorite comedians. We'd watched the movie a few times, and Cara would always talk about how her father would let her chase him around, pretending to be the Bald-Headed Bear of Claire County while she jumped on his back and pinned him to the floor.

"We didn't know when you'd get home," Cara apologized. "There's soup on the stove and bread and crackers on the counter. Dad brought some of Mom's garlic butter. It's in the refrigerator."

"No Mauser?" I asked.

"Jimmy is at your dad's tonight," Cara explained. Jimmy was Genie's son. He spent most nights in his Tallahassee apartment at a group home for people with Down Syndrome, but whenever he had the chance to spend the night with his mom, he always made sure that his favorite black-and-white moose would be there.

"I see Alvin is taking advantage of Mauser's absence." Alvin was stretched out on the couch with his head resting on Henry's leg.

"He's a good boy," Henry said.

When the movie was over, I went outside with Cara and told her about my visit with Pete and Sarah.

"I'll go over there this weekend," she offered.

"I don't know if that will help or hurt."

"You know who my parents are. Mom has spent most of her life befriending broken people. Several years ago, Mom and Dad let a young man who'd had a bad motorcycle accident stay in their yurt. The accident had left him with cognitive issues, which led to anger and depression. Every task was harder for him than it used to be. Mom would constantly be over there helping him, or taking him some food or clean clothes. He seemed to hate her for it. I'd hear him screaming at her to leave him alone."

"Sounds awful for him and your family."

"I asked her why she did it. Wouldn't it be better to let

him be by himself? She told me that as long as he was mad at her, then he couldn't be mad at himself. I didn't really understand what she meant until I had a friend who would get depressed. Like the young man Mom was helping, my friend's depression was born of an anger that was focused inward."

"What happened to the guy?"

"Eventually he got better. Never fully recovered and always had bouts of depression, but even now, when he's falling into a deep depression, he'll show up at Mom's door. Anyway, what I'm saying is, it's better to let someone be mad at you for caring about them than to ignore them."

"I see the logic. I just don't know how well it's going to work on Pete," I told her.

"I don't care how mad he gets at me. He's our friend and I'm not going to let him be alone. We can't stop him from being sad, but we can make sure he's not sad and alone."

I pulled her to me and hugged her tight, kissing the top of her red hair. I still didn't know how I'd been lucky enough to find a woman as caring and loving as Cara.

Later, I wrote my report on Nicholas Archway's death, then pulled out the reports from the Simmons murders. Those murders had been so gruesome, it made me wonder why I felt like there was a comparison to be made between them and Archway's death. I went back and forth until I finally decided I was seeing things that weren't there. Gut feelings weren't facts.

I kept waking up every couple of hours that night, feeling anxious about the hunt for Neil Manning. A part of me was worried that he was going to evade capture, and another part was worried that he could be stalking us. A voice in the back of my head kept urging me to get out of bed and go look for him. I tried to ignore it, but it wasn't easy.

CHAPTER SEVENTEEN

Without a restful night's sleep, I walked into the office on Friday feeling more like it was late afternoon than early morning. I wanted to drink some coffee, eat a donut and wake up before I tackled my to-do list.

Life had other plans. As soon as I entered CID, I saw Mick Klein standing by his desk.

"I need to see the pictures from the FBI capture of the fugitives," he shouted across the room, hurrying toward me.

Shocked by this confrontation, I didn't know what to say. As he advanced with a determined look on his face, I managed to open my office door and step back.

"Let's go into my office," I said as I tried to clear the morning fog from my brain.

"I need to see those pictures," Mick demanded again once he was inside.

"What's this all about?" I asked, attempting to regain the initiative.

"I… Look, it's a long story. If I can see the pictures, I'll have a better idea."

"No," I said, and he started to bow up at me. "I don't mean you can't see the pictures, but we're going to slow down. You need to start at the beginning and tell me why you have to see evidence in a case you aren't involved in."

I saw his inner conflict as he stared at me. I'd been there myself more than once. He was wondering if he would get what he wanted sooner by giving in and explaining himself, or by remaining stubbornly uncooperative.

"Fine." He clenched his jaw. "It's that burglary report you've been so obsessed with."

I thought about arguing that I hadn't been obsessed, but that I had just wanted him to do his job. But I wisely kept my mouth shut and let him speak.

"I know who committed that burglary. His name is Andre Roberts. He's my confidential informant. I've worked with him for almost ten years. I recognized his MO, so I went out to pull him in and get back the watch and money he'd stolen. Not the money, of course, that would be gone, but I might get the watch and the other little stuff."

"This is your CI?" I asked with raised eyebrows.

"He backslides about every six months. He never burglarizes an occupied house, and only steals money and watches. He's got a thing about watches. Anyway, it's usually not a problem, I just go bring him in and charge him. Trouble was, this time I couldn't find him. Nowhere. Ten years and I've always been able to go out and find him within a couple of hours. He's a forty-year-old black man with a speech impediment who wears a trench coat all year long. He's usually hard to miss."

I knew who he was talking about now. "Folks call him Trench, right? Isn't he deaf?"

Mick nodded. "Yes, that's his street name, and no, he's not deaf. Most people think he is 'cause his speech sounds like a person who was born deaf. What really happened is he lost most of his tongue when he was a child. A wound got infected and the doctors amputated about half of it. Anyway, I couldn't find him and didn't want to turn in the report until I did."

"So? What's that got to do with the fugitives?"

"A friend with the police told me that the meth they

found at the scene had a nickel in each of the jewel bags."

"Maybe. I hadn't heard about it." To be honest, I hadn't paid much attention to the drugs they'd found.

"Andre's cousin makes meth. The nickels are his trademark, and also his street name. According to Andre, his cousin does it so if the cops are chasing him and he throws the bags into the water, they'll sink."

"That's meth logic," I commented.

"The story going around is that the fugitives got a delivery from someone."

"Let me guess. Andre delivers for Nickel."

"It's been known to happen," Mick admitted.

I sat down behind my desk and booted up my computer. While I waited to log in, I turned the monitor enough that Mick could see it. A few minutes later, I pulled up a shared folder and we were looking at photos from the crime scene.

"Those are his cousin's drugs," Mick said confidently.

"Which brings up the question of where's Andre."

"Dead or gone to ground," Mick said solemnly. "I guess you think it's crazy that I care what happens to him." He made it sound like a challenge.

"No, not at all. My old CI, Eddie Thompson, has actually turned into a good friend, believe it or not. Even before he got cleaned up, I appreciated what he did for me."

"Andre has his flaws. Still, he's given me good tips sometimes at a risk to himself. A few times when he's seen a crime that he just doesn't think is right, he's told me flat out. No negotiating. No give or take. He just gives me the information. He saved one woman's life by reporting her boyfriend to me."

"You've looked for him in all his usual bolt holes?"

"Every one of them that I'm aware of. I've talked to anyone who's ever claimed to know him, and no one has seen him for days."

"Could he have gone that deep?"

"I've never known him to."

"What about his cousin?"

"I wanted to make sure the drugs were his first."

I stood up. "Want some backup?"

Mick nodded and headed for the door without another word.

"We'll take my car," I told him. "Grab your vest and other gear." If we were going to visit a meth dealer, then we would need to take precautions.

Vests on and badges visible, we pulled out of the parking lot. I called Phil Eccles and told him what we were doing.

"You want more backup?" he asked.

"I'll let you know when we get to the house." Nine o'clock in the morning was not a bad time to be hitting a drug house. Most of the residents would be in a zombie-like state, if they were even awake at all.

"I checked with vice," Mick told me when I hung up with Phil. "They gave me an address. Last they knew, the cousin wasn't manufacturing. Most of the meth is made south of the border now."

"Still need to make sure there aren't any chemicals or fentanyl lying around. If we see anything, you know the current protocol."

"Back out and call hazmat to clear the house."

"Did you see the bulletin on that new drug that's even more potent than Fentanyl?"

Mick nodded. "It's scary. It's one thing knowing that you're going into a house where there could be a human threat. That's what we signed up for. But I don't like these substances where you touch them, and next thing you know, you're flat on the floor looking up at some mustache-wearing EMT wanting to tongue-dance with you."

"And that's if you're lucky enough to wake up." I felt like we were having a bonding moment, so I decided to push it. "This probably isn't the right time to bring this up, but what do you have against me and my dad?"

I could feel the temperature in the car drop by ten degrees.

"It's what you all have against me," Mick said sullenly.

"Come again?" I asked, confused.

"Your dad hasn't liked me since I showed him up on the Simmons case. If he'd solved the murders, then it would have been him moving into CID."

"Dad didn't *want* to be in CID," I told him. "I talked to him about the Simmons case. I got the feeling he was glad you had his back. You can't think he'd rather have let the daughter get away with murder?"

"Don't blow smoke in my face." There was bitterness in his voice. "Why am I still covering burglaries after all these years? How did you get moved straight into violent crimes?"

I was stunned at how deep-seated his resentment was.

"Mick, I think you're a victim of your own success. For a lot of departments, home burglaries are relegated to the solve-or-not pile. They wait until there are half a dozen in one area and then figure out which kid or delivery driver or ex-con is responsible. It's different in Adams County. We seldom have more than two burglaries in any neighborhood because you're on top of your game."

"I have a network of informants, I keep a list of the different MOs, I keep an eye out for who's getting out of jail. I've got about a dozen tabs on a spreadsheet where I keep track of it all. It's not rocket science. Honestly, it's boring as hell sometimes."

"So why haven't you told my dad?"

"'Cause he... I thought he held a grudge against me."

"What made you think that?"

"A few years ago, when I pushed Lieutenant Johnson to move me around, he said your dad wanted me to stay on burglaries."

"Yeah, Dad wanted you to stay on burglaries because you do a great job! Johnson wanted you to keep working them too. But I'd bet you a silver dollar that if you'd gone to Dad and asked him, he would have moved you into violent crimes and I'd be doing burglaries."

Mick was silent while he processed what I'd told him. We were only a block away from the drug house, so it was time to table the conversation anyway.

"Circle the block," he told me while he pulled out his phone and called the owner of the property. With the owner living two hundred miles away, the house had been vacant for several years, allowing the meth heads to move in. The owner gave us permission to check on the house.

The house was in better condition than I would have expected. It was made of block and painted a light blue that was now a mix of grey dirt and green mold. All of the windows that we could see from the road looked to be intact and, while the yard was overgrown, it hadn't gone completely wild. I assumed that the county's code enforcement unit had been riding the owner to keep the place from becoming too much of an eyesore.

"I'll park a block behind the house and we'll approach it on foot through the neighbor's yard. You want front or back door?"

"Back," he said.

We trotted quickly through the neighbor's yard. Fortunately, there wasn't a fence to negotiate, only a spotty hedge. As soon as we'd pushed our way through the hedge, we became more cautious. After making sure the yard was clear, Mick went to the back door and waved me on. I hurried around the side of the house, hunching down to keep from being seen through the windows.

At the front door, I knocked and was pleased to see that the lock on the door had been broken. When there was no answer, I took a quick picture of the lock before pushing the door open. Then I radioed dispatch and reported a probable break-in. With my gun in hand and a flashlight in the other, I announced that I was entering the house.

Nobody scrambled out of a window, shot at me or yelled that I was violating their rights. Mick joined me and we cleared the house room by room, finding nothing but dirty clothes, food wrappers, bottles, cans, drug effluvium and trash. Not surprisingly, the house smelled like drugs and human waste.

"Clear!" I said from the back bedroom where there was a nasty collection of blankets and a discarded backpack.

"Clear!" came Mick's response from the kitchen.

We met up again in the living room.

"Looks like it's been a couple of days since anyone has been in here," I said. I'd put my gun back in its holster and was using my mini flashlight to look around the living room, which still held a few pieces of furniture the owner had left in the house when they moved out. All of it was trash now. No one but a drug addict would consider using it.

"Andre's cousin has a bad reputation," Mick said. "Since this was known as his dive, no one else is going to use it, even when he's not here."

"Let's pick through the house and see if we can find any clues to where they went or where your CI is," I suggested.

I used a telescoping probe I'd brought with me to pick through the clutter on the floor, being careful not to touch anything. During my career, I'd disturbed thousands of roaches, hundreds of rats and dozens of possums, raccoons, squirrels, cats, dogs and snakes.

"I'll check out the trash in the other rooms." Mick sounded as enthusiastic about the task as I was.

I found nothing in the living room and had moved on to the kitchen, which was cleaner than I would have expected. There weren't any dirty dishes in the sink since the squatters hadn't cooked anything and the water wasn't turned on. Which was also the reason why the bathroom was a toxic experience that I dealt with quickly while holding my nose.

"I've got something," Mick said as I finished up in the bathroom.

"Good. Let's go outside. I need some fresh air." I went to the front door and took several deep breaths.

"I found three of these scattered around in the back room." Mick handed me a card that read: *Free Massage*. There was also a name, Pixie, along with a phone number and website address.

"I'm sure there's a list of extras at various prices," I

muttered. "Toss a coin, loser calls?"

"I'll do it." He took out his phone and dialed the number. "Pixie, I'd love to meet up and get a free massage. I got cash for extras. Call me back." He disconnected and looked at me. "Voicemail. Ugh, I feel like I need a shower."

We weren't even back to my car when his phone rang.

"It's Pixie," he told me and answered. "Yeah, sure, I've got money for a motel room. Cool. An hour? Yeah. At the truck stop. How much? Sure, I just got paid. Yeah, me too." He hung up and looked at me. "I'll be earning combat pay for this."

"We need to find another car," I said as we reached my unmarked that practically screamed law enforcement. "Our vice squad should have something we can use."

Since we were a small department, our vice squad consisted of six patrol officers who worked vice as a special duty operation. The sergeant, Malcolm Yates, worked vice full time while the other deputies volunteered hours from their patrol duties when the watch commander authorized it.

Yates was gung-ho and always ready for action, but sometimes he could be a bit of a jerk. Honestly, he made me a little nervous and I avoided working with him unless I had to, but today we needed his help.

"What you need?" he asked when we tracked him down back at the office.

"A car that says 'I'm just a car,'" I told him. "You know, the kind of car that Mick here would look comfortable in if he was driving by to pick up a prostitute."

Yates snorted and I got an eyeroll from Mick.

"I got just the car for you. It was confiscated in a drug sting a year ago. We keep it at the public works department so it stays fresh."

"Fresh" was the term for cars that hadn't been spotted and noted by the bad guys. Once we'd actually caught a drug dealer taking pictures of all the cars in our parking lot so they could recognize them. As dumb as the majority of criminals were, there were a few who actually worked hard at their criminal careers.

Yates gave us the keys and I drove Mick out to the public works parking lot to pick up his 2018 Hyundai Elantra.

"Makes me feel sporty," Mick said with the proper amount of sarcasm as he folded himself into the car. He'd put on some clothes from a gym bag he kept in his car and now looked like the manager of a fast-food restaurant who was looking for a little fun.

"You look perfect."

"I knew you hated me," he joked in a way that made me feel like the ice was melting.

"I'll meet you at the Roads Best Motel," I said.

"Don't wait more than a couple of minutes to come in," he said slightly desperately.

"I'm sure you can fill the time while you're waiting for me," I said, and he scowled. "I'll be right behind you," I assured him.

Mick headed to the truck stop to pick up Pixie while I drove ahead to the motel. We wanted to get her into a room where she couldn't make a run for it, and where we'd have a charge we could use as leverage. Prostitution wasn't a big charge, but I was sure she'd have drugs with her too, which would begin to look like time in jail if we wanted to push it.

I parked at the motel and scanned the parking lot. If Nickel the drug dealer was also pimping Pixie out, he might be nearby keeping an eye on her.

Ten minutes after I parked, Mick drove up with Pixie in the car. Even from across the parking lot, I could see that she was thin to the point of anorexia. Her hair was stringy and her clothes were dirty.

The Roads Best was an old-school motel, two stories with exterior doors to the rooms. Mick had asked for a room on the second floor so she'd have less of a chance at getting away if she tried to run. Though, when we'd been planning this, I'd assumed she'd be in better physical shape.

I let them get into the room and counted to thirty before getting out of my car. When I knocked on the door, I could hear a woman complaining inside. Mick opened the door.

"Twosies is extra," Pixie slurred from the bed.

"I'm glad to see you." Mick shook his head. Behind him, Pixie threw off her shoes and was dropping the straps of her dress. "Put your clothes back on!" Mick said when he turned and saw what she was doing.

"We aren't going to have any fun with my clothes on," Pixie whined. Up close, I could see the meth sores on her face and, when she smiled, I could count at least three gaps where teeth should have been.

I took out my bifold and showed her my badge.

"There ain't no police discount!" she told us.

"I'd like to see some ID," Mick said, showing her his star.

"Is this like a roleplay thing? I can do that." She tried to sound coy, but it came out in a nauseating simper.

"No. You are under arrest. Now show me some ID," he insisted.

"Shit! I got a state ID in my purse." She reached for the bag.

"Stop!" I ordered.

Mick took the bag and gave the contents a quick search before handing it back to her. She dug around and pulled out a state-issued ID. I wasn't surprised that she didn't have a driver's license. In fact, I was relieved to find out she didn't have a license to operate a motor vehicle. In the state she was in, she wouldn't have qualified to ride a tricycle.

Mick looked at the ID and handed it to me. I pulled out my radio and called in: "Wants and warrants for Petra, no middle name, Benton, date of birth, seven, twenty-two, two thousand."

Marti in dispatch told me that Petra had an outstanding bench warrant for a failure to appear in court for a minor drug offense. She had her head in her hands, muttering curse words as I finished the call.

Mick went through her purse again. In the end, he laid out two prescription pill bottles with names other than Petra Benton and several jewel bags with various drugs. Four of the bags had nickels in them.

"You're looking at time in jail. Enough time that you'll be clean and sober when you come out," I said like it was a selling point.

"I can't do time. No, no, no." She rocked back and forth.

"We can help you out with that," I told her. This was only partly true. We didn't have any discretion with the bench warrant. In order to let her go on that, we'd have to lie in our reports and say she escaped. I wasn't going to do that. All the other charges were in our hands, victimless crimes that we could charge her with… or not.

"Please. I can't go to jail."

"Where's Nickel?" Mick asked.

At the mention of Nickel's name, she looked up at us.

"I ain't sayin' nothin' about him." She closed her mouth tight like a toddler who wasn't going to eat their green beans.

"At this point it's not optional," I said.

"Come on, Larry, that's not true," Mick said, falling into a good-cop, bad-cop routine. "She can refuse to tell us anything and go to jail for say…" He flicked through the drugs on the bed. "…five, ten years."

"For that?!" she screamed, staring at the drugs.

"That's enough to qualify you as a dealer," I told her.

"No, no. Nic… no, no." She fell over on the bed and curled up in a fetal position.

"There *is* a way out," Mick assured her. "We can keep this conversation confidential, where Nickel will never know who pointed us to him."

"No, no." More moaning.

"Go to jail or give us a little information. The choice is simple," I explained.

Petra uncurled and wiped at her eyes.

"Come on. This can all be over and you can get back to your… business." Mick smiled.

"He'll kill me," she stated, still lying on her side.

"We won't let him know it was you," I promised, thinking: *Besides, you'll be in jail, so you won't have to worry about him.*

"Just tell you where he is?"

"That's all."

"Oh, why does everything go wrong for me?"

I didn't point out that she'd most likely brought ninety percent of her problems onto herself.

"This can be fixed with just a few words from you," Mick encouraged.

"Just where he is?"

"Right."

"He's staying at Fire's place."

That nickname rang a bell. Fire was known for setting dumpsters alight whenever he needed to create a distraction. I knew of at least one arson arrest for him and numerous petty theft charges.

"Where does Fire live?" Mick asked.

"He's got a place by the Ditch."

"More detail," I urged.

"I don't know. It's kind of yellow."

"Do better or we'll make you ride over there with us," Mick warned her.

"A block from the Fast Mart. Behind it, like. There's a big, fenced yard next door with a couple big dogs."

I looked at Mick and we both knew the general area.

"Is Nickel there now?" he asked.

"Guess," she muttered.

"Did you text him that you had a customer?"

"He makes me do that," she complained.

"Text him that you're done and have some money," I told her.

"He'll know it's a lie when I don't have no money."

I took out a couple of twenties and laid them on the bed, knowing she wouldn't really need them.

"Text him."

Like a petulant child she grabbed her phone from the bed and grumpily messaged him.

In less than a second, the response from Nickel came

back: *Bring it to me.*

"I assume that means to Fire's place?" Mick said.

"He'd have told me if he wasn't."

"We're going to take you in on the outstanding bench warrant," I told her, at which point she became all kinds of indignant.

"You told me I wouldn't go to jail if I told you where Nickel was," she fumed, throwing in enough colorful language that it almost made me blush.

"We're protecting you. Being arrested will give you a great excuse for not showing up at Fire's house with the money."

I could see her calculating all the pros and cons. It was obviously a mental strain.

"It's just the warrant?"

"Yep. And sooner or later that was going to catch up with you, so we're doing you a favor," Mick said, still playing good cop.

"Okay," she agreed.

As if she had a choice.

CHAPTER EIGHTEEN

We radioed for backup and handed Petra off to Deputy Sanderson before returning the vice car to public works. Back in my car, we headed for the Ditch, one of Calhoun's most notorious neighborhoods and Fire's current residence. We found the house easily enough. From the outside it looked in worse shape than the other home where Nickel had been squatting.

We switched up who would take the front door and who would take the back. As I waited, I assessed Nickel's possible escape routes. I was pretty sure he wouldn't jump the fence into the yard next door, where two Rottweilers were pacing. The yard on the other side was blocked by a seven-foot fence. From what I remembered of Nickel, he stood around five-foot-eight and carried a good three hundred pounds, not counting the gold chains around his neck, so climbing the fence was unlikely. Feeling confident of my choice, I stepped into the shadow of a large camelia bush in the backyard and waited. I didn't want to stand right by the door as the porch was rotted and covered in junk. If I had to tackle Nickel, I wanted to do it in the yard where we would have a softer and safer landing.

Sure enough, Nickel burst out of the back door and

stumbled down from the porch. He looked right and left before heading my way. I didn't even have to jump him. I simply stepped out from behind the bush and yelled, "Sergeant Macklin, stop!" With a girly scream, he tripped, fell and tried to scramble back up before I pounced on him.

"I didn't do nothin'!" he shouted as he struggled against me, echoing the words of almost every criminal I'd ever apprehended.

"I'll be glad to talk to you about that when you settle down," I huffed as I attempted to pin down his arms. "Give up," I warned him.

He made a few more futile efforts to get loose before he went limp.

"Why you gotta do this to me?"

"We want to talk to you, that's all."

"Do you care about the others in the house?" Mick asked as he walked over to us.

"Nope," I told him.

"Good, 'cause they're refusing to open the door without a warrant."

"Aww, man, y'all didn't have a warrant?" Nickel cried.

"Guess there's a lesson in that for you," I told him.

"Then you got no right to hold me."

"If you remember correctly, I identified myself and ordered you to stop. So you were fleeing an officer of the law."

"No way. You didn't give me time, man. Look at me. I can't stop on no dime."

"Rules are rules."

Mick put on gloves and went through Nickel's pockets. There weren't any drugs, just a wad of cash.

"Looks like a couple thousand dollars," I observed. "I'm going to let you sit up. If you run, I won't chase you, but you'll be leaving a bunch of cash behind for no reason."

"You goin' to arrest me?"

"Talk, we just want to talk," I said.

"Yeah, yeah, I hear ya."

I let go and stood up. Awkwardly, he rolled over, sat up and gave a little shake of his head.

"Man, y'all messed me up," he complained.

I turned back toward the house, where a face at the window disappeared as soon as they saw me looking.

"Your friends aren't doing much to defend you," I pointed out.

"Man's got to look out for your own self. Now what you all bangin' on me for?"

"Where's your cousin?" Mick said with attitude.

"Who? I got lots of cousins." He didn't sound convincing.

"Andre."

"What about him?"

"Where is he?" Mick leaned into Nickel's face, forcing him back.

"Man, I don't know."

"When was the last time you saw him?" Mick pressed.

There was a long hesitation before Nickel said, "I can't remember."

"Bullshit!" Mick spat. "Where is he?"

"Why you care so much about him?"

"We've got a warrant with his name on it," Mick lied.

"That punk?" Nickel sounded incredulous.

"Maybe for holding *your* drugs," I suggested.

"I don't know anything about drugs." He looked offended.

"If you're going to play games, then we're going to play too. And if we play, I promise you that the last move you make will be to go directly to jail without collecting your two thousand dollars," Mick warned him.

"You're cranked." He waved us away.

"I swear if you don't start talking, we'll get real with you. You know what I'm talking about? I'm talking FBI. I'm talking U.S. Marshals. I'm talking long stretches in a maximum-security prison," Mick threatened.

Nickel looked shaken. "That's crazy." His voice was soft,

and I heard a tinge of fear.

"Your signature nickels were found in bags at a crime scene where an FBI agent was shot, two dead bodies were found and another fugitive was killed. Bad mojo for you. I suspect that it was drugs you sold that killed one of the fugitives. And it was possibly your drugs that inspired the other fugitive to shoot the FBI agent." Mick was being careful not to mention that the FBI agent hadn't been seriously injured. "Don't you think the FBI would like to meet you?"

"This is... No, man... I just... Come on." Nickel was looking left and right, desperate for a way to escape.

"All you need to do is talk to us. Tell us where Andre is."

"But that's the problem. See, I sent Andre out there." He was shaking his head vigorously back and forth. "He never came back, see. I don't know where he is. I got scared they would come after me. See?"

"I don't see," Mick argued. "I don't see how you could let your cousin disappear and not even take a step to find him."

"I did. Really, I did. I sent Pixie out to talk to people. He still had some of my money."

"Who asked you to send drugs out there?" I asked.

"Andre. They contacted Andre and gave him half the money and a note."

"Where's the note?" I asked, feeling a rush of adrenaline at the prospect of a piece of real evidence. But he dashed my hopes immediately.

"They made me send it back. The deal was the drugs and the note for the rest of the money."

"And you haven't seen Andre since you sent him out there?" Mick asked.

"I know." Nickel looked a little ashamed of himself.

"What have you done to find him?" Mick's tone and posture were menacing.

"I... I told my aunt," was Nickel's lame answer.

"Think! Where would Andre hide?"

"I've been thinking for days. He's got like a thousand dollars of my money." Nickel cringed as though he expected Mick to hit him.

"If you don't know where he is, who would?" I asked, stepping in closer.

"Maybe his sister. They're tight."

"Name and location," Mick growled.

"Anita. She's married. The guy's name is Posner. Anita Posner on Merchant Avenue. She's got a nice house. Won't even talk to me."

"Shows taste and good sense," Mick said. "Which house on Merchant?"

"The two-story brick. Let me think, 4523 or 4513, something like that. I swear it's the only two-story brick house on the block."

"We better find her there." Mick held up the bundle of cash he'd pulled out of Nickel's pocket. "This is so dirty. I should burn it."

"Hey, you can't—"

"I wouldn't make it a challenge," I warned Nickel.

"Yeah, no, hey, man," he stammered with his eyes glued on the bills.

Mick threw them at him.

"I don't have the time to legally take this from you." He pointed his finger straight at Nickel, who was fumbling to pick up all the bills from the ground. "But if anything has happened to Andre, I'm going to make the time to put you in prison." Mick turned away. "For a long time," he added over his shoulder.

Nickel wisely kept his mouth shut.

"Thanks for all the help. We're going to go bust them now!" I said loudly enough that his friends in the house could hear me. "I hope they believe you ratted people out," I said *soto voce*.

"They know me better than that," Nickel said, clearly trying to convince himself of the fact.

We got back in my car and headed over to Merchant

Avenue. It was part of a ten-block, historically black neighborhood where middle-class black business owners had lived before integration. Most of the people living there now were professionals of one type or another—doctors, lawyers and professors who commuted to Tallahassee.

I looked at my watch. What were the chances we'd find Andre's sister at home on the Friday before Memorial Day weekend? I figured it was worth a shot.

The house was the largest on the block, with a yard full of flowers spread out under the pine trees. My estimate of our chances rose when I saw the BMW parked in the driveway. I pulled in behind it.

"I didn't know Andre's sister had this kind of money," Mick said, surprised.

"Let's go knock and see who's home."

A teenager with sharp eyes answered the door.

"We'd like to talk to Anita Posner," I told him.

"You with the police?" he asked.

I took out my bifold and showed him my star and ID. "I'm an investigator with the sheriff's office."

"Is this about my uncle?"

"Is your mother here?"

"Is he dead?"

"We're looking for him," I told him.

"That's what Mom's doing. She left about an hour ago to drive around looking for him."

"What's your name?"

He seemed to think about this for a minute. "Tindell."

"Thank you, Tindell. Would you give us your mother's number so we can call her?"

"No. But I'll call and tell her you're here," he offered and pulled a cell phone from his back pocket.

"That would be great."

He made the call and told his mother who we were and that we were standing at the front door.

"She wants to talk to you." He handed me the phone.

"Who are you?" There was an edge of panic mixed with

frustration in her voice.

I explained who I was and that we were looking for Andre. Ten minutes later, she pulled into the driveway. She was driving a Range Rover, which made me wonder who drove the BMW.

Anita Posner was impeccably dressed and walked with a determined stride toward us. Even though her shoes probably cost more than my entire wardrobe, there was a disheveled look about her that came from worry and lack of sleep.

"Who told you my brother was missing?" she almost yelled at us as soon as she was on the porch.

"I've been looking for him for several days," Mick told her.

Tindell was still standing at the door. His mother looked at him and waved him back into the house.

"Let's go inside," she said in a tired voice and followed her son.

We were right behind her. The inside of the house wasn't as over-the-top opulent as I thought it would be. There were a few antiques and paintings on the walls, but the furniture looked used and comfortable.

"Now tell me what's going on," she said after guiding us into the living room.

"When was the last time you saw Andre?" I asked, and got a look that could have withered a rose on the vine.

"No!" she shouted and stepped in close to me. "You need to tell me what's going on with my brother right now." Her anger was palpable.

"I'm sorry, Mrs. Posner," Mick said. "I'm a friend of your brother's."

She turned to him and gave him an odd look.

"What?" she asked, incredulous. "You expect me to believe that?"

"I'd like to think I am. He's helped me out on more than one case. I've seen him do some unselfish things to help others."

"My brother?" Her anger had changed to confusion. "Are we talking about Andre?"

"I've been looking for him since I saw a burglary report that had some of his earmarks."

"Now *that* sounds like my brother," she said, then put her hands over her face. "No, no. I shouldn't say those things. I'm just worried." There was a pause, and she dropped her hands and looked at us. "I don't understand. How does he help you?"

"He's helped the sheriff's department out a number of times. Andre has issues but, and I mean this, I think he's got a good heart," Mick told her.

"This is so messed up. I should be the one saying things like that. Unfortunately, he's done so many stupid things and hurt those of us that want to help him."

"Nickel sent us to you," I said.

"Ha! That man is half of Andre's problems. Why don't you arrest him?"

"We have… repeatedly," Mick reminded her.

"Are you really Andre's friend?"

He nodded. "I'm doing everything I can to find him. I'll tell you that he's gotten himself into a dangerous situation this time."

"Do you know of anyone that might have asked him to buy drugs?" I asked.

"I'm sure that list is several pages long. Fortunately, they aren't the type of people we hang around with. Andre knows how much I hate drugs and his so-called friends."

"Did he ever mention Neil Manning?"

"That name is familiar." She thought about it. "Didn't he kidnap a woman? I think he owned a truck stop or something out by the interstate?"

"That's roughly what happened," I said, not bothered that a few of her details were skewed.

"Andre wouldn't be around someone like that." She sounded appalled.

"What about Lester Stevens or Doyle Waugh?"

"No, I don't think so. Like I said, he knows how I feel so he won't talk to me about his druggie friends."

"When was the last time you talked to him?" I asked.

"Sunday afternoon. He wanted me to take him to Tallahassee on Wednesday. When I didn't hear from him, I called and texted him."

"Would he normally get back to you?"

"Always." She looked down at her feet, gathering her thoughts. "Andre has stolen from us and done some bad things, but I've never doubted that he cares about his family. The drugs just have a grip on him. Besides, he needs me to drive him places sometimes. The doctor, dentist, places like that. Because of his speech problems, he likes to have me along to help him communicate. Most people assume that he's deaf when they first meet him. He has a special number he gave me. I don't know how he manages to keep his cell phone."

"I pay for that phone. Or I should say, the sheriff's office pays for it," Mick told her.

Anita looked at Mick again with a curious expression on her face.

"I didn't know that," she said quietly. "I guess there's more to Andre than I know."

"He never mentioned that he has a sister," Mick said. "I think he likes to compartmentalize his life."

"*That* I do know about him. There have always been people he let believe he was deaf and others that he'd explain what happened to him when he was young. I think he's embarrassed that he lost most of his tongue."

"Had he been acting different in any way lately?" I asked.

"No... Well, maybe a little more... I don't know, optimistic maybe. Optimism is not one of his usual attributes. The trip on Wednesday was an example. He wanted me to take him to a store to buy new clothes. I thought he was going to ask me... Wait... You were asking about someone buying drugs from him. See, he didn't say he wanted me to buy him clothes. Instead, he said *he* wanted to buy some clothes. He must have thought he was going to get money from somewhere. I didn't think about it at the time 'cause I just figured he'd hit me up for the money when we were committed to going to Tallahassee." She looked thoughtful.

"He could be naïve," Mick said.

Again, she looked at him like Andre had formed a bond between them.

"That's right," Anita confirmed. "He has a childlike quality about him. When he was younger, I thought it was because he didn't socialize much, but as he got older, I understood that it was just him and that no amount of being let down or cheated would change him. There's a part of me that envies that."

I thought about asking if she knew of any place where Andre might be lying low, but she'd obviously already looked everywhere she knew. There was no point in us telling her about the drugs and the fugitives. It would only skyrocket her anxiety.

We all exchanged information and promised to keep in touch and to keep looking for Andre.

"What do you think?" I asked when Mick and I were back in the car.

"She doesn't know any more than we do. Less probably." He was staring out the window as though he expected to see Andre walking down the sidewalk.

"I'm going back to the office. You can continue to follow up on any leads if you want."

"I've about run the course. I've got a few more informants that might have heard something," he said. "After that…"

"I'll talk to my old CI. He still hears the gossip from time to time. He might have some ideas about where Andre could have gone to ground." I almost added, *If Andre is still alive.*

CHAPTER NINETEEN

Back at the sheriff's office, I headed straight for Phil Eccles. I wanted to see if he'd added anything to his map and to bring him up to date on the situation with Andre.

"We had a stolen car that I thought had possibilities," Phil told me, pointing to a spot on the map about two miles from where the van had wrecked. "It was stolen from an isolated house on the edge of the wildlife management area, but it's turning into a big nothing. Patrol found it in a ditch south of town near the Misty Moon Nightclub. The interior was trashed. Discarded Red Bull cans, blunts and two stolen purses."

"Our playful youth."

"There were plenty of fingerprints, so at least the case is going to solve itself."

I filled him in on our search for Andre.

"You should have brought Nickel in," he scolded.

"Nickel isn't going anywhere, and Mick and I both think he's told us all he knows. Better to let him sit out there another couple of days. We'll hit him up again on Sunday and see if he's gotten word about Andre's whereabouts."

"Makes sense. He's going to have more luck scouring the denizens of the drug world than you will, I suppose."

"I think I should bring Padilla up to speed on Andre and Nickel's involvement."

"Are you sure they won't go in like a herd of buffalo and send everyone to ground?"

"No. But they have access to resources we don't and can get results quicker than we can. With the clock ticking, I think it's worth the risk. Also, I might be able to bargain our information for theirs."

"You think they still have something we don't?" He frowned. "That's a stupid question; of course they do. What I meant to ask was: Do you think they'll give us anything useful?"

"We won't know unless we try."

"Agreed."

We looked at the board and talked about a dozen incidents that could, but most likely didn't, have any significance in our hunt for Manning.

"What keeps getting under my skin is Manning's mysterious benefactor. Who likes him enough to take all those risks in order to break him out of prison and keep him in hiding?" I asked.

"A woman," Phil said. "That's my guess. I'm sure the FBI has already scoured all his correspondence while incarcerated. What about his time on house arrest? Could he have communicated with a woman then? One that became so enamored with him that she'd break him out of prison?"

"You could be on to something." I thought about it. "I've heard of insane cases where a woman has fallen in love with some prison rat and helped them. There was that highly respected female corrections officer that helped a monster. White, I think it was. Casey White. Her name was Cindy or Sherrie or something."

"Vicky," said Phil after a quick trip to Google.

"That's right. From Alabama." I shook my head.

"Manning's girlfriend would have to be someone that hasn't come up on the FBI's radar."

"And can operate a backhoe."

"*Steal* one and operate it. That's starting to seem farfetched."

"Don't underestimate the power of a woman in love," I said.

"Good point. Since his arrest, the only time he's had a chance to contact someone on the outside without the FBI picking up on it is when he was out on bail. Get Padilla to let you search his house. Maybe there's a clue they've missed."

"No matter who's helping him, he's probably out of the county by now."

"If he was smart. But I re-read the reports from his arrest, and he strikes me as someone who's motivated by thoughts and emotions that are alien to normal people. So who knows?"

"I can't disagree with that. Is there anything else I can do?"

"Get me out of this office. I'm going stir-crazy. I never thought that becoming a lieutenant would mean being chained to a desk." There was deep frustration in his voice. I knew how much he'd enjoyed being a deputy in the field.

"One way or the other, this is going to be over after this weekend," I said.

"It's a long weekend," he reminded me.

"I'm afraid it's not going to be long enough to find Manning."

"Have you settled your differences with Mick?"

"I believe I've made some progress. I'm thinking of making some changes in how we run CID."

"When you're ready, we can discuss it. How's Pete?"

I told him about my visit the night before.

"When bad things happen to you, it's hard not to take it personally. I'll touch base with him and keep my fingers crossed that the new surgery works out. When is it scheduled?"

"I don't think they've gotten that far."

"He's welcome to work as many hours as he wants. Just remember that it needs to be office work until he's given the okay to go back on full duty."

I was headed back to my office when Darlene called.

"It's lunchtime. What can I bring you?"

"Are you coming back to work for the sheriff's office?" I asked eagerly.

"Not today. But I want an update on the hunt for Manning and thought I wouldn't come asking for favors without bringing a bribe. Beef or chicken or whatever you want, provided I can pick it up from the taco truck."

I gave her my order, and thirty minutes later she was standing in my office with a bag of tacos and chips.

"I was hungrier than I thought," I said, wolfing down a chicken-and-mushroom taco. The local taco truck wasn't afraid to try unusual but tasty combos.

"So what's the inside scoop on the hunt for Neil Manning?" Darlene asked.

"Same as the outside scoop. Zilch, nada." I took a drink of my iced tea. "We're looking for Andre Roberts, better known as Trench. Our intel is telling us that he transported the drugs to the house where the two dead fugitives were holed up."

"Isn't he one of Mick's CIs?"

"How'd you know that?"

"Mick and I worked on a couple of cases together," she said as though this was common knowledge.

"Why don't I remember that? Other than a few questions about each other's cases, I don't remember you ever working with him."

"Might have been when you were down at the coast with your family." She took another taco out of the bag.

"Anyway. Yes, that's the Trench we're talking about."

"And you can't find him? That must have Mick pretty upset. He's pretty protective of him."

"Yeah, I was surprised by their... friendship, frankly."

"I think it's because he had a friend when he was growing up who had some physical deformities. The other kids went all *Lord of the Flies* on him and harassed the boy. From what

Mick said, he spent a lot of time stepping in and defending him. In fact, according to Mick, that was part of the incentive for him to go into law enforcement."

"How did I miss all this? Mick's right. I did shut him out." I shook my head.

"They don't call you High Horse for nothin'."

"Gee, thanks."

"I'll make sure my team is on the lookout for Trench. It's a bad sign that no one has seen him. There have been times I've thought there were two of him, I've seen him around so much. He does odd jobs at a couple of places. I know the Fast Mart guys pay him to clean up around the dumpsters and to tear up boxes occasionally. A few other businesses will pay him for an hour's work if he cleans up their parking lot."

"You're right. He's one of those people who's always in the background… until they aren't." Suddenly, I had a thought. "Hey, you're a woman."

"Thanks for noticing," she said, jokingly pushing out her chest.

"Phil had an idea that Manning might have talked a woman into helping him escape. What do you think?"

She looked up at me with a thoughtful expression. "There are a few of my fellow femalians that have no taste. They'll actually seek out the most inappropriate mates they can find. There was that prison guard in Alabama, for instance."

"Yeah, that was the example that Phil and I came up with."

"I thought Manning was banned from using any computers, phones or other devices?"

"He was. But remember, you can get cocaine in jail if you want it bad enough."

"You have a point, Mr. Peabody. So, yeah. If he could get the word out, he could probably find someone stupid enough to help him. It doesn't even surprise me anymore how stupid and crazy some people can be. What about the female guard who was killed? Has anyone looked into her background?"

"The FBI cleared her. From what they said, she didn't have any contact with him or the other prisoners before they picked them up in the van."

"If they said it, then they're probably sure," Darlene admitted.

"Which leaves us with: How do we hunt for a woman that might not even exist? Oh, yeah, and we only have until Tuesday before the FBI is gone." The task was daunting.

"Think it through, Matlock. We know that there was an outsider who helped the three men escape. But two of the men were left to their own devices."

I held up my hand to stop her. "And I think this other party laid out a smörgåsbord of drugs so those two would kill themselves."

"Which makes some sense if the outsider just wanted to help Manning. He or she would be better off if the other two escapees died."

"Because at that point they are witnesses to who he or she is."

"Then why not kill them at the scene of the breakout?" Darlene had slipped into the mode of a professor helping a dull student.

"If you let them live, then they'll run off and provide a distraction for the Feds and any local law enforcement out looking for you."

"Any proof that the mystery person *wanted* them dead?"

"I think they were given enough drugs that they were likely to overdose... or at least take enough that it would be more likely they'd get themselves caught or killed."

"After being in prison, their tolerance would be low and their desire high. Overdose would be a strong possibility."

"Which is what happened to Lester Stevens," I said. "This also suggests one reason why Cortez's phone was on and half hidden. The outsider wanted the Feds to catch up to them. Probably told them to hide out at the house and gave them the shotgun."

"Yep, which would ramp up the odds that the fugitives would be killed when the Feds showed up at their doorstep." Darlene tossed her last taco wrapper back in the bag. "So who's the mastermind, Manning or the mysterious other?"

"Until you asked, I hadn't even thought about it. I'd assumed it was Manning."

"Ass of you and me."

"Yeah, thanks for that. If I was a betting man, I'd still make it sixty-forty in favor of Manning. Still… that's a lot of strategizing and planning from inside a cell."

"So turn it around. If the brains of the operation is the person on the outside, then what do they want?"

"If it's a love interest, then they want Manning."

"Okay, Cupid, what are the other alternatives?"

"I see where you're going with this. We're talking motives. Love is one. Money is another. Also revenge. It's interesting that we haven't found Manning. Maybe he's dead."

"Or being tortured as we speak."

"That's a happy thought. You really are brightening up my Friday." I finished my iced tea and put the cup down. I was tempted to eat the ice, but from our days as partners I knew how much the sound irritated Darlene. Besides, I was getting excited about this line of thought.

"Following the motive might give us the person who was helping Manning," I said. "Love will be a tough one to prove. We need to find out how he could communicate with someone on the outside. As for money, unless Neil has some stashed away, his dad's got most of it. And even if money was the motive, it still goes back to how he was able to communicate with someone to get them to help him."

"And revenge?" Darlene asked.

"That's the best from an investigatory standpoint. We can look into all the people he wronged who might want revenge. Maybe this whole thing wasn't done to *help* Manning, but to hurt him. Wow! I've been blind and now I can see." I was excited. I felt like I had a path to follow.

"It might not be the right answer, but it's the answer that gives you tangible goals."

"Of course, Terri Miller's family would be at the top of the list for people he's wronged. I wonder if Padilla and her crew have thought of this?"

"It's counterintuitive because you would think that the person helping him to escape was actually there to *help* him."

"I'm sure that the other two fugitives thought the person was helping them too. The more I look at this, the better I like it." I looked at Darlene with admiration. "We always did work well together."

"Yep, you were a great Hooch to my Turner." She smiled and stood up. "I got to get back to work. The troops are buzzing me." She held up her phone and turned to the door. "You take care of the trash?"

"No problem," I said, already formulating my next move.

CHAPTER TWENTY

I checked to see if Pete was at his desk, but I was disappointed to see that he hadn't come in. Trying not to think about what this indicated about his mental health, I picked up my phone and called him, keeping my fingers crossed that he'd answer.

I was pleased to hear that he sounded willing to take on some work. I explained the logic behind the possibility that the person who helped Manning escape was seeking revenge.

"That's not the most ridiculous theory you've had," he said.

"Darlene walked me through it," I admitted.

"That explains it," he said, and I heard the smile in his voice, more of the old Pete.

"I want you to go through the Manning case and pull the names of anyone who might want vengeance for the crimes he committed against Terri Miller... or anyone else, for that matter."

"Does that include your dad and you?" When I didn't say anything right away, he said, "Just kidding. I'll get on it." He had access to all the files from his laptop at home.

"If you find anything interesting, get back with me."

"If it's a real lead, you have to promise to take me with

you to check it out," he said. I could tell he wasn't kidding. I thought about what Phil had said about waiting until he was cleared for full duty.

"Guaranteed," I assured him. If we ran into trouble when we were just driving around town together, then the lieutenant couldn't blame me for that.

There was a text from Julio when I got off the phone: *Sister is coming here in an hour.*

Let's meet in the small conference room, I responded.

I jumped on the reports I needed to review while I kept an eye on the time. I tried to concentrate on each report, but my mind kept going back to my conversation with Darlene. Was I captivated by the revenge angle because it gave me a new avenue to pursue, or did it really make sense in light of the evidence? What seemed clear was that the person helping Manning had wanted Waugh and Stevens dead. There was no telling what that meant for Neil Manning.

If I flipped it back to Manning as the mastermind, I could also see him wanting the other two dead. He was an egomaniac with no regard for anyone else's life. If he had convinced someone to help him, he might have already killed his liberator. At that thought, I just shook my head. This was turning into one of those puzzles where the more you looked at it, the more complex it became. I knew that with the clock ticking down, I needed to pick a few trails to follow and stand by my choices.

I walked down to the conference room and heard Julio speaking with a woman in the lobby. I stopped and turned toward the foyer to see Julio holding the door for a short, petite woman who looked a few years younger than her brother.

Julio introduced me to Justina Cortez-Russell. Her eyes were red and puffy.

"I don't understand what happened to my brother." She looked directly into my eyes as if hoping I had all the answers.

"I'm sorry for you loss." It was always hard to know what

to say to a grieving relative.

We followed Julio into the conference room where we all took seats around the table.

"Deputy Ortiz said that my brother was killed. Was it a robbery?"

"From what we know now, we think he was killed for his car," I said.

"But he would have just given them his car."

"They probably didn't want to leave any witnesses."

"These men were escaped convicts," Julio explained.

"They came to the bank?"

"No, this happened in the woods." As soon as I said it, her brow cleared.

"I see. That makes sense," she said. "And these men are dead?" She looked at Julio, who must have already told her.

"Yes, both of them," Julio assured her. I exchanged looks with him. He knew I would have to tell her that there were other men who could be involved who were *not* dead.

"I don't want to cause you any more grief. However, I need to tell you there is a possibility that others were involved in your brother's death," I said.

"Others who aren't dead?" she asked, catching on quickly.

"One was another prisoner. And we don't know if the person who helped them escape is a man or a woman."

"I see." She looked down at the table where her hands were clutching at each other.

"We need to catch these other people, so we need to ask you some questions." She didn't look up. "Is that okay?"

Finally, she gave me a determined look and nodded.

"I don't know how I can help, but if there are bad people out there who have hurt my brother, I want to see them locked up in jail."

"Did your brother ever mention having any enemies?"

"No." But there was a slight hesitation that made me wonder what she was thinking.

"You sound unsure?"

"No, no. I just wasn't sure what I wanted to say about… It might sound like a criticism of my brother, but he could be distant. Well, that's not the right word. I mean he was maybe… aloof. No, that isn't the right word either. He didn't get close to people. So he didn't make enemies, but he didn't make many friends either. I think his passion for hunting was as much about getting away from people as it was about the sport."

"Thank you for that," I said sincerely. "We need your honest opinion of your brother. Everyone we've talked to said he was an excellent bank manager, and no one has had a bad word to say about him."

"What about his ex-wife? How did she feel about him?" Julio asked. Even though we had eliminated her because of an airtight alibi, it didn't mean she couldn't have orchestrated this as a way to kill her ex-husband. It was farfetched, but not impossible.

"Lisa? No, she still cares about him. The divorce was all about his detachment. I believe he loved her; he just couldn't show it." She looked down at her hands again. "I should tell you that his early life was different from mine. Our mother went through a hard time after he was born. They didn't call it postpartum depression back then, but that's what it was. Just weeks after he was born, she ran off and was gone for almost two years."

"That must have been hard on your father and brother," Julio sympathized.

"Dad must have understood because he took her back, and five years later they had me. Their marriage was never picture-perfect, but they made it work. There was real love there. What I'm trying to explain is that, as a baby, Roberto was handed over to nurses that my father hired. He was very busy running his law firm. Not having a real mother for those first couple of years seemed to have affected him. Also, our father may have blamed him at first for our mother running away."

"Sounds like your father could be emotionally distant

too," I commented.

"True. Roberto had more than one reason for being the way he was."

"Did your brother talk about any problems at the bank?" I asked.

"He seemed very happy with the job, and he loved being up here where he could fish and hunt whenever he wasn't working."

"Did he ever talk about the people working at the bank, or the customers?" Julio asked.

"He did mention that one of the bank's customers had done a very bad thing. Kidnapping and murder, I think."

"What did he say about the man?"

"Nothing else. It was like you would mention seeing a car accident, something horrible that you stared at for a minute."

We talked to her for another fifteen minutes without learning anything that was going to help us. When we were done, Julio went through the procedures for claiming her brother's body from the morgue before escorting her out to her car.

Julio came back to my office with his notebook so we could go over our notes again. After sharing the revenge theory I'd developed with Darlene, I turned our focus back to the murders.

"Let's look at both murders as just that, murder cases. What have you learned about the death of the guard, Florence Murray?"

"Dr. Darzi's autopsy didn't reveal anything we didn't already know. She suffered minor injuries from the crash and from the backhoe opening up the van. What killed her was the brutal beating to her head. Dr. Darzi estimated twenty or more individual blows. Any one of them could have been fatal. After just two, her chances of survival would have been nil."

"Sounds personal," I said, and Julio nodded.

"Murray lived here in Adams County. A year ago she worked as a temporary replacement for Bert Hodges at the bank. He had surgery and was off work for two months," Julio said.

"Then it's possible she crossed paths with Neil Manning." I thought about this. "Is there a real connection between the two of them or was this just a coincidence?"

"I've talked to her friends and the people she worked with at Silver Security. They didn't have anything but nice things to say about her. No one remembers her talking about Neil Manning. And the FBI didn't find any connections between the two of them."

"Yeah, but the FBI didn't mention that she had worked at the same bank Manning used."

"Even if she was part of it, there still had to be another person operating the backhoe," Julio pointed out.

"You're right, which means bringing Murray into the equation just complicates an already complicated set of circumstances. How long has she worked for Silver Security?"

"Five years. They have a contract with a number of banks, like the First Bank of Calhoun, to provide security."

"Bert told me that the bank let him stay on after they contracted with Silver Security. He didn't mention that Murray had been a replacement for him while he was on medical leave. Where did Murray live?"

"In a house just north of the city limits. I did a search of the residence and turned the computer over to Lionel. She lived with her elderly mother. It's awful, really. Now her brother is trying to figure out how to take care of their mother."

"This is just a big nothing sandwich," I muttered, then asked Julio, "Thoughts?"

"If revenge is the motive, then the murder of Florence Murray doesn't seem to fit." He looked up at the ceiling. "Unless the prisoners killed her, and her death was just coincidental."

"We keep bumping into coincidences. I know they happen. I just hate relying on them for answers to big questions like why someone was killed. Never mind, I think we've talked this to death for now. You're on call this weekend so I can reach you if I need you."

"Yeah, I wanted to ask you about that. I talked to Lynn and she's willing to take my shift and on-call duties for tonight, tomorrow and tomorrow night. If it's okay with you, I'll cover Sunday, Sunday night, Monday and Monday night."

"As long as you're both happy with the arrangement and no one is taking so many hours that overtime comes into play, I'm fine with it."

After Julio left, I called Padilla and arranged to meet with her at four-thirty, which gave me just enough time to get some non-Manning work done.

When I drove over to the command center, I noticed that the parking lot looked considerably less crowded. Padilla met me at the door of the RV.

"They've already pulled some of the special-unit personnel from under me." She wasn't in a good mood. "I hope you've got a trail with some blood on it."

"A couple of things, but nothing that has the dogs running." I continued her hunting metaphor.

"Come on in."

When we were seated, I told her about Andre's and Nickel's connection to the two dead fugitives.

"That ties up a loose end. Or it will when you find this Andre character. I'll put out an alert to my men to look for him. You have a picture?"

I texted Mick, who quickly sent us both a picture of Andre. Padilla forwarded it on to what was left of her team. Technology has its upside.

"I want to go through Neil Manning's house," I told her.

"Why? We've searched it twice and come up empty."

I explained that I wanted to cover the romance angle. She frowned but nodded.

"Okay. We were looking for contacts, but not specifically

romantic contacts, so maybe you'll see something we didn't. At this point, I'm prepared to throw everything at the wall."

"Have you looked into Terri Miller's family?" I asked.

"Everyone we could find was alibied. The revenge angle felt right at first, we just couldn't find a hook." She gave me a wicked smile. "We even ran down alibis for you and your father."

"I would expect nothing less." I tried to smile but felt a little let down that the FBI had already considered revenge as a motive. "If his father didn't pay someone to break his son out of prison, and it isn't about revenge, then we're left with love or…" I shrugged.

"If the driver of the van had seen a little more, then maybe we wouldn't be in this situation," Padilla groused.

"Or if Silver Security had cameras inside and outside of the van. The fact they didn't gives weight to the idea of an inside man or woman."

"We've gone over that possibility with Charles Maxwell. Everyone on their payroll looks clear. I say that, but we know that people talk, and every one of those employees have half a dozen close friends and relatives and each one of them has half a dozen more."

"Loose lips sink ships." I felt a sense of fatigue when I thought of all the trails that we'd already gone down, and all the unexplored trails that seemed to be more and more obscure.

"Rudy Manning's phone and electronics were clean. No odd correspondence with his son or anyone else. His business is so extensive that we had to get him to explain some of the emails and texts. And it will take weeks to go through his finances. They're just a little more extensive than mine," she joked, which was a rarity. I could tell that she was also sensing the hopelessness of the situation.

"All of this would be a moot point if we could just stumble upon Manning's hideout. You're the expert when it comes to hunting fugitives. Where do they normally go to ground?" I asked.

"Where they're comfortable. Near friends or family. We've covered all those bases with Neil Manning. My men have done basic checks on everyone he's worked with or had any kind of relationship with in the last five years. The Manning family isn't that large, so we've covered all the aunts, uncles and cousins."

"Where else?"

"If you have a woodsman, then they might try and go to ground in the forest. There's plenty of that around here."

"Manning is not the outdoorsy type."

"That was our conclusion too. If he had a particular lifestyle then we might look in those circles, but his only lifestyle was manipulation of people. He hasn't been gone long enough for us to think about occupations. If we're looking for a fugitive who's been missing long enough that we can assume he or she would need money, then we look at the types of jobs they're familiar with. A truck driver will usually go back to driving a truck. A nurse will find a nursing job when they need money. But like I said, he hasn't been gone long enough to be looking for work."

"What about money? Where is he getting cash?"

"We assume it's from whoever helped him to escape. The person spent money on drugs and a shotgun for the other two fugitives. Like you, we think freeing Manning was the whole point, so it stands to reason they are supporting him now. There's also the possibility he had a stash of some sort, though we haven't found any sign of it on the computers or phones that were confiscated when he was arrested. Does that mean it's not possible? No. His father or someone else could have set up an account and given him the cyber keys to it."

I snapped my fingers. "Could that be the reason someone helped him escape? Maybe Manning *does* have some cash stashed away."

"The problem there is that his finances were reviewed extensively after his first arrest. If he hid money, then he did a great job of it."

"I can vouch for that," I admitted.

"I can think of a million ways to find someone, but none of them will work in this case."

"Like what?"

"Does he need special medication? No. Is he addicted to gambling? No. Does he like a special type of boyfriend or girlfriend. No."

"He liked to keep girlfriends tied up in shipping containers. But I doubt that's something many people would be eager to do." I sighed. "We have to be missing some clue or angle we haven't exploited."

"He might have found a bolt hole and be hunkering down, waiting for us to give up," Padilla admitted.

"That's a depressing thought." I frowned. "What did the autopsies on the two fugitives show?"

"Nothing we didn't already know. Lester Stevens died of an overdose, possibly fentanyl, and Waugh died from two well-placed nine-millimeter rounds to the chest and forehead. He also looked to have been high as a kite when our agent shot him."

She walked me back to my car. "You can get the key to Manning's house from his dad. I don't think he'll give you any problems. If he does, remind him that the house is in Neil's name and that Neil is a fugitive from justice. Oh, and if Neil's lawyer is present, tell him to kiss my ass."

"So you like him too." I grinned.

"He's put up some ridiculous roadblocks that have made it a lot harder to do our job. Let's just say I won't be disappointed if I never have to work with him again."

CHAPTER TWENTY-ONE

Rudy Manning was alone when I got to his house.

"Come in." His words were slurred, and he swayed a little as he led me into the house. "What do you want now? A pound of flesh? My first-born son?" He turned and faced me. "Oops, you already got that."

"Mr. Manning, I'm not going to apologize for arresting your son. He has committed horrible crimes."

"Yeah. Think I don't know that? Think that doesn't haunt my dreams? Congratulations, you've birthed a monster." He cursed and dropped down in a chair beside a half-full bottle of whiskey.

"I came by to get the key to Neil's house." A part of me wanted to get out of there as fast as possible, while another part, not the best part, wanted to see if I could get him to tell me anything while he was drunk.

"Yeah, yeah, whatever. It's somewhere," he said, not being helpful at all. He poured a finger of whiskey into a double shot glass he'd pulled out of thin air. In a gulp, the amber liquid was gone, and Manning smacked his lips. "That's the stuff that helps me to sleep. Or maybe I should say, pass out." He raised the empty glass in my direction.

"I just want to get the key. After that, I'll leave you

alone."

"Very gracious of you, sir. You just take everything I got and leave me alone." He fumbled with the shot glass before grabbing the bottle and filling the glass up again.

"Can I call someone from your family?" I said as kindly as I could.

"Call my son! I want my son…" His voice trailed off bitterly before he downed more whiskey.

"The key," I reminded him.

"The blasted key." He tried to stand up but fell back down into the chair. On his second try, he remained standing and pushed himself off toward the foyer. He stopped in front of a coat tree carved out of some exotic dark wood. It looked like a natural tree with branches arching out in all directions. An artist had spent a great deal of time making a beautiful piece of furniture just to have it reside in this unhappy home. There were little Hobbit-like drawers in the tree, and Manning opened several before finding the right one.

I reached my hand out for the key.

"I blame everyone but myself when I speak. But at night, all the voices in my head blame me." He dropped the key into my hand. "Please don't kill my son. He may be a monster, but he *is* my son." Manning fell to his knees. "I'll beg you. Would you like that?"

"Come on, get up." I took his elbow and gently pulled him to his feet. I thought of a dozen things I could say, but none of them would mean anything to him. I half carried him back to his chair. By the time I got him there, he was sobbing. I took the bottle and shot glass away and left them on a bar in the dining room. The sound of his weeping followed me out the door.

I headed over to Neil Manning's house, confident that I wouldn't find anything worth what I'd just been through.

The sun was touching the trees as I pulled into the driveway. I could hear the sounds of kids and families as I walked up to the house. The FBI's van was still parked up the street, and their sticker still warned me that I was forbidden to enter the crime scene. I ignored it and walked inside.

The house smelled musty. A flick of a switch proved that the lights still worked. As Padilla had told me, the FBI had not been neat as they rummaged through Neil's stuff. The rooms looked like a family of bears had passed through.

As I walked from room to room, I saw wires hanging out of the wall where we had removed TVs, phones and routers. When Neil had been placed on pretrial house arrest, the court had ordered that he couldn't have access to any electronic devices that could be used to communicate across the internet or by phone. Nothing had been replaced.

In the spare bedroom, there were now only desks running along one wall where once there had been banks of screens which he'd used to monitor his captive and everywhere else that he considered his domain. He had hacked into the security cameras at the trucking company so he could watch the employees. I wondered if that was a clue. Could he have been somewhere right now monitoring us, watching the efforts of law enforcement as we tried to find him?

Boxes of evidence had been taken out of the house when he was arrested, so there weren't many personal items left to sift through. There were a few geek magazines, law books and notes on his case. Apparently, he'd been trying to educate himself on the law as it applied to his criminal activities.

Frustrated, I headed home.

Cara and Henry were playing gin rummy at the dining room table when I came in. Ghost was doing his best to steal cards from the deck and the discard pile, while Alvin lay at Henry's feet and snored as only a Pug can. Ivy was on the back of the couch in the living room, slowly twitching her tail. She didn't like company, no matter who they were.

"There's stew in the pot on the stove," Cara said while studying her cards.

"Great." The smell of the stew was intoxicating. I could already tell that I would be fighting off a nap after I ate.

"Any luck finding the bad guy?" Henry asked while moving cards around in his hand.

"Nope," I said, spooning up a bowl of stew.

"You sound exhausted." Cara picked a card from the discard pile.

"I've been racking my brain trying to find an angle on this."

"I thought it would just be a matter of waiting until he sticks his head out of the trenches," Henry said. "With all the camera surveillance and credit-card tracking they have these days, he's bound to show up sooner or later."

"He's too dangerous to wait him out," I said.

"Gin!" Cara laid her cards on the table.

"Hmmm. I guess I can't complain if my best student beats me." Henry laughed.

I tried to relax and enjoy the good food, the company and the laughter, but I was haunted by Rudy Manning's breakdown, and the thought that his spawn was out there waiting on his chance to bring grief to someone else. Maybe us.

"What can I do?" Cara asked as we sat on the couch later that evening.

"Tell me what I'm missing."

"Let it go," she told me.

"Easier said than done."

"Let it go."

She kissed me. And again. With Henry snoring in the guest room, I let her lead me back to our bed. It wasn't earth-shattering, but for a while I let myself go and rocked gently in her arms.

I woke up on Saturday with the jitters. I hated that it was a holiday weekend and our time was running out while most people enjoyed picnics and went to the beach. On Monday,

Dad and a number of our deputies would be participating in the annual Memorial Day ceremonies held at cemeteries throughout the county. As important as it was to remember those who had died serving our country, I couldn't help but feel that it would be time lost in the search for Neil Manning and his accomplice.

Henry had volunteered to help me clear a fence line that had grown thick with small oaks, vines and weeds. I chopped and hacked and pulled at the debris in an effort to exorcise my frustration. It wasn't working.

"Let's take a break," I told Henry who, though he had more than two decades on me, had barely broken a sweat.

"You need to go to work," Henry told me as I wiped sweat from my face.

"No, I need a rest," I laughed.

"Not this kind of work. You need to go look for your fugitive," he told me. "You aren't relaxing. You're only pretending to take the day off, and you're becoming more stressed. Go to work. Cara and I are fine. I'll have something on the grill when you want to take a break." He patted me on the back while half pushing me toward the house.

"I think you're right." I had mixed feelings about going back to more fruitless investigating, but like Henry said, I wasn't really taking the day off, anyway.

Cara was very understanding. "What are you going to do?"

"I want to talk to Dr. Darzi and get a look at the bodies," I told her. "I should have done that yesterday. I have no idea if I can talk Darzi into coming to the morgue just to satisfy my curiosity."

"What do you think you'll find?"

"Nothing. But I've done everything else I can think of."

"It's Memorial Day weekend. Darzi may not even be in town," Cara said.

"True. Only one way to find out."

I pulled out my phone and hesitated as I looked at Darzi's personal number in my contacts. Calling on a

Saturday morning *and* on a holiday weekend would burn up a lot of credit with Darzi. With a sigh, I tapped the phone's screen.

"You better have one interesting dead body, my friend," Darzi answered.

"Actually, it's *your* dead bodies I'm calling about. I want to talk about the recent autopsies of Cortez and Murray."

"No, no. This is Saturday. Memorial Day weekend. I'm not on call and my family is having a cookout. It can wait." He sounded adamant.

"Time is running out for us to find Neil Manning."

"Looking at those bodies isn't going to help. I've sent my reports. I think you're aimlessly looking around in the hopes you'll stumble upon a clue."

I couldn't argue the point.

"What will it take to get you to come in and show me the bodies?"

He was quiet for a moment, and I heard his kids laughing and playing in the background. One of them asked who he was talking to.

"Bring Mauser to my house today," Darzi said.

I wasn't sure I understood him. The doctor wasn't one of Mauser's biggest fans. "Dad's dog?"

"Yes, that's right. That's my price. My kids love him. You bring him to our cookout and let the kids see him, then I'll go to the morgue with you."

Now it was my turn to think. "I'll check with Dad."

"What are you doing today?" I asked when he answered my call.

"Genie is down at the beach with some of her girlfriends, so I'm just getting a few chores done. Why?"

"Do you and Mauser want to go to a cookout?" I made my voice sound as happy and chipper as I could.

"Is Henry doing the grilling?"

"Henry is grilling, but that's not the cookout I'm talking about. You've been invited to Dr. Darzi's family cookout."

"Really? Why didn't he call me? Are you and Cara and

Henry going?"

"Well… Darzi and I are going to go over to the morgue while you and Mauser enjoy the cookout." I cringed, anticipating his reaction.

"What?" I was encouraged that he didn't sound mad yet.

"Here's the deal. I want to have Darzi go over the autopsies of Cortez, Murray and Stevens. In exchange, I have to bring you and Mauser to entertain his family while we're gone."

There was a long silence on the other end of the phone.

"Is this going to help find Neil Manning?"

"Probably not. I just don't have any other ideas."

"The food better be good."

"I'll be at your place in half an hour."

When I got to Dad's house, he'd loaded the van with Mauser's usual travel bag full of treats, water and waste bags, and Mauser was already on leash touring the front yard. Dad had dressed for the occasion in an Adams County Sheriff's polo and tan shorts.

"That outfit would be complete with leather sandals," I joked.

"You don't wear sandals around Mauser."

Mauser was decked out in a new red, white and blue collar and smelled like he'd recently had a bath. As always, he was excited at the prospect of an adventure, and he almost ran me over on his way to the open door of the van.

"First you schedule us for a Sunday school visit and now you negotiate a deal with the coroner. Since when did you decide to become Mauser's manager?" Dad asked as he drove.

"I'm bargaining with what I have," I told him.

"I read over your reports."

"I didn't leave anything out."

"That's what I was afraid of."

"I feel like there's a mastermind behind all of this, but I

haven't been able to pull the curtain back to see who it is. I can't even figure out the reason why."

"Rudy Manning?"

"No." I told him about my recent experience with Manning's father.

We went down the same paths that I'd already thoroughly plowed with both Darlene and Julio.

"It all comes down to emotions or money," Dad said, not telling me anything I didn't already know.

"And Manning doesn't seem to have had the opportunity to use either one to manipulate a third party."

There was a whine from Mauser as he hung his head over the seat and drooled on my shoulder.

"I know, big guy. It's a holiday weekend and we should be enjoying it instead of talking about work. If this was a normal situation, I'd be on your side," I told Mauser. "But you're going to have plenty of people to worship you and feed you treats when we get to Darzi's house."

The coroner lived in a large Colonial in one of Tallahassee's older subdivisions. Our arrival was met with much oohing and aahing from a phalanx of children.

"Welcome to my home," Dr. Darzi told Dad and shook his hand.

"A pleasure."

The kids listened to Dad's instructions and were very respectful of Mauser as they came up one by one to pet and gush over his size. When he opened his mouth in his trademark silly grin, his two-inch-long canines caused a few kids to run screaming before they stopped and turned back, laughing.

After Darzi introduced us to his two dozen relatives gathered around the backyard pool, we left Dad and Mauser at the party and headed for the hospital. I felt snug and secure as I settled in the passenger seat of Darzi's Audi A8 which he gracefully maneuvered through the streets at seven miles over the posted speed limit.

"Not afraid of the Tallahassee PD?" I asked.

"Nine, I'm fine," Darzi quipped.

We weren't surprised to see that the hospital's emergency room was full of holiday accidents and poorly timed illnesses.

"I prefer working with the dead," Darzi said as we walked to the morgue. "You can put them back in the drawer when you want to take a break."

The intern working the front desk put down his phone to greet us when we came in.

"I won't be here long," Darzi told him, and the man looked relieved.

We walked down the hallway to the storage room. Inside, Darzi activated one of the three monitors around the room and logged into his files.

"You want to see Murray and Cortez, right?" His eyes were glued to the monitor.

"Yes. Let's start with Murray. This is truly a fishing expedition."

"Most of my family love that dog, but my Aunt Pimi and cousin Ishaan think he's unclean. It horrified them that I invited him to the cookout, so that's a bonus for me. You have paid in full for your fishing trip."

After taking a minute to review his notes, Darzi went over to a drawer and pulled it open.

"Not a pretty sight. I tried to leave her in better shape than I found her, for the funeral home's sake."

He unzipped the bag, and I remembered how gruesome the assault on Florence Murray had been.

"Someone sure wanted to make sure she was dead," I said.

Darzi pulled up photos taken at the scene as he went over his notes from the autopsy. I noticed the bloody Silver Security uniform and wondered how Maxwell was squaring this with the company. I'd seen him several times hanging out with the FBI agents, but I hadn't talked to him since the first day.

Darzi showed me the gouge in Murray's arm.

"My judgment is that this happened when the bucket on the machine cracked open the van."

"So that happened first?"

"Yes. Only an educated guess from the circumstances and the amount of bleeding." He shrugged.

We moved on to the body of Roberto Cortez.

"One shot from the shotgun. Very close," Darzi said, showing me the shot pattern on Cortez's chest.

"There's no real way of knowing if the shotgun that Waugh had was the one that killed Cortez. We can analyze the pellets to see if they came from similar ammunition, but all that would tell us is that they shop at the same Walmart," I said with a frown.

"There were some other marks on Cortez's body consistent with being hit and forced into the back of his car," Darzi said, pointing to spots on the head and back.

"Not surprising. Cortez strikes me as a man who wouldn't go along easily."

"Along those lines, we've sent the coins in his hand to be tested for DNA, but your odds of learning anything from that are slim." Then he pointed to another report on the screen.

"Neither Murray nor Cortez had any alcohol in their systems. We'll have to wait for the rest of the lab tests to come back before we can comment on other drugs." Darzi raised his eyebrows. "There are times when an autopsy is just an autopsy, not the conclusion to a case."

He glanced up at the monitor. "Don't we have another body here from Adams County?"

"An unattended death," I told him. "Nicholas Archway."

"Yes, the older gentleman. Would you like to see him?"

I almost said no, but thought: *In for a penny in, for a pound.* "Why not?"

"Okay, I'll pull up the file." Darzi studied it for a moment. "The good news is that I can concur with the natural-death conclusion." I heard a slight hesitation in his voice.

"But?"

"No *but*. Like all conclusions, it is based on the totality of information. There are a few items that could point in another direction, that's all."

"Such as?" I was curious now. Anything to distract me from the frustrating hunt for Neil Manning.

Darzi went over and slid Archway's body out of its drawer. After unzipping the body bag, he pointed to very slight marks on Archway's arm.

"That could be where someone gripped his upper arm. Or it could be where he bumped into a doorway. He's an older gentleman, so…" Darzi shrugged. He opened the bag wider, and this time he pointed to a spot on Archway's thigh. "Same here. Either, or."

"What about his face?"

Darzi looked at me and then at Archway's face.

"Again, he's older, his skin is thin and there are a number of areas of actinic keratosis on his face that make it difficult to discern other types of abrasions. I don't see anything that raises a red flag," he concluded.

"Bloodwork?"

"Basic bloodwork didn't show anything unusual. And since this is an unattended death, I didn't order any further lab tests."

I remembered the piece of plastic I'd found, and a thought took shape in my mind.

"Do you have the crime-scene photos I sent you?"

"Here." Darzi pulled up a folder of pictures on his monitor.

"Look at the bathroom cabinet."

Darzi pulled up a couple of photos. "OCD," he pronounced.

"Those sleeping pills. Could one or two of them put a man in a deep enough sleep that you could cover his face with, say, a bag or a piece of plastic and smother him without leaving a lot of trauma?"

"Of course. At his age, certainly. That would be

consistent with the marks on his thigh and arm. But without more evidence, I won't even list his death as inconclusive. From all the evidence, this is a natural death."

"Yeah, you're right. I need to let it go. Like I need to stir up murders that aren't even murders."

CHAPTER TWENTY-TWO

We drove back to the house and found Dad and Mauser living it up by the pool. Dad was receiving enough reflected glory from Mauser that the kids had volunteered to bring him beer and food. The two of them were enjoying themselves so much that it took me an hour to convince Dad to drive me back to Adams County.

I was deep in thought when I left Dad's. Something was nagging me about one of the autopsies, but I couldn't put my finger on it. With no clear direction, I drove to the sheriff's office, then sat in the parking lot, going through all the texts and voicemails I'd received that morning. Most were things that could wait, but one item stuck out. It was a text from Mr. Griffin. *Got a call from Archway's neighbor. Could be important.*

I considered calling him, but since I wanted to talk to Eddie anyway, I drove on over to his house. Mr. Griffin and Eddie were doing yardwork when I pulled up.

"You missed some weeds over there," I joked with Eddie, who was sweating profusely.

He glared at me. "Thanks for all the help."

"I'm glad you stopped by," Mr. Griffin said. "I got a call from Harold. He remembered something Nick said, and he wanted me to let you know." He saw me take my phone out of my pocket and shook his head. "He can't hear well over the phone. Best if you go over there. Do you want me to come along?"

"Only if you want to," I told him.

"I'll let you do it. I'm about done-in. I'll call and let him know you're coming."

Mr. Griffin went inside the house, and I turned to Eddie. "Do you know Trench?" I asked him.

"Sure. I knew him when I was using, and now he comes by the library and does odd jobs occasionally."

"He's missing. Took drugs to someone and now he's been gone for a few days."

Eddie looked thoughtful. "Yeah, I guess I haven't seen him lately."

"Where would he go if he was hiding out?"

"Trench doesn't really go to ground much. When I was using, I'd hide any time I owed someone money or had screwed something up. Trench is different. He works all the time to make a few bucks, and a lot of what he does is legal. Sweeping, picking up pecans, cutting grass, cleaning up parking lots. He likes to be out doing stuff. I think 'cause of his... speech problem, he doesn't like to talk to strangers. But he *does* like to see people, if that makes any sense. You think something bad has happened him?"

"Maybe. His last drug delivery may have taken him to some very bad people." I shrugged. "We just don't know."

"Maybe someone he works for is helping him hide out."

"That's a thought." It actually made a lot of sense. "Can you think of all the places he's worked?"

"I guess I could come up with a list. The library would be on it, but I can tell you he's not there. I've sort of been the go-between with him and the head librarian, so I'd know if he was around. Let me think." He looked up as though the answers might be written in the fluffy white cumulus clouds drifting overhead. "The Fast Mart, the coffee shop across from the courthouse, the bank, the theatre... and I've seen him cleaning cars at the funeral home. I'll try and think of any others. The people at the coffee shop, the theatre or the funeral home are your best bet."

I thanked him and drove off to see Harold Powers. He was waiting for me on the front porch and waved me on into the house.

"My daughter is in the kitchen. Would you like some water or a Coke?"

"No, thank you. Mr. Griffin said you had something to tell me."

He looked furtively back toward the kitchen.

"It's about a woman," he said, leaning forward and half whispering. "I would have told you when you asked me about Nick the first time, but… well, it's kind of private. Between friends, you know?"

"I don't think he'd mind you telling me under the circumstances," I assured him.

"That's what I decided." He took a deep breath and looked back at the kitchen door again. "Nick had a woman who was interested in him. Came by his house a couple of times."

"Who was she?"

"I don't know. Nick didn't say. Just that she was pretty and he kinda got ahead of himself, I think. See, a guy can forget his age. Thinks he's a young man again. Especially if a woman starts paying attention to him."

"When did he tell you about her?" I asked.

"Not till it was over. I got the feeling the whole experience embarrassed him. He… you know, he tried to keep up with her. He said he felt like a fool and finally told her it wasn't going to work out."

"He broke it off with her?"

"I got the feeling Nick thought she might be looking for a sugar daddy."

"Did Nick have money?" I asked, remembering how Harold had reacted the last time I'd asked him.

"I know he was more than comfortable. Broke his heart

when his nephew died and he didn't have anyone to leave his house and money to. Guess he thought this woman had figured out he didn't have any family."

"Did he give you any description of her?" I don't know why I cared. It wouldn't have made any sense for her to kill him if he hadn't married her or rewritten his will. Then an idea occurred to me. "Did he keep money in the house?"

"No. Never. Well, maybe five hundred dollars. You know, emergency money. But he was always talking about how keeping money in your house is dangerous. Bad guys can get wind of it and then you've got a target on your back."

"He wasn't wrong."

Harold nodded. "Nick kept all his money in investments or in the bank. Even kept his nice watches and the like in a safe deposit box at the bank. If there was a big to-do we were going to attend, he'd say he had to get his dress watch from the bank."

If he was murdered, then it probably hadn't been to rob him. Unless the killer didn't know he kept his money in the bank.

"When was he seeing this woman?" I asked.

"He mentioned it to me about two months ago. I guess a little bit before that."

"Can you tell me anything he said that might help identify her?

"He said she was pretty. Don't know what that means." Harold lowered his voice and leaned in again with a glance back toward the kitchen. "I look at women these days that I would have called a granny thirty years ago. A man's standards change over time."

"I guess she lives here in town."

"I'm sure he met her here. He never traveled anywhere."

"Did he use the internet much?"

Harold shrugged. "He was better than me. His nephew helped him out. Set up his computer and got him email and such. Nick lost interest after Taylor died. Last few years, he just watched TV, read books and kept his house spotless."

We talked for another few minutes without me getting any additional information I could use. When I left his house, the nagging feeling that I had a clue right in front of me continued to grow.

Cara called to let me know that Henry was firing up the grill and I told her I was on my way. I could smell the bratwurst as soon as I got out of the car.

"Got these from a friend of mine." Henry pointed to the grill. "His cousin has a beautiful farm and makes them from his great-great-grandfather's recipe."

"Perfect for kicking off the summer," I told Henry. "Thank you!"

Cara had made a big bowl of potato salad and cooked green beans and ham. By the time I'd finished eating, I'd almost forgotten about Neil Manning and the murders. I helped clean up and then planned to do a little work on my laptop, only to find myself dozing off on the couch. When I woke up, it was almost dark and Cara and Henry were playing gin again.

I shook off the nap and listened awhile as Henry and Cara talked.

"I should have gone by the bank yesterday," I heard Henry say.

"What?" I asked.

"I said I should have picked up some money for the weekend. I'll go by the ATM first thing in the morning. They can run out of cash fast on a holiday weekend."

"The bank." I didn't know why that caught my attention. "Archway kept his money at the bank."

"Yeah, most people do," Cara said, playing a card. "Who's Archway?"

I told them about Nicholas Archway's death. "And Roberto Cortez was the manager of the bank," I told them.

"You knew that." Cara waited for Henry to discard.

I got a glass of tea and stood by the table, half watching them play and half letting my mind stir around ideas.

"The guard who was killed had worked at the bank… and the Mannings banked there."

"There's only one bank and a credit union in town," Cara reminded me.

I snapped my fingers. "Andre cleaned up their parking lot." *Andre did a lot of odd jobs*, the voice in my head reminded me. *Still, this is the first solid connection I've found between all the players*, I told the voice. *Archway isn't a player*, the voice assured me. *But that's a lot of coincidences*, I thought. *This is a rural community. Everybody shops at the same stores and banks at the same banks*, the voice reminded me.

I looked at my phone, wondering if my half-baked theories were ready to share. Instead, I sat down at my laptop and did quick background checks on Bert Hodges, the bank guard, Curtis Warner, the assistant manager, and Catalina Knight, the head teller. None of them had a criminal history. Credit checks were also clear, and Googling their names didn't reveal anything I didn't already know.

I picked up the phone and called Charles Maxwell.

"No, you aren't bothering me," Maxwell said, sounding a bit tipsy. "I've been living on the edge… looking over the cliff I'm about to be pushed off of."

"Are you okay?" I asked.

"I'm taking a lot of blame for this fiasco with Manning and the other escaped prisoners. I told them when we brought them in that the transport company needed to come up to par. Do you think that helps? Nope. Makes it worse."

"I wanted to ask you about the guard in the truck, Florence Murray. Was there anything hinky in her records?"

"No. We went over her life with a fine-tooth comb. So did the FBI. She talked too much. That was the worst anyone said about her."

"What about Bert Hodges?"

"Who?"

"Hodges, the guard who works at the First Bank of Calhoun."

"Name's familiar. I… Yeah, he retired from the police

right around the time I became chief. There was a kerfuffle because of his disability pay. Bad back, hips, maybe both. I don't handle bank security, but I know who you're talking about."

"Can you check on him?" I asked.

"If I can get off the couch, I'll go do it now." I heard him groan as he got up. "Glad you called. I've been sitting around here crying into my beer all afternoon." A minute later: "Give my laptop a second to wake up."

"Take your time," I said, wanting him to hurry.

"Got to log in." Time ticked by. "Bert Hodges. Yes, he's been our employee for about two years. He looks clean. When we were contracted to handle the bank's security, there were concerns about his health and his request with the city for arbitration over his disability. Ultimately, his disability payments were reduced when he went to work for the bank. Had surgery about a year ago. No, all looks good. Why are you asking about him?" Maxwell's voice was sharper now.

"A trail I'm following led me to the bank, that's all."

"Okay." He sounded unconvinced. "Look, if you get anything going, it would mean a lot if you let me come in on it."

"Sure." I felt a little sorry for him. "Could you go ahead and give me Bert's current address?"

As I hung up, I decided I was comfortable taking Bert off of my suspect list. He'd never seemed viable, anyway. That left Curtis Warner and Catalina Knight.

Could Catalina have been the woman who had tried to hook up with Archway? The idea seemed crazy. Catalina's looks were way beyond my league; why would she even consider an old man like Archway? He may have had a little money, but could it have been enough to make a professional like Catalina turn gold digger? It seemed unlikely.

That left Curtis Warner. Had he wanted Cortez's job so badly that he'd developed some elaborate scheme involving multiple murders? That was farfetched.

"I'm going out," I told Cara and Henry.

"It's late. Can't your hunch wait until tomorrow?" Cara got up and came over to me.

"I need to be working."

She gave me a hug. "Okay, go. We'll be fine."

"I promise I won't be long." I smiled. "Unless I get on a hot trail."

"I knew that. Good luck." She gave me a kiss.

"Lock the door when I leave."

When I got out to the car, I called Lynn Lewis and told her that I might be looking for a way to get into trouble.

"I'm on call," she assured me. "Everything's been quiet, though the night is young." I could hear her puffing on a cigarette.

"I just wanted to make sure you were around if I need backup."

"I'm just a phone call away."

CHAPTER TWENTY-THREE

I started toward town without a concrete plan. Finally, I decided I'd start by scoping out the homes of the three bank employees with possible connections to the murders. Even though I'd already ruled out Bert Hodges as a suspect, I had his address, and it wouldn't hurt to talk with him.

Bert lived in a hundred-year-old tobacco warehouse that had been converted into apartments. I knocked on the door several times and finally Bert shouted for me to wait a minute. When he opened the door, his hair was mussed and he was wiping the sleep from his eyes.

"Sorry, always take a nap after dinner. What's wrong?" he said when he realized that a deputy knocking at his door might be more than a social call. "Something happen at the bank?"

"Everything is fine," I said, wearing my best disarming smile. "I'd just like to ask you a few more questions."

"Workin' the case on a holiday weekend. I'm impressed." He backed away from the door and ushered me inside.

The apartment was impressive. The renovation of the building had taken great care to preserve the feeling of the old barn while adding walls of old brick and thick heart-pine beams. The ceiling rose up two stories with a staircase leading to a loft. In the back was a well-appointed if cozy kitchen.

"They give me a break on the rent," Bert said when he saw my reaction to the apartment. "I'm the official unofficial security for the place. Have a seat." He pointed to a sagging old couch. "And tell me what you want to know."

"How well did you know Florence Murray?"

"Not well. She took over while I was havin' my surgery. I only met her once or twice, but I've seen her come into the bank a few times since. I think she banks there."

"How well did you know Nicholas Archway?"

"Who?" He frowned.

I scrolled through the photos I'd taken of Archway's corpse and held one out to Bert. As an ex-cop, I knew I wouldn't be showing him anything he hadn't seen before. "He died this week."

"Oh, him. Yeah, I saw him in the bank a lot. Never knew his name. Quiet old guy. Sorry to hear he's dead. He came into the bank two or three times a week. Now that's old-school. Kids these days run their whole lives out of their phones." He scoffed at the idea.

"Did you ever talk to him?"

"What are these questions about?"

"I'm trying to fill in some gaps. A few items of interest tie back into the bank. You're not a suspect," I assured him.

"Okay, I guess." He settled back in his chair. "I said hi to him most days. Might have commented on the weather, that sort of thing. Nothing more."

"Did he regularly talk to anyone else at the bank?"

Bert suddenly smiled.

"He did! *Now* I remember. A few months back, I saw him talking to Catalina every time he came in. Not surprisin'. I could give you a list of a dozen guys and a few girls that flirt with her. What was odd about it was that Catalina gave him more time than the others. She always does a little flirtin', but this time she seemed to take it a little further. I saw them walk out of the bank together three or four times.

Then, after a few weeks, it changed. He didn't even make eye contact with her. It looked like she tried talkin' to him a couple of times, and he just nodded or gave her a one-word answer."

"What do you think was going on?" I asked.

"Danged if I know. An old fart like him with her? If I thought that was possible, I'd've been whistlin' up her skirt myself."

I was confident I'd identified Archway's secret girlfriend. But what did it mean?

"Did she ever flirt with anyone else like that? You know, beyond her normal flirting?"

"After that weirdness with the old guy, she looked like she was goin' after Mr. Cortez. Now that made sense. When he started workin' there, I half assumed there would be an office romance at some point."

"Why was that?"

"Simple. They were both tens in a world of fives and sixes. Just stood to reason."

"But nothing happened?"

"Like I said, Mr. Cortez, he was kind of a… cold fish. Maybe that isn't fair. More like that sort of thing didn't interest him. Not that he had an interest in guys or anything. Just didn't want any romance. I've had a couple of friends who were like that after the first couple of ex-wives."

"But Catalina tried?"

"Not when he first got there. When he didn't show any interest, she dropped it. Then after the old guy, it looked like she was goin' after Mr. Cortez again hot and heavy. After a couple of weeks, it stopped. I don't know if he said something to her or she just gave up."

"What about Curtis Warner? Anything between him and Catalina?"

"Those two are thick as thieves, but it's professional. Office politics stuff. Any work issues and you know those two are going to be on the same side."

By the time I left Bert's, I'd been able to put a few pieces of the puzzle together, but the image still didn't make any sense.

My next move was to drive over to Catalina's house. I called dispatch and got her address. She didn't live far from Neil Manning, but her subdivision was smaller and priced for first-time homebuyers. The lots were a decent size, but the builders had used modestly priced materials and none of the homes were over fifteen hundred square feet.

The porch light was on at Catalina's house, but the rest of the house was dark. I parked on the street and watched it for ten minutes. Then I got out and walked up to the door, knocking but not expecting anyone to answer. I wasn't wrong. I thought about walking around the house, which wasn't strictly allowed under Florida law. I could have done it, but I wouldn't have been able to use anything I saw or heard as evidence in a case. It didn't matter. I was sure no one was home.

Back in my car, I headed toward Curtis Warner's house. His neighborhood was several steps up the economic ladder. His house was a two-story Federal-style set back from the street. Unlike at Catalina's house, there were plenty of lights on. I could see an SUV in the driveway, but I couldn't make out the license plate from where I'd parked in the street.

I got out and walked up the drive far enough to read the tag on the car. The other houses nearby were dark, and I was confident that I could walk back to my car with no one wondering about the weird guy walking up and down the driveway.

I got back into the driver's seat, opened my laptop and entered the tag number. Sure enough, it was Catalina Knight's Toyota in the driveway. Now my curiosity was piqued. If there had been other cars in the driveway or on the street, then I could have convinced myself that it was an office holiday party. But I was pretty sure that this was personal, and that was interesting.

Now I had a dilemma. I could walk up to the door and ring the bell, keeping everything on the up-and-up. But doing that would also alert them that I was on to… whatever it was they were doing. On the other hand, I could do what I knew I shouldn't do and snoop around the house, where anything I learned would be moot as far as a judge was concerned.

I picked up my phone and called Lynn again, briefly explaining the situation. "I might need some backup."

"So you don't want to call dispatch 'cause you're being naughty." I could hear the smirk in her voice.

"I'll give you a get-out-of-trouble-free card if you just agree to head in this direction and stand by," I told her.

"Sure. I'm finishing up at an attempted carjacking that turned out to be more of a domestic dispute."

"Hang back. I don't want to flush the pigeons," I told her.

"Assuming you have any pigeons," she said. "Unless there's evidence you aren't telling me about, you don't have enough to get a warrant of any kind."

"Exactly why I'm doing a little snooping."

"You ever heard of the fruit of the poisoned tree?"

"I solemnly swear that I won't use anything I find out to get a warrant in the future. Remember, this isn't just a murder case. We *are* trying to apprehend a dangerous felon."

"Humph. You can argue all you want, but you're still walking on thin ice."

I suddenly heard what she was saying, and I thought about my current position in the department.

"You know what? You've convinced me. I've got to set a good example. I can't be the guy that cuts corners anymore. I'm now the guy who *punishes* the deputies that cut corners."

"That's not exactly what I… I said I'm coming over there," she backpedaled.

"No. I changed my mind. I'm going to knock on the door. I'll learn a lot from their reaction and everything I find out will be usable." I paused. "Still, if you wanted to head this way, I might need a second investigator."

"Can do. Are you still going to give me the get-out-of-trouble-free card?"

"No," I said and hung up.

When I got to the front door, I hesitated with my finger poised to ring the bell. I decided I would act surprised when I learned that Catalina was there. Maybe Warner would pretend that she wasn't in the house. *That would be interesting*, I thought, pressing the bell.

I had to ring the bell twice more before I heard Warner's voice on the other side of the door asking who was there.

"Sergeant Larry Macklin. I know it's late, but I have a few questions I was hoping you could answer."

There was a long pause before I heard the deadbolt turn.

"Sorry, come in," he said with a strained smile.

Warner was wearing a button-down shirt and slacks. His forehead bore a sheen of sweat as he stepped back and invited me inside.

"We can talk in the den," Warner said as he led me into a room that was all dark wood, unread books and floor-to-ceiling windows.

"I'm surprised to see you. Not just because of the time, but I can't imagine I have anything else to tell you about Mr. Cortez." His smile was stiff and held in place by force of will.

"Actually, I wanted to talk to you about the death of Nicholas Archway," I said nonchalantly.

The look on his face gave everything away. He recovered quickly, but the game was up. He'd clearly had a part in what had happened to Archway, but what, how and why, I didn't know.

"Mr. Archway was a nice man and a good customer. I was sorry to hear of his death." The words were stiff and forced.

"How well did you know him?"

"Only as a customer."

"What about Catalina?" I asked and watched him flinch.

"You'd have to ask her."

"Why don't you ask her to come into the room and I

will."

I thought he was going to deny that she was there, but instead he smiled a little and said, "Sure."

A few minutes later, the door opened again, and I was staring at the beautiful visage of Catalina Knight, who was holding a revolver. It was a Colt, a large bore, one of their snake models, a Python or Anaconda. Looking down the barrel made it look even larger than it was. The stainless steel reflected the lights in the den. The gun looked so out of place in her hands that I was confused for a moment.

"You didn't give us a choice," she said. "Don't even think about moving. I'm perfectly capable of pulling the trigger."

"This is not going to help you. I told people where I was going." Well, I'd told one person, at least.

"We'll see." Warner came over to me. "Raise your hands high."

I hoped that he would step between me and Catalina, but no such luck. He was very careful as he took my gun and phone from me. He set them on an end table and patted my legs down until he found my Beretta Nano strapped to my ankle.

If I hadn't asked Lynn to come back me up, I would have tried to put up a fight, but it would have been a desperate chance. Still, a desperate chance was better than any chance I'd have once I was disarmed and tied up. Now I was putting all my faith in Lynn.

I was feeling both vulnerable and foolish. My preconceived ideas had gotten me into this mess. I'd assumed that people in a nice house with good-paying jobs would have acted reasonably and not like the stupid, desperate criminals I was used to dealing with.

Warner pointed my phone at my face and opened it. *Stupid face recognition*, I thought. He scrolled through my texts. "Doesn't look like he texted anyone about coming here."

"I radioed in from my car," I lied.

He looked at the last phone number I'd dialed and hit the

message button. It took him a minute to read through the messages and figure out who I'd called.

"He did call another investigator before he came to the door," Warner reported.

"Let's tie him up."

Together they were able to tie me up without giving me a chance of escaping. Catalina was obviously the one in charge. Warner did what she said and only occasionally made suggestions. Unfortunately, Catalina was also the smarter, more aggressive and decisive of the two.

With my hands tied tightly behind my back, I was gagged and made to kneel on the floor. *Anytime, Lynn*, I thought.

"Watch him," Catalina ordered and then left the room.

With a sock stuffed in my mouth, I didn't even have an opportunity to talk my way out of this mess. My only hope was that Lynn would start to wonder what was going on and come to the rescue.

Ten minutes later, Warner, clearly unnerved, went to his desk and pulled out a full-size Beretta handgun. Time ticked by slowly as I watched him pace up and down, looking more nervous by the minute. Every once in a while, he would casually point the gun at me.

I was beginning to wonder if I'd put too much faith in Lynn. There were other possibilities for rescue. My car was parked outside and had a GPS locator that dispatch could use to pinpoint its location. The apps on my phone could also give the department my location. Feeling increasingly desperate, but knowing I couldn't fight back, I decided that time was my friend.

CHAPTER TWENTY-FOUR

After what must have been close to an hour, I heard a door open and slam. There were two voices in the hallway. One was Catalina's and the other gave me hope… until I realized what they were saying.

"We can work a deal if you put a stop to this now," I heard Lynn say.

"Is that you, Cat?" Warner yelled, his voice high and nervous.

"Yes, keep it down," she called back. A minute later, she pushed Lynn into the den while holding a gun on her.

There was a scrape across Lynn's forehead and her hair was matted with blood. She looked at me and shook her head.

"Who's this?" Warner asked.

"The other investigator. The one he called before showing up. Her name's Lynn Lewis. Now tie her up," Catalina instructed. I noticed that Catalina had Lynn's handgun stuffed in her pocket.

"Two! What are we going to do with *two* of them?" Warner was close to panic.

"Tie her up," Catalina hissed.

"You work at the bank, both of you," Lynn said, making

eye contact with Warner. "I told her we can get this all cleared up if—"

Catalina cut her off. "And stuff a sock in her mouth!"

Warner had already retrieved the roll of rope he'd used to tie my hands. With a rough push, he forced Lynn into a chair. He'd set his gun down when he picked up the rope, and I saw Lynn's eyes as she calculated the distances between herself and Catalina and Warner. There was a triangle formed between the gun on the desk, Warner at her back and Catalina, who was smart enough to be across the room. She was holding the big-bore revolver in both hands in a shooter's stance.

As Warner leaned in to take Lynn's hands, she reached up and grabbed his shirt. In a swift move, she pulled him off balance and he fell to the floor.

As she started to move toward Warner's gun, Catalina shouted, "I'll kill you both, I swear!" The words were cold and hard. "Put your hands up, now!"

Lynn hesitated and it was over. With Catalina's gun at her head, she put up her hands.

"Can't blame a woman for trying."

"Get up!" Catalina told Warner, who was stumbling to get to his feet.

Five minutes later, Lynn was tied and gagged in a chair five feet from me.

"What are we going to do?" Warner asked, visibly shaking.

"First, hobble them," Catalina said.

"What?"

"Tie their feet together. Take a two-foot piece of rope and tie one end around each ankle so they can't make a run for it." She explained all this through clenched teeth like an exasperated teacher to a purposefully ignorant child.

"Sorry, I've never taken anyone hostage before," he whined as he got more rope.

"Neither have I, but I've got enough sense not to let these two escape." Her words had less of an edge. "You need to calm down and start using your brain. We don't have much time to fix this."

"How can we fix it?" He finished tying Lynn's feet and moved to mine.

"I'll tell you when you're done."

I had a feeling she didn't want to let us know their plans until we were secure.

"Now what?" he asked, standing up.

"We stick to the plan."

"But what about them?"

"We'll do the same thing to them we're going to do with Manning," she said.

"But… Can we go ahead and kill them?"

"Are you stupid?!" she shouted. "Leave it to me. Do what I say. Okay?"

"Yeah, yeah. I just want this over with," Warner said meekly.

"We need to move fast before the cops start looking for these two. Come on, let's get them in the car."

We were ordered to our feet and shuffled out to the garage. Lynn and I were shoved into the back seat of Warner's Mercedes. For the second time that day, I was getting to ride in a luxury sedan. Catalina, carrying a bag and her very big gun, climbed into the passenger seat and Warner backed out of the garage.

For the next half hour, we sat in the back of Warner's car. He followed along behind while Catalina moved our cars to two different locations a couple of miles from his house. If I hadn't had the gag in my mouth, I would have pointed out all the ways this wouldn't work to Warner, who was the weak link in this conspiracy.

With the cars disposed of, Catalina's next move was to use our phones to confuse things. Her plan for getting rid of the phones wasn't bad. She explained the details to Warner as he drove to the truck stop near the interstate.

"I'm going to stay in the car with these two. You're going to go out and put each of the phones on a truck. Do it at the pumps. You don't want trucks that are going to be here for hours. Just place the phone somewhere in the undercarriage. Ideally, they'll fall off in an hour or so."

She took each of the phones and used our faces to open them. "I'm going to turn off all the power-saving features. When you place the phone, make sure it's on and turn it upside down so the light can't be seen. I've already turned off the sound. The battery should run out in a couple of hours."

As he pulled into the truck stop, Catalina turned to us. "I want you two to lean over and keep your heads below the seat. If you raise up even an inch, I'll blow both of your heads off."

Ten minutes later, we were moving again. I watched Lynn wipe her injured head on the back of her seat and followed her lead. Even without the blood, I tried to rub off some of my hair and skin. Anything to leave DNA in the car. They could explain our DNA being in Warner's house, but the car would be a lot harder to explain.

I listened as they talked softly to each other in the front seat.

"The plane's big enough, isn't it?" Catalina asked.

"I told you. It's a Cessna 208B Grand Caravan. They use it for skydiving, so the weight is no problem. Once we're a few hundred miles out, we can dump them out the door. I did what you said and reserved it for our trip two weeks ago, and I even said there will be people coming back with us to justify the size of the plane."

"Good. The reservations in New Orleans were also made two weeks ago. When we get back, we'll tell everyone we're engaged so there won't be any suspicions about why we were traveling together."

"Are you sure the passcode will work?" Warner asked.

"Yes. The virtual wallet has never been used since Archway bought the original thousand bitcoins for his nephew. They were in the birthday card, just like he said they were."

"Twenty million dollars." Warner whistled.

"Ten each. We'll go our separate ways after a year."

"And we've taken care of everything else. Manning fixed the video feeds for us, right?"

"Yes. I told you, we're good. We just have to get rid of these two," Catalina said with surprising calm.

"They'll know they came to my house."

"So what? Their phones are on their way to who-knows-where and will probably never be found. Their bodies are going to plummet ten thousand feet down to the Gulf. Whatever is left of them will be eaten by sharks."

"Yeah, I even charted out the shipping routes to avoid."

"And it doesn't matter what the police suspect. They won't be able to prove anything. Not beyond a reasonable doubt. Remember, Neil Manning will still be missing. Everyone will think that he could have been involved in Macklin's and Lewis's disappearances."

"That makes sense." Warner sounded calmer.

"When the dust settles, we can go wherever we want in the world and have enough money to live the way we want."

While they were talking, Lynn and I had been quietly working our faces together, gently pulling the rags from each other's mouths. If we survived, I was going to give her a hard time about her cigarette breath. After a lot of effort, we finally had enough of the rags in our mouths to make it look like we were still gagged, while being ready to spit them out when the right time came. We tried to wiggle around and untie each other's hands, but it was too awkward.

We were getting close to the Tallahassee airport.

"You can pull into the hangar, right?" Catalina asked.

"Yes, I've got the key. When I said I wanted to leave at eleven on Saturday night, they said no one would be there but that the plane would be fueled and ready to go. I've already filed my flight plan."

A few minutes later, we pulled up in front of the hangar and Warner got out and unlocked the door. He pulled the car inside and I hoped we'd get a chance to fight for our lives before we got on the plane. The thought of fighting in a plane at ten thousand feet might sound exciting while watching a movie, but frankly it made my bowels loosen. Did Lynn know how to fly a plane? I sure as hell didn't.

Once we were inside the hangar, Catalina and Warner got out of the car. I watched as Warner got a set of steps and wheeled them to the side of the plane, then climbed inside. Two minutes later, the skydiving door on the side of the plane rolled up and Warner hopped out onto the tarmac to push the steps to the other door.

While Warner was opening up the plane, Catalina went to the back of the car and we heard the trunk open. Warner came back to the car, and they carried what was obviously a body wrapped in black plastic over to the plane. I didn't think it was a huge leap to assume it was Neil Manning's body.

They heaved the body up and into the back of the plane. Once that was done, Warner climbed up the steps and dragged the body out of sight. When he exited the aircraft again, I noticed that he had to duck a little as he came through the back door. I formed a quick plan.

Warner and Catalina returned to the car with determined looks on their faces. I'd just had time to fill Lynn in on my idea, hoping that she'd understood what I was saying around the sock in my mouth.

"Get out of the car," Catalina ordered. Once again, she had the revolver in hand and pointed straight at us.

We stumbled out of the car as best we could with our hands tied and feet hobbled.

Warner pushed me toward the plane. I'd debated which would be best: me entering ahead of him or him going first. I had to settle for what I got and hoped that Lynn could play her part.

I made gestures indicating to Warner that the hobbles were going to prevent me from climbing the steps up to the plane.

"Fake it till you make it." He shoved me and almost sent

me to the ground.

Okay, I thought, miffed at him playing the tough dog with me now. *You're going to get everything I can give.*

Slowly, I climbed the steps. There was a flimsy handrail that I carefully braced myself against as I took each step. This was working for me, because I wanted Warner right behind me when we got inside the plane.

Once I was in, I shuffled forward a couple of feet before I turned just enough to see when he ducked and got his head inside the craft. At that point, I spat out the gag and threw every bit of my weight at him. His head was about ten inches from the door frame when I body-slammed him and his head hit the bulkhead with a crack. I'd thought it might break his neck, but instead it was just hard enough to daze him.

The momentum of my attack sent both of us flying out of the plane toward the concrete. I tried to keep him between me and the ground since I couldn't use my hands or feet to brace myself. I came down on his chest and heard him expel a woosh of air. He broke most of my fall, but after I hit him, I flipped quickly to the right and cracked my own skull against the concrete hard enough to see stars.

Behind me I heard a scream, but I ignored it. I'd told Lynn that we each had to concentrate on taking out our own captor.

Dazed but not out, Warner half stumbled to his feet, gasping for air and bleeding from the back of his head. His gun had slid across the floor of the hangar and I expected him to make a move for it, but instead he lurched toward the stairs into the plane. With my feet still hobbled and my hands behind my back, I had to roll around and struggle to get to my feet.

Warner was up the stairs and into the plane before I could get to him. When he turned to slide the door down, I was on my knees halfway up the steps. I fell into the plane and tried to knock him off his feet by swinging my torso around. In a panic, he jumped back away from me and ran toward the front of the plane.

I managed to get the rest of the way inside the plane and was able to pull myself up on a bench seat. By the time I was moving toward the cockpit, I heard the engine turn over. *All that effort and the bastard might still be able to take off*, I thought. A surge of panic went through me as I fought back images of fighting with Warner as the plane dove and rolled through the air.

I was within ten feet of the cockpit when I felt the plane jerk forward as the sound of the engine wound higher. The motion caused me to go down to my knees. I pulled myself back up and stumbled the rest of the way to the cockpit, where a bloody and disoriented Warner was pushing the plane forward. I threw my body at him, knocking him forward and onto the throttles. The plane picked up speed.

A second later there was the sound of a thousand car wrecks as the plane plowed into the side of the hangar and abruptly stopped. I pulled Warner down off of the controls as pieces of metal came scissoring through the windows. The engine screamed loudly, then there was sudden silence.

I lay there for a minute expecting an explosion. When I lifted my head, I saw Warner's torn and bloodied back. Just when I'd decided he might be dead, he groaned and tried to turn over.

"Move, you bastard, and I'll strangle you right here," I told him.

There was no lack of jagged pieces of metal in the cockpit, and I quickly sawed my hands free, then my legs. I dug through Warner's pockets until I found his phone. Luckily, I could dial 911 without having to unlock it.

While I made the call, I started back out of the cockpit, dragging Warner with me. He was practically catatonic, so I shoved him into a seat and headed quickly for the back door while telling the Leon County dispatcher enough to get help headed our way.

I stuffed his phone into my pocket and jumped out of the plane. I was scared I'd find Lynn dead, but what I actually saw was just bizarre. Lynn was lying on top of Catalina with her ear in her teeth. The back of Lynn's shirt was ripped and bloody. Every time Catalina moved, Lynn would bite down on her ear and bump her head against Catalina's head, which in turn hit the concrete.

I rushed over to them. "Are you okay?"

"No. My back is on fire thanks to this hellcat," Lynn said after I'd helped to pin Catalina down so Lynn could let go of her ear.

Catalina was spitting mad, and it took some convincing to get her to settle down. I helped Lynn untie her hands while I sat on Catalina.

"What about Warner?" Lynn asked.

"He's in bad shape. His gun is over there." I pointed to where it still lay on the ground. "But keep your eye on the plane."

We could hear sirens in the distance. Neither Lynn nor I had handcuffs, so I remained sitting on Catalina, who was spewing a never-ending and very imaginative string of curse words.

"I sure could use a cigarette," Lynn said.

"Those things'll kill you," I responded.

"Now you think you're Schwarzenegger with the one-liners." She smiled.

When the EMTs and law enforcement arrived, we turned Catalina over to the deputies and pointed toward the plane, where they found Warner still in a daze. We walked around on rubbery legs, trying to compose ourselves while the first responders threw questions at us.

Finally, I borrowed one of the deputy's phones to call Cara and my dad. Dad had already gotten wind of something happening at the Tallahassee airport that involved me and Lynn. By the time I talked to him, he was halfway there with his lights flashing and siren full blast.

CHAPTER TWENTY-FIVE

I spent the rest of the holiday weekend doing paperwork and talking to investigators from half a dozen agencies, including the Leon County Sheriff's Office, the NTSB, the Federal Aviation Authority, the Tallahassee Airport, the U.S. Marshals, the FBI and our own internal affairs department.

Curtis Warner had suffered serious lacerations, including where a piece of metal had sliced a deep groove across his shoulder, and he'd lost a lot of blood. Thanks to me, he also had a severe concussion. Catalina had a concussion and several bites across her hands, face, ears and back. Lynn explained in her statement that her teeth and her body mass had been her only weapons and she'd used both liberally.

I took a little time off on Monday to join Dad at the memorial ceremonies. It was always humbling to stand before the graves of men and women who had died defending our country and our Constitution. It put my petty complaints and problems into perspective when I imagined a soldier facing the beaches of Normandy or IEDs hidden in the sands of Afghanistan.

On Tuesday morning, once everyone had reviewed my report of what happened, I was allowed to sit in on an interview with Warner. It was one of several in a long string of interviews, and Padilla was in charge of this one. The State Attorney, a U. S. Marshal and Warner's attorney were also present.

"Catalina Knight says you were the mastermind," Padilla told Warner. In truth, Catalina had shut down like a clam.

"That lying…" He went off with a string of uncomplimentary terms for his co-conspirator until his lawyer convinced him that he wasn't helping himself. "How can she say that? She's the one who told me about the bitcoins."

"How did she find out about them?"

"She worked the safe deposit boxes. When a customer came in and wanted to get to their box, she was the one who opened the vault and escorted them to their box. She would insert the bank's key and the customer inserted theirs. She took the box out and placed it on the table. The bank employee is supposed to leave at that point and give the customer privacy to dig through their box, but you know how it is. A lot of the customers just want to grab one item, and they'll tell you just to wait so they don't have to come get anyone to put the box back in its drawer."

"And she saw Archway's bitcoin passcode?" Padilla asked.

"No. She would chat up some of the guys. Some liked it, some didn't. Cat is very sensitive. She knows who wants her to flirt and who doesn't. Archway liked it. He even flirted back. She said he got very chatty and didn't want her to leave the vault while he went through his box. Obviously, this was an opportunity for him to have her full attention. One thing he talked about was his nephew, who had died eight years earlier. The nephew had been a tech savvy guy who helped Archway with his computer and taught him about email and all that back in the day. Anyway, the nephew died just before his birthday. Turns out, Archway had bought his nephew a thousand bitcoins as a birthday present. At the time they were valued at about forty cents each. So roughly five hundred dollars.

"Archway bought them 'cause his nephew had showed him what cryptocurrency was and how to buy the coins. Archway put the passcode and information in a birthday card for the nephew. Well, a month later he finds out the nephew has been killed in a car accident. Archway is grief-stricken about the loss of his only living relative. The card is just sitting on his dining room table until one day he puts it in his safe deposit box. Not because he thinks the bitcoins are worth more than the five hundred dollars he paid for them, but because the card in the envelope represents all the hopes he'd had for his nephew's future. Or some such crap is what he told Catalina. Without his nephew or anyone to keep him up to speed on cryptocurrency and the internet, the old guy never figured out that he had twenty million dollars in his box."

"But Catalina figured it out and decided to seduce him to get the passcode?"

"Bingo. But it seems she might have pushed too hard. He got cold feet about the relationship and cut her off."

"That probably didn't make her happy," Padilla observed.

"That's an understatement. Once she figured out that the old man had a fortune in his box and didn't even know it, she made up her mind to get it one way or another."

"So she came to you?"

"No, first she tried to sidle up to Cortez. See, she knew that she'd have to have the bank manager in on it to get into the safe deposit box without the owner."

"He rebuffed her advances?" I asked.

"Cortez didn't have any interest in an office romance. Anyway, he seemed immune to her charms."

"Then she came to you?" Padilla asked.

"Yeah, my bad luck." He rubbed his eyes. "She had this elaborate plot mapped out where she would kill Cortez and I would become bank manager. Of course, she knew that Archway would have to die too. Beyond that, she didn't have much of a plan."

"You improved on it?"

"I knew they were going to be moving Neil Manning. After she worked security at the bank, Florence still came back in all the time and talked about what she was doing. When she found out that she was going to be transporting Manning, it was all she could talk about, with him being a local villain."

"And you knew Neil Manning?"

"Yeah, the bank manager before Cortez didn't like Neil and always made me deal with him. I wouldn't say I liked him, but we got to be something like friends. He set up my home security system. I knew he was smart with computers, and we would need that to pull off what Catalina had in mind. See, there are cameras throughout the bank. We couldn't be seen entering the bank or the vault after hours. Or even during the day without good reason. In the old days, it wouldn't have been too difficult a problem, but our cameras upload in real time to Silver Security's main office. I figured Manning could figure out how to bypass the cameras. Breaking him out of jail would also help with the other elements of our plan. We could make it look like the prisoners killed Cortez."

"Were you the one that operated the backhoe?" Padilla asked.

"I paid my way through college doing construction work. Thanks to Florence, I knew the route they were taking. And I knew where I could get the backhoe. The bank was financing the construction job that was put on hold, and I'd been out to the site a few times. With it shut down, I figured I had a couple of days before anyone missed it."

"So you killed Florence Murray because she recognized you," I said.

"No. I was wearing a ski mask the whole time. Manning killed her. He told me she recognized my voice, but I think he just wanted to kill her," Warner said, and I suspected he was telling the truth. From what I'd seen of Warner, he wasn't the kind of guy to beat a woman to death. Neil Manning was.

"Who killed Cortez?" I asked.

"That was…" He looked at his lawyer, who gave a small nod. "Catalina. She knew about him going scouting in the forest. All of us did. He talked hunting *ad nauseum*. It was just luck that he happened to be in the same area that day. Catalina called him and told him that her car had broken down on the dirt road near where we staged the accident. This was an hour before the transport van was due. When he arrived, she used the shotgun to get him into the trunk and then… she shot him."

"You weren't there?"

"No. Not then," he said.

We all looked at each other. He was a rotten liar, but would we be able to prove it? Maybe, maybe not. They had been very careful with their cell phones. Tracking them would have been the best way to put him at the scene when the killing took place. The next best way would be to get Catalina to point the finger at him. Time would tell.

"What about Nicholas Archway?" Padilla asked.

"Catalina convinced him to let her come by. When she did, she dosed him with his own sedatives, got him in bed and smothered him using a piece of plastic wrap and a pillow."

"The plastic was for…?" I already knew, but I wanted him to say it.

"She'd watched some true-crime show where the coroner picked up fibers from a pillow in the victim's throat, convincing them that it was murder."

"What about Neil Manning?" I asked.

"Catalina had always planned on killing Manning. She didn't like him. There'd been some friction when he used to come into the bank. We set him up in a foreclosed house, not much different than the one we used for the other prisoners. Once he'd helped us bypass the bank's security, she shot him."

"And you were going to drop him in the Gulf of Mexico," Padilla said.

"We figured if he was never caught and no one knew he was dead, the focus would remain on him. The great part of the plan is no one would have ever missed those bitcoins. No one even knew they were there. We could have dropped Manning's body in the Gulf, come back and cashed in whenever we wanted with no one the wiser."

The interview moved on to the events of Saturday night. There were several times that Warner tried to evade responsibility for some of the crimes that had been committed. He seemed to have forgotten that while we had gags in our mouths, Lynn and I were able to see and hear everything that had happened. Catalina Knight and Curtis Warner were likely going to spend the rest of their lives behind bars.

After the interview, I went to see Mr. Griffin.

"How's Harold doing?" I asked when we were sitting at his kitchen table with glasses of ice-cold tea.

"Trying to adjust to his new reality. His daughter had to explain to him what bitcoins are. I'm still not sure he really understands. Heck, I don't really understand how it all works. What he *has* figured out is that he's going to be able to take care of his daughter, grandchildren and great-grandchildren."

"I guess without any other relatives, Harold was a natural choice for Nick to leave his estate to. Harold always had Nick at his family's holiday get-togethers, so Nick must have felt that they were as close to family as he was going to have."

"Of course, he didn't know he was leaving them twenty million dollars."

"I think he's probably smiling down from heaven right now," Mr. Griffin said. "He'd appreciate you catching the witch that killed him too."

On Wednesday, I was lounging in bed enjoying my leave of absence, which was mandatory after the events of the weekend. There would be an internal review and until it reached a decision, I was required to sleep in.

"I've got to go into town to arrange something, if I can," I told Cara as she got ready for work. Henry had gone home on Monday, giving Cara and me a few days to relax and recover alone.

"You're still on leave," she reminded me.

"I know. This is only tangentially related to work. I don't want to jinx it until I see if I can make it happen."

"I always worry when you're being mysterious." She laughed.

"I promise this is just a small favor for a friend. I'll tell you all about it if it works out."

I called Mick Klein on my way to town. "How's Andre?"

We'd finally figured out that Andre had been responsible for the break-ins that had occurred near the house where the fugitives had been killed. It had taken a while, but Mick had eventually found him hiding out in an old shed. Waugh had stolen the drugs from him without paying the rest of the money, shooting at him in the bargain. Andre had escaped, but not without several pieces of buckshot in his butt and thigh. He'd been scared to death, not only of the fugitives, but also of his cousin. He was afraid Nickel would kill him for losing the drugs *and* the money.

"He'll be fine," Mick told me. "His sister is letting him stay with her for a couple of days, but he'll be back on the street soon."

"Glad he's going to be all right. It's a real shame you couldn't solve those burglary cases," I told him meaningfully.

"Yeah, I guess I'll complete my report now," Mick said, sounding grateful.

After talking with Mick, I made several stops in town to pull all the pieces of my plan together. Once it was done, I filled Cara and Dad in on what I had in mind, receiving their enthusiastic support, which I'd never doubted.

On Friday morning, I showed up at Pete's house, ostensibly to bring him up to speed on everything that had happened. When I got there, he was sitting in his recliner, looking irritated. Sarah had spent the hour before I got there badgering him to get cleaned up and put on decent clothes. He'd argued that it was only me coming by, so why bother. Finally, she'd lied and told him that I'd offered to take them both to lunch at the Palmetto.

"That's a lot of killing for imaginary money," Pete whistled once I'd told him all that had happened.

"It's only imaginary until it isn't."

"And how did you figure it all out?"

"I didn't. What I figured out was that all roads led back to the bank."

"You can't be too upset that Manning is no longer a problem."

I looked down at the floor. "I can't believe I'm saying this, but I have mixed feelings after seeing what this has cost his father. Neil Manning was a monster, but he was a monster who was loved by his father."

"What's that noise?" Pete sounded annoyed.

"Don't know. Sounds like a bus." I tried to look surprised.

Pete got up using a crutch and moved toward the windows.

"It's a couple of school buses," he said, confused as the buses parked in front of his house. "What the hell…"

Sarah came out of the kitchen and gave me a knowing look. A couple of vans pulled up behind the buses.

"They're from the elementary school." Pete turned from the window and started toward the front door.

"That's odd," I said and gave Sarah a wink.

Pete fumbled with his crutch and the doorknob.

"Let me." I stepped past him and opened the door.

Outside, groups of elementary-school children were lining up as teachers and staff set up tables in Pete's front yard.

Mr. Campbell, the principal, walked up to us. He held out his hand to Pete.

"Hope you don't mind, but we decided to hold our end-of-the-year party on your front lawn. It's because of you and what you did that all of us can be together and have this party," the principal told him. I'd made it very clear to Campbell that he shouldn't say I had anything to do with this.

"Come on, that's crazy." Pete was looking at the ground and I heard a hitch in his voice.

"We know you made a great sacrifice for us." As Campbell spoke, his voice got louder, and teachers and students got quiet and moved forward. "All of us wanted to let you know that we appreciate what you did. We'll never know whose life you saved or which of us you kept from spending years in pain or grief." He stuck his hand out again and took Pete's hand, shaking it vigorously. "Thank you."

Pete was fighting back tears as teachers came forward and urged the kids to do the same.

Box lunches were served as many of the children's parents showed up and thanked Pete. Dad arrived with Mauser, which took the attention off of Pete for a while as all the children clamored to have their picture taken with the big dog.

I took the chance to walk over to Pete when no one else was around.

"In law enforcement, you often don't meet the people you've helped the most, and they never know what you did for them. I think all these children and their families will remember what you did that day. Whatever the future holds for you, you'll never have to wonder if you made a difference in the world," I told him.

Pete looked up at me with tears in his eyes and a smile on his face. "I knew you were behind this, and I hate you for it."

"I know you do." I smiled and jokingly punched him in the arm.

Larry Macklin returns in:

Independence Day's Search
A Larry Macklin Mystery–Book 20

ACKNOWLEDGMENTS

As always, thanks to my wife, Melanie, for her editing skills and support; to H. Y. Hanna for her inspiration, assistance and encouragement; and to all the fans of the series. Larry never would have come this far without all of you!

Original Cover Concept by H. Y. Hanna
Cover Design by Florida Girl Design, Inc.
www.gobookcoverdesign.com

ABOUT THE AUTHOR

A. E. Howe lives and writes on a farm in the wilds of North Florida with his wife, horses and more cats than he can count. He received a degree in English Education from the University of Georgia and is a produced screenwriter and playwright. His first published book was *Broken State*. The Larry Macklin Mysteries is his first series and he released the Baron Blasko Mysteries in summer 2018. His most recent series, the Mortician Murder Mysteries, was launched in 2022.

The first book in the Macklin series, *November's Past*, was awarded two silver medals in the 2017 President's Book Awards, presented by the Florida Authors & Publishers Association; the ninth book, *July's Trials*, was awarded two silver medals in 2018. Howe is a member of the Mystery Writers of America, and was co-host of the "Guns of Hollywood" podcast for four years on the Firearms Radio Network. When not writing, Howe enjoys riding, competitive shooting and working on the farm.